THE BEASTS OF BLOOD & SPIRIT

A NICOLE BERETTI THRILLER

LUKA T. JACOBS

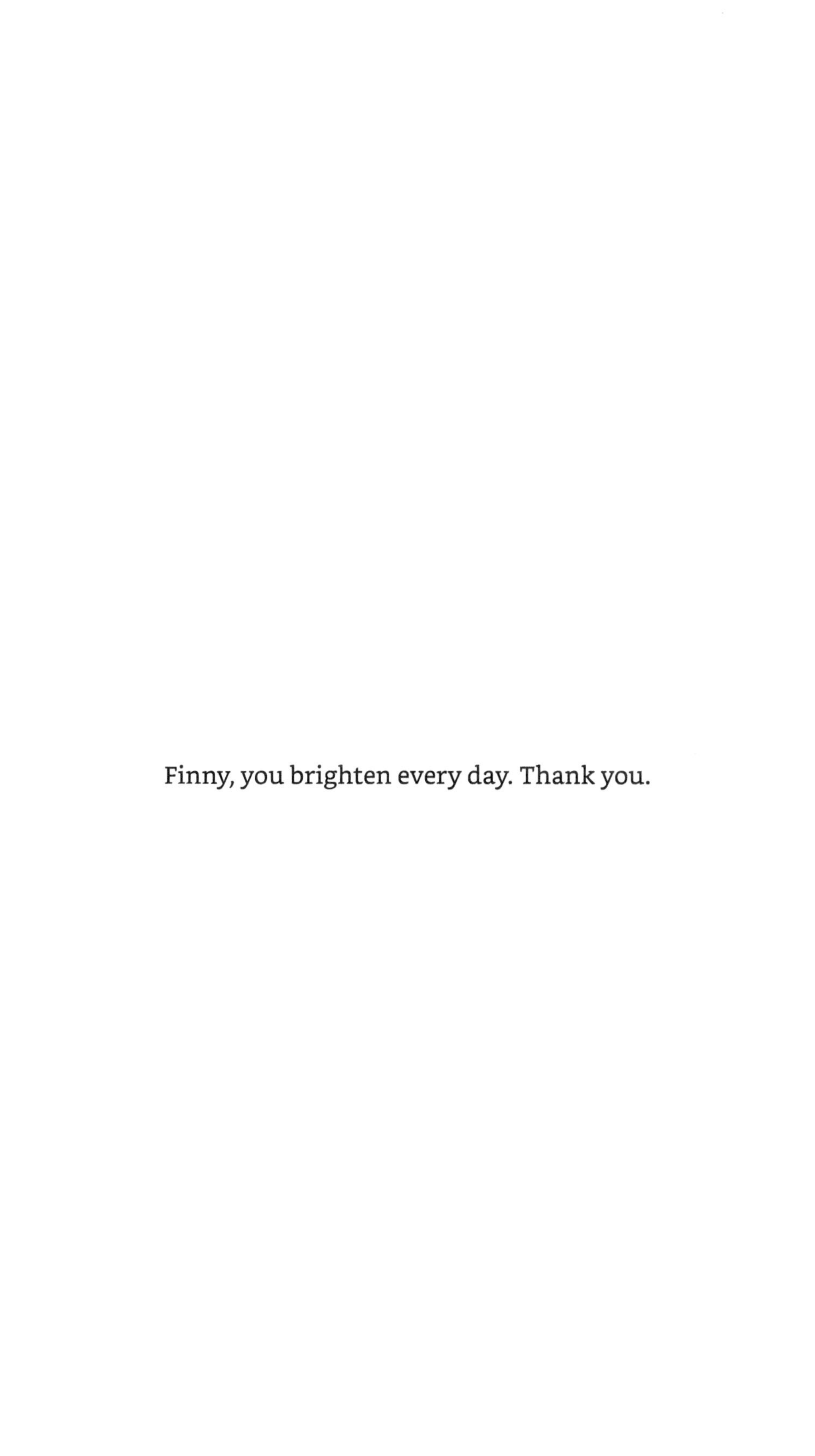

Finny, you brighten every day. Thank you.

FROM THE AUTHOR

Dear Readers,

Thank you for diving into my latest book, *The Beasts of Blood and Spirit*. With this story, I pushed myself to explore new layers of suspense and mystery, blending the familiar cryptid theme with fresh and unexpected twists. Writing it was both an enjoyable and challenging experience, and I hope it kept you hooked and eager to turn each page until the very end.

It's readers like you who inspire me to keep crafting these stories and exploring the unknown alongside Beretti and Jacobi. Their journey is far from over, and I can't wait to share what's next.

Stay tuned! There's always more lurking in the darkness!

Warm regards.

Luka T. Jacobs

CONTENTS

PROLOGUE

The forest was his sanctuary. Deep in its shadows, where the light barely penetrated, he thrived. The Dogman had lived many years alone, carving out an existence that suited his needs and no one else's. His kind had always been family-driven, packs bound together by instinct and survival. But not him. He had severed those ties long ago.

He could still remember the moment he left them. The pack's rules had chafed against his growing hunger for freedom. They were too bound by tradition, too focused on the collective. He wanted to hunt on his own terms, roam where he pleased. And so, one night, while the others slept, he slipped into the darkness and didn't look back.

In the years since, he'd learned to thrive in isolation. He

followed his instincts, prowling the vast woods and rocky hills. Each night, the forest became his domain, and anything that entered it was his prey. The absence of his family didn't weaken him. It emboldened him. He was stronger now, faster, sharper. He had no one to answer to, no one to share his kills with.

Yet, deep in the recesses of his mind, he sometimes felt it: a faint, nagging emptiness. It was not loneliness, not exactly. It was the memory of connection, a fleeting shadow that passed over him and was gone before he could examine it too closely. He had trained himself to ignore it, dismissing it as weakness. He didn't need anyone. He had the forest, the hunt, and the fear he inspired in those he encountered.

The hairless ones intrigued him the most. Fragile, predictable, and amusing in their ignorance, they were his favorite prey, but only under certain circumstances. He avoided them if they carried their thundersticks, having learned early that they could kill even him from afar. But if he encountered them in the forest, unarmed and unguarded, he would stalk them. He studied them first, watching for signs of weakness or foolishness, waiting to strike only when he was sure.

Tonight, he moved silently through the underbrush, his claws pressing into the damp earth. The moon was full, casting a faint light through the canopy, but he kept to the shadows. He didn't need the light to see. His eyes, golden and unblinking, cut through the darkness with ease.

He came to an abrupt halt, captivated by a certain scent. Though subtle, it was undeniable. The hairless ones. There were traces of firewood, the oily tang of metal, and the musk of sweat. His nostrils flared as he inhaled deeply, pinpointing the direction. His movements were cautious yet fluid.

He crouched low, hidden by dense foliage, his focus fixed on the dwelling ahead. There was something about this particular place, something unexplainable, that lingered at the edges of his mind. The air here seemed heavy, thick with sorrow and despair that seemed to seep from the walls. It wrapped around him, unsettling in a way he couldn't fully understand.

The pull wasn't logical, but it was relentless. He stayed, crouched and watching, drawn not by hunger or curiosity but by an invisible force that tugged at him like a leash. It wasn't the hairless ones themselves, though he could smell their presence. It was something deeper. A sense of grief, of loss, that reached into him and stirred feelings he didn't know how to name.

He let out a low rumble, too soft to be heard but enough

to vibrate through his chest. This strange connection unsettled him, prickling at instincts he didn't fully trust.

A faint noise from inside broke the stillness. His ears perked, alert to the scrape of a chair and the murmur of voices. He remained motionless, his golden eyes locked onto the house.

His claws scraped lightly against the frozen ground, a restless habit he barely noticed. The urge to move closer gnawed at him, to press his snout against the thin glass and watch their faces twist with fear when they realized what lurked outside. But he held back. Not yet.

Instinct and experience kept him still. He was the predator, but even predators had to be cautious with the hairless ones. They were unpredictable, clever in ways his kind had learned not to underestimate. His amber eyes flicked over the house, searching for anything out of place. He would wait.

As he retreated deeper into the forest, the strange pull lessened, replaced by the familiar rhythm of survival. The house would still be there tomorrow, and the day after that. He had plenty of time to figure out why it called to him, why the despair it radiated felt so intimately familiar.

But tonight, his hunger demanded his attention. His muscles tensed as his nose lifted to the air, searching for the scent of prey. There was no room for hesitation now. The hunt was calling him, and he would answer.

For now, he would watch, and he would wait.

And when the time was right, they would know what it meant to fear the darkness.

ONE

Ethan Pendleton stared out the smudged passenger window of the sedan, his hands clutching the strap of his backpack. Outside, the Maine countryside unfolded in shades of muted green and gray. Eastern Hemlock trees loomed tall on either side of the winding road, their branches heavy with the memory of last night's rain. Somewhere in the distance, a crow cawed, its sound swallowed by the vastness of the forest.

His grandmother, Lillian, drove in silence. She was a small woman, but there was a quiet strength in the way she carried herself. Her face bore the lines of experience rather than age, a testament to a life that had thrown its share of challenges her way. Despite everything, there was warmth in her gaze, a steadiness that made it clear she had endured and come through the other side.

"You'll have your own room," she said suddenly, breaking the quiet. Her voice was calm, even soothing, but it didn't match the strain in her eyes. "It's not much, but I've made it nice for you."

Ethan nodded, not trusting his voice. The truth was, he didn't care about the room. He didn't care about moving to Evernight. He didn't care about anything right now. His mind was still trapped in the wreckage of the accident, replaying the moment he was called to the principal's office, the quiet scrape of the chair as he sat down, and the solemn expression on the officer's face as he delivered the news.

Your mother didn't make it.

The words had come like a punch to the gut, leaving him breathless and disoriented. Now, two weeks later, the world still seemed unbalanced, as if its axis had shifted, leaving him in a reality that didn't quite fit.

Lillian's house appeared modest, tucked at the edge of a quiet street with a small backyard that stretched toward the tree line. The trees stood at the rear of the property, their branches almost void of all their leaves. Small and single-story, the house was well cared for despite its age. The gravel driveway crunched beneath the tires as the car came to a stop, the house settling into view with an air of quiet resilience.

It looked nothing like where he was from in Chicago. Back home, he lived in an apartment with no yard, no towering trees at the edge of the property, and no quiet stillness that made everything feel too open and too exposed.

Ethan sighed heavily, climbing out of the car, the cool air hitting him immediately. He pulled his hoodie tighter around him and slung his backpack over one shoulder. Lillian was already at the trunk, pulling out his suitcase with surprising ease.

"Come on," she said, nodding toward the house. "I'll show you around."

The inside of the house was warmer than Ethan expected, with the faint smell of cinnamon lingering in the air. The floors were hardwood, worn smooth in places, and the walls were lined with photographs. Most were black and white, showing faces Ethan didn't recognize, their expressions frozen in time. One photo caught his eye of a man standing next to a much younger version of Lillian. She was smiling in the picture, the man's arm draped protectively over her shoulder.

"That's your grandfather Christopher," Lillian said, following his gaze. Her voice softened, taking on a wistful tone.

"What happened to him?" Ethan asked, surprised at how easily the question slipped out.

Lillian hesitated, her fingers brushing the edge of the frame. "He passed a long time ago. It's… a story for another day." She straightened, her expression shifting back to its usual firmness. "Come on. Let's get you settled."

Ethan's room was small but cozy, with a twin bed tucked into the corner beneath a single window that looked out over the backyard. There was a desk, an old wooden one with scratches and dents that hinted at years of use. Near one corner of the desk, the name "Diana" was faintly etched into the wood. Ethan ran his fingers over the letters, and the last memory of his mother flashed in his mind, sharp and bittersweet.

A bookshelf stood along the wall, half-filled with titles ranging from mystery novels to gardening guides. A worn quilt, patched in places, was draped over the bed, adding a touch of warmth to the otherwise simple space.

Ethan walked to the bookshelf, letting his fingers trail

over the faded spines of the books. Their titles had faded, but he caught glimpses of names like *The Hardy Boys* and *Reader's Digest Gardening Tips.*

On the desk, an old-fashioned lamp with a green glass shade stood, its cord snaking down to a dusty outlet. Curious, he opened the desk's single drawer and found a few pencils, a cracked ruler and a small stack of yellowed notepaper.

As he stood there, he subtly noticed the chill in the air. The room was colder than the rest of the house, the kind of cold that settled into his skin, just enough to make him aware of it.

Ignoring it, he moved to the window and peered out at the backyard. The neatly cut grass glistened with dew, and beyond it, the forest loomed. The trees seemed to stretch endlessly, their shadows weaving together in the light. Ethan shivered and pulled the curtain closed.

Overwhelmed by the day, he dropped his backpack and sat on the bed. The mattress creaked slightly under his weight, but it was soft. Lying back, he stared at the ceiling, where faint water stains formed patterns that looked almost like maps. He traced them with his eyes, letting his thoughts drift.

The last thing he remembered was the sound of the distant crow, its call fading into the quiet of the room.

"Ethan, dinner's ready," Lillian's voice cut through his sleep.

Ethan blinked awake, disoriented for a moment before the details of the room came back to him. He sat up slowly, rubbing his eyes, and glanced at the window. He sensed the forest's overwhelming presence bearing down, despite the curtains drawn. Something about the woods unnerved him.

"Coming," he called, as he tried to shake his brain into gear. Pushing himself off the bed, he ran a hand through his hair and made his way down the hall, the faint aroma of chicken and potatoes pulling him toward the dining room.

The dining room was lit by a single chandelier, its light flickering slightly, as if unsure of its purpose. Ethan recognized the chicken and mashed potatoes Lillian prepared; the meal brought back memories of his sparse childhood visits.

"So, how is your room?" Lillian asked, pouring gravy over her potatoes.

"It's nice," Ethan said, though the word didn't seem adequate. He poked at his food, his appetite absent. "I think I was here once or twice when I was little. Why didn't Mom ever bring me back?"

The question landed heavily, and Lillian's hand paused mid-air before she set the gravy boat down carefully. Her expression didn't change much, but Ethan caught the flicker of something in her eyes, sadness, maybe, or regret.

"Your mother and I... we didn't see eye to eye on a lot of things," Lillian said slowly, as if weighing each word. "She thought it was best to keep some distance. I didn't agree, but it wasn't my decision to make."

Ethan frowned. "What kind of things?"

Lillian's lips pressed into a thin line. "That's not something we need to get into tonight," she said. "What matters is that you're here now, and this is your home for as long as you need it to be."

Ethan nodded, though the answer left him unsatisfied. He took another bite of mashed potatoes, the flavors dull in his mouth. Across the table, Lillian's gaze lingered on him for a moment before shifting to the window behind him, her expression unreadable.

"It's quiet out here," Ethan said, attempting to steer the conversation to safer ground. "Not like the city."

"You'll get used to it," Lillian replied, her tone softening. "The quiet can be comforting once you've settled in. Helps you hear the things you might otherwise miss."

Ethan wasn't sure what she meant, but he nodded anyway. The rest of dinner passed in relative silence, broken only by the clink of silverware against plates.

That night, Ethan lay in bed, staring at the ceiling. He turned onto his side, pulling the blanket up to his chin, but sleep refused to come. His thoughts lingered on Lillian's words and the gaps they left behind, like puzzle pieces that didn't quite fit.

And then his mind turned to his mother. He thought of her laugh, the way she used to ruffle his hair, and the stories she told him before bed. The memory ached, vivid and raw, leaving a deep hole in its wake. He was practically alone now. He didn't remember his father and had only met Lillian a few times before. She was kind, but a stranger in so many ways.

And now, he had left all of his friends back home. The ones who knew him, who understood him without explanation. The ones who would have been there, cracking dumb jokes to make him laugh even when nothing was funny. Here, in this unfamiliar town, everything felt distant, like he was stuck in someone else's life. His own felt like a scattered puzzle with missing pieces, and he couldn't see the picture it was supposed to make.

Would he go to school here? Would he make any friends? Could he ever like it here, or learn to like the forest that loomed so close to the house?

The questions spiraled, unanswered, tangling in his mind until it felt overwhelming. He pulled the quilt tighter around him, seeking comfort that wouldn't come.

Finally, exhaustion crept in, dragging him into restless sleep as the weight of uncertainty lingered like a shadow in the dark.

TWO

For days, the Dogman moved swiftly and purposefully through the forest, his mind a whirlwind of restless energy. Hunting brought little relief. Each kill filled his stomach, but the pull in his chest refused to fade.

The house.

It lingered in his mind, clear and unshakable. Its modest frame stood at the edge of the tree line, its presence thick with something unexplainable. He didn't understand why it consumed him, but each day when he woke, the pull grew stronger, sharper, impossible to ignore.

By the fourth day, he gave in.

The growing tension inside him made the forest feel

confining. His claws pressed into the frozen earth as he followed an invisible thread pulling him forward.

The feeling wasn't just sorrow or despair. It had changed, deepened into something raw and consuming.

It wasn't his.

Grief settled inside him like a storm, twisting through his thoughts. Beneath it lay anger, cold and relentless, more cutting than anything he'd experienced before. He had never hunted the hairless ones unless they crossed his path, but now the thought of them sparked a burning rage.

Whatever had been left in that house had awakened something in him, and it demanded action.

When he reached the edge of the forest, he crouched low, hidden among the brush.

The house stood quiet, its backyard stretching to the tree line. The pull toward it was overwhelming, almost suffocating. The air seemed thick with grief and rage, and beneath it all, he sensed the presence.

One of his kind.

It wasn't alive, not entirely. It seemed like a fragment, left behind and crying out for help, or vengeance.

The Dogman's claws flexed against the ground as the anger surged. The presence's fury mingled with his own, twisting his instincts into something darker. He had long avoided hunting the hairless ones on purpose, but now he saw them as enemies.

His golden eyes scanned the house. He couldn't see the hairless ones inside, only faint shadows moving behind the windows. He didn't know if they carried thundersticks.

The pull from the house had changed him. It had warped his instincts, filling him with an unnatural need for vengeance. Any hairless one he encountered now would pay the price, guilty or not.

But not yet. Acting now would be reckless. With a low growl, he turned and moved deeper into the forest, though the pull to the house dragged at him with every step.

The sorrow and anger didn't fade. They clung to him like a shadow, growing stronger with each passing moment.

Tonight, he would hunt and regain his strength. The house would still be there tomorrow, and the pull would still be waiting for him.

Whatever had been left behind, whatever had been done to his kind, he would make it right.

And if the hairless ones crossed his path in the meantime, they would face his fury.

This wasn't over.

He would return.

THREE

Adeline Morris buttoned her coat as she stood on her front porch. "Come on, Grace," she snapped, yanking gently on the pink leash. Her three-month-old Groodle, dressed in an equally pink jacket, sat stubbornly on the welcome mat, her big brown eyes full of reproach. Adeline sighed loudly, crossing her arms.

"You'll look adorable," she said. "People will talk about how stylish we are. Now, let's go." She tugged on the leash again, and Grace whined, reluctantly stepping onto the frosty lawn.

Adeline didn't care much for dogs, but appearances mattered. The Groodle was a recent addition, a calculated move inspired by a man she had noticed at the park. He had a dog too, and Adeline figured getting one herself would provide the perfect excuse to approach him. She imagined their dogs playing together while she made polite conversation, picturing how impressed he'd be by her stylish little companion. It was just one more way to maintain appearances without putting in the effort.

As she adjusted her scarf with a tug, her mind flickered briefly to the man from the park. Would he be there this morning? She marched forward, dragging Grace along to keep pace. The morning air was icy, the sun just beginning to rise over the quiet streets of the small town of Evernight.

The few neighbors who were out waved or called greetings, some warming their cars or saying goodbye to their partners before work, but Adeline ignored them. She had no interest in their small-town pleasantries or mundane chatter. She worked at an art gallery, surrounded by culture and refinement, something people around here wouldn't understand.

Grace whimpered again as they passed a row of tidy houses, her tiny legs hesitating. Adeline stopped and looked down at her. "Oh, for heaven's sake," she snapped. "What now?"

Adeline's attention flicked to a crow that landed on a

nearby branch. She glanced at it but quickly dismissed it, focusing on her reluctant dog.

The Groodle didn't respond, her gaze fixed on something ahead. She whimpered again, this time backing up. Adeline followed her line of sight but saw nothing unusual in the early morning light.

"Keep moving," Adeline commanded, giving the leash a quick tug. Grace yelped, the sound echoing down the quiet street, and then, to Adeline's shock, slipped out of her collar. With a startled bark, Grace turned and bolted back toward the house, her tiny pink jacket flapping.

"Grace! You useless mutt!" Adeline shouted after her, but the dog disappeared around a corner. Adeline huffed, clenching her fists. "Fine! You'll be in trouble when I get back!" As she stood fuming, she noticed a neighbor across the street watching her from their driveway. "What are you looking at?" she yelled. The neighbor quickly averted their gaze and went back to their car.

With the leash dangling in her hand, Adeline hesitated for a moment, debating whether she should turn back to retrieve Grace or continue her walk. Pride won out quickly. She huffed and resumed walking down the winding street, mumbling under her breath, "Dogs should come trained already."

As Adeline strolled down the street, mentally critiquing the homes she passed, a loud squawk shattered the morning quiet. She flinched, snapping her head toward the sound.

A crow had landed on a streetlamp just ahead, its sleek black feathers stark against the pale morning sky. It cocked its head, fixing her with an unblinking stare before letting out another grating call.

She let out a quick breath, scowling. "What?! You following me now?" she said, shaking her head.

The crow flapped its wings slightly but didn't budge, its caws relentless.

Adeline rolled her eyes and turned away, dismissing the bird as she resumed her silent assessment of the neighborhood.

Minutes later, rounding a bend in the street, she noticed something. A shadow moved against the slant of a roof, backlit by the rising sun. Adeline squinted as she tried to make out what it was. A large, dog-like figure stood silhouetted on the roof of a nearby house, its form unnaturally still. The morning sun glinted off its fur, and its head tilted slightly, as if watching her.

Adeline froze, her heart pounding. "What in the…" she whispered, her voice trembling. A chill of genuine fear crept down her spine. It wasn't just the size of the thing that unnerved her. It was the way it seemed to be studying her, unmoving and unblinking.

Adeline took a step back, and the creature shifted. She didn't wait for it to move again. *How the hell did a dog get on the roof?* she thought to herself, her voice shaking as she hurried down the street. Her eyes darted to the empty porches and closed blinds. No one was outside now. She banged on the nearest door, desperate for help.

"Hello? Is anyone home?" she called, her fist pounding against the wood. There was no answer. She turned and scanned the street again. The creature was gone. Her stomach twisted with unease.

Stepping down from the porch, Adeline glanced around frantically. She'd just started toward the neighbor's gate when a low, deep growl rumbled from the bushes nearby. A hot wave of anxiety coursed over her body as she turned to face the noise.

The bushes rustled, and the growl grew louder. Adeline stumbled backward, her feet sliding on the frosty ground. Her pulse pounded as she steadied herself. "Go on, get!" she shouted, trying to sound firm, though her voice wavered with fear.

The crow let out one final squawk and took off from its perch, its black wings flapping noisily as it disappeared into the sky.

Before she could react, the creature leapt from the bushes with frightening speed. It was massive, its glowing amber eyes locking onto her as it lunged. Adeline's scream was cut short as its jaws clamped onto her face with a sickening crunch. Blood sprayed across the snow as the beast dragged her back into the bushes, her body limp and lifeless.

The street fell silent once more, the rising sun casting a serene glow over the neighborhood. The only sign of what had transpired was the bloodied snow.

FOUR

Sheriff David Carter adjusted his beanie as he stepped out of the patrol car, the crisp November air clinging to his beard. The cold was a sign of the long winter ahead, but he barely noticed. After a lifetime in Maine, the chill was nothing new.

For the past fifteen years, he had served as sheriff of the small town, earning the respect of both his deputies and the townspeople. His reputation wasn't just built on experience but on his steady presence and level-headed approach to even the worst situations. In his fifties, he remained as fit as he had been in his thirties thanks to early morning runs and a disciplined exercise routine. He believed strength and endurance weren't just about staying in shape; they were necessary for handling the pressures of the job.

The sheriff greeted his deputies with a nod as he stepped onto the lawn. It wasn't until he moved closer to the bushes that he noticed the grim discovery lying within.

The victim's body was barely recognizable. Most of her face was gone, torn away in ragged strips that left raw, jagged flesh. One leg was severed below the knee, the missing portion nowhere to be found. Deep gashes carved through her torso and arms, crisscrossing her pale skin with brutal precision. Blood soaked the frost-covered grass, painting a macabre trail that led back toward the yard.

Deputy Carla Ramirez stood nearby, her breath clouding in the cold air. "Sheriff, this one's… different," she said.

Sheriff Carter tugged on a pair of gloves as he turned towards her. "I'd say so. Any ID yet?"

Ramirez nodded toward Deputy Kyle Jefferson, who approached with a plastic evidence bag. Inside was a driver's license, smeared with blood. "Found this in her jacket," Jefferson said. "Name's Adeline Morris. Twenty-nine years old. She lives two blocks from here. I took photos of the scene before I touched anything."

The sheriff held the bag up, studying the picture. The woman in the photo smiled brightly, her features full of life.

A stark contrast to the mutilated remains in front of him. "Adeline Morris," he mumbled.

Jefferson cleared his throat. "Sheriff, the homeowner's over by her car. She's pretty shaken up. She was the one who found the body this morning."

The sheriff nodded, his expression softening. "Alright. Thanks, Jefferson."

He turned and walked toward a young brunette woman standing near the edge of the yard, her arms crossed tightly over her chest despite the thick jacket she wore. Her face was drawn, and she shifted her weight nervously as the sheriff approached.

"Ma'am, I'm Sheriff David Carter," he said gently. "Can you tell me what happened?"

She nodded, her voice shaky. "I wasn't home last night. I stayed over at my boyfriend Joe's place. When I got back this morning, around seven, I pulled into the driveway and saw…" She paused, swallowing hard. "Blood. Right there in the yard." She gestured to a large patch of red-stained grass. "There were drag marks, too. I…I followed them, and that's when I saw…" Her voice faltered, and she looked away, her hands trembling. "Her foot. Sticking out of the bushes."

The sheriff waited a moment before continuing. "You didn't hear or notice anything unusual when you left yesterday?"

She shook her head. "No, everything was normal. I didn't hear anything strange."

"Do you have a doorbell camera? Security system?"

The woman winced. "No, but I've been meaning to get one. I'll get one now."

Sheriff Carter nodded. "You're doing fine. Just hang tight for a bit longer."

The coroner, Dr. Myra Chase, arrived a few minutes later, her assistant in tow. Chase moved with her usual no-nonsense efficiency, pulling on gloves, and crouching near the body to begin her examination.

After several minutes, she straightened, removing her gloves with a loud snap. "Well, Sheriff, this doesn't look like your average homicide."

"What are we dealing with?" the sheriff asked, stepping closer.

Chase frowned, glancing back at the body. "The injuries

are consistent with an animal attack. These gashes?" She pointed to the deep claw marks raking across the victim's torso. "Definitely claws. The missing face tissue and the severed leg suggest feeding behavior. Whatever did this was big."

"A bear?" Ramirez asked cautiously.

"Could be," Chase admitted, "though bears are usually hibernating by now." She gestured to the blood-soaked yard. "Something heavy moved through here, but there are no distinguishing paw prints."

"What about a wolf?" Sheriff Carter asked, his voice tight.

Chase hesitated. "It's possible, though unusual. If it was a wolf, it's a mighty big one. The bite radius on her hip isn't normal. And..." She pointed to the victim's hands. "No defensive wounds. She didn't fight back. Whatever did this caught her completely off guard."

The sheriff stared at the remains, his eyes narrowing. "Unusual doesn't mean impossible. Let's keep all options on the table until we know more."

The deputies worked methodically, combing through the bushes and the yard for evidence.

"Sheriff!" Jefferson called, holding up a set of keys. "Found these buried under some leaves."

The sheriff took the keys, examining them briefly before nodding. "Bag them. They might be hers."

As the investigation wrapped up, Chase and her assistant carefully loaded the body into a black bag and wheeled it into the waiting van. Chase gave Sheriff Carter a grim look before stepping away. "I'll know more after the autopsy. But Sheriff... whatever did this, it didn't stop to think. It just killed."

"Let me know as soon as you've got something," Sheriff Carter said.

The sheriff turned back to Ramirez and Jefferson. "Anything else?"

Ramirez gestured toward a deputy near the fence line. "One more thing. Jefferson found a dog's lead and collar caught on the fence over there. Looks like it broke loose. No sign of the dog itself, though."

The sheriff's expression shifted as he glanced toward the fence, curiosity flickering in his eyes. "Bag it for evidence, just in case. It might mean nothing, but let's not assume."

Ramirez nodded. "Got it sheriff."

The sheriff exhaled heavily, his gaze shifting back to the scene. "Alright. Before you head back to the station, check with the neighbors. Ask if anyone saw or heard anything. Somebody around here might have noticed something, even if they don't realize it yet. Once that's done, get everything logged and let's see if we can track down this woman's relatives."

"Yes, sir," Ramirez replied.

Sheriff Carter approached the homeowner one last time. "Thanks for your patience," he said. He reached into his pocket and handed her a business card. "We'll be out of here shortly, but if you think of anything else, call me directly."

The woman took the card with trembling fingers, glanced at it briefly, and nodded. "I will. Thank you." She paused, then looked up at the sheriff and asked, "Will you... will you find out what happened?"

The sheriff met her gaze. "I'll do my best."

As he walked back to his vehicle, the sheriff glanced one last time at the blood-stained bushes. The coroner's words echoed in his mind: *It just killed.*

FIVE

Ethan woke to the sound of 60's music playing softly on a radio in the kitchen as he shuffled to the bathroom. A glance at the clock on the wall told him it was nearly nine in the morning. His grandmother, Lillian, was nowhere to be seen.

The house seemed emptier without her, the silence stretching out like a thin sheet over his nerves. He checked the front door; it was locked. The back door was too. Maybe she'd gone out early and forgotten to leave a note. He frowned but decided not to dwell on it.

Instead, he focused on breakfast. He dug through the cabinets and found a loaf of bread, popping two slices into the toaster. Butter and jam sat on the counter, remnants of

Lillian's breakfast, maybe. He slathered his toast and ate at the kitchen table, staring out the window at the backyard that bled into the dark line of trees. Something about those woods set his nerves on edge. Perhaps his unfamiliarity with the wilderness stemmed from his city upbringing. It could have been something deeper, something he couldn't quite express.

Once he finished, he washed his plate and got dressed and brushed his teeth. The day was cool but pleasant, so he grabbed his hoodie, sliding it on as he stepped out the front door. Ahead, the street was quiet; only the occasional bird chirp and distant chainsaw hum broke the silence. The road was flanked by houses, each bordering the same thick forest.

As he walked, his sneakers crunching against the gravel edge of the road, he noticed movement up ahead. Two kids on bikes, weaving lazily back and forth across the street, their laughter carrying on the breeze. They spotted him almost immediately and stopped, one of them leaning on his handlebars while the other spun slow circles on his bike.

"Hey," the boy on the stationary bike called out. He had messy blond hair that stuck out from under his baseball cap and a wide grin. "You new around here?"

Ethan nodded, stuffing his hands into his hoodie pocket.

"Yeah. Just moved in with my grandma."

The other boy skidded his bike to a stop beside his friend. He was shorter, with dark curly hair and freckles. "What's your name?"

"Ethan," he replied.

"Cool," said the blond boy. "I'm Nick. This is Ryan."

Ryan waved but didn't say anything. Nick dropped his bike to the ground with a loud clatter and walked over, giving a casual nod. "Nice to meet you. This place is alright. Mostly, we just ride bikes or hang out."

Ethan shook his hand briefly, unsure of what to say.

Nick nodded, and the three boys continued walking. Ryan stayed quiet, riding his bike slowly alongside them, while Nick filled the air with chatter. He described his favorite places in town, pointed out a house where he claimed the neighbor had a vicious dog, and told Ethan about the best spot to grab ice cream in the summer. He talked about the local school, the best places to grab snacks, and the teacher everyone hated. Ethan listened, occasionally nodding but contributing little.

When they reached the end of the street, Ethan pointed

toward the forest. "You guys ever go in there?"

Nick exchanged a glance with Ryan and shrugged. "Yeah, sometimes. We fish, hike, and go hunting with my mom or dad when it's not, you know, freezing."

Ryan nodded, slowing his bike. "It's pretty cool. There's a lake and some trails. Lots of stuff to mess around with."

Ethan glanced at the dark, still trees in the distance. "Doesn't freak you out?"

Nick snorted. "What? Trees? Nah. Maybe at night, but during the day it's fine."

Ryan tilted his head toward Ethan. "Where are you from, anyway? You sound, like, not from here."

"Chicago," Ethan said, still eyeing the forest. "This is… different."

Nick grinned. "I'll bet. You don't have woods like this in Chicago, huh?"

"Not really," Ethan admitted.

Ryan smirked. "You'll probably like it when it warms up. In the spring, we'll take you out and show you the woods, if you're not too scared." He laughed, pedaling ahead a little.

Ethan rolled his eyes but couldn't help a small smile. "Yeah, we'll see."

Nick grinned and motioned ahead. "Come on. There's this old shed down the next street. It's creepy, but it's empty."

Ethan shook his head. "Maybe later. I should probably head back."

"Hey, if you're sticking around, we should hang out sometime. Maybe watch some movies or something," Nick said, his grin broadening as he gave Ethan a light punch on the arm. Ryan pedaled off ahead, calling for Nick, who jogged back to grab his bike and follow. "Catch you later, Ethan!" Nick called over his shoulder as their voices faded into the distance.

Ethan stood there for a moment, staring after them. He turned and began walking back toward his grandmother's house, his gaze drifting toward the forest as he went.

Maybe Nick and Ryan liked the woods because they were used to them. Maybe it was just him because he'd never lived anywhere near woods before. Still, the sight of the trees made his stomach twist.

He paused on the front porch, looking back at the forest one last time before stepping inside.

SIX

A few blocks from the crime scene, the neighborhood looked calm and orderly. The houses were modest but well-kept, with neat yards and tidy porches. Sheriff Carter pulled his cruiser to a stop in front of one of them, the address matching the one on the victim's driver's license.

A car sat in the driveway, its windows frosted over. The house itself was small and inviting, with a row of dormant flowerbeds lining the front porch.

Movement near the door caught his eye. A young dog stood there, its cream-colored fur faintly dusted with frost, a pink jacket snug around its small frame. The dog shivered, its dark eyes watching him cautiously.

The sheriff stepped out of the cruiser and approached slowly, crouching a few feet away. The dog didn't have a collar, and its size matched the one found tangled on the fence earlier.

"Hey there, girl," he said softly, keeping his voice calm. "You're Grace, aren't you?"

The dog tilted her head slightly, taking a cautious step forward.

"It's okay," he said, holding out his hand. "I'm not gonna hurt you."

After a few moments, the dog crept closer, sniffing his outstretched fingers. When she finally pressed her cold nose to his palm, the sheriff reached out gently and scooped her up. She trembled in his arms, but she didn't resist.

Carrying Grace, the sheriff circled the house. The lawn was neatly trimmed, and the bushes looked undisturbed. The car in the driveway was locked, its frosted handles untouched.

He checked the windows and doors as he moved, ensuring everything was latched and secure. The back door was locked, as was the gate to the fenced yard. Nothing seemed out of place.

At the edge of the property, the forest loomed, its leafless trees forming a natural border. Sheriff Carter glanced at it briefly before turning back toward the house. The gruesome scene from earlier lingered in his thoughts, but here, everything appeared quiet and untouched.

Returning to the cruiser, he placed Grace gently on the passenger seat. The dog curled up immediately, her small body still trembling but beginning to relax.

"You'll be alright," he said, starting the engine. "Let's get you warmed up."

****

Back at the station, the familiar buzz of phones and mumbled conversations filled the air. Shelly Adams, the dispatcher, glanced up from her desk, a smile forming across her face as she noticed the dog in the sheriff's arms.

"Well, who's this little one?" she asked, standing.

"I think her name's Grace," Sheriff Carter replied. I found her on the deceased's doorstep after I left the scene.

Shelly's expression softened immediately. "Oh, poor thing. She must've been terrified." She reached out, scratching the dog gently behind the ears. Grace leaned into her touch, her tail giving a tentative wag.

"She doesn't have anywhere to go for now," the sheriff said. "Can you keep an eye on her until we figure things out?"

"Of course," Shelly said, taking the dog from his arms. "She'll be in good hands. Don't worry."

Shelly carried Grace to her desk, retrieving a folded blanket from a drawer and laying it out. Grace sniffed around before settling down, her tail wagging faintly.

"Let me grab her some water," Shelly said, disappearing into the break room.

The sheriff stood for a moment, watching as Grace curled up on the blanket. When Shelly returned with a bowl of water, the dog lapped it up eagerly.

"She's a sweetheart," Shelly said. "I'll keep her comfy until we've sorted things out."

"Thanks, Shelly," the sheriff said, removing his beanie and running a hand over his head. "Let me know if you need anything."

"You got it, sheriff," Shelly said with a smile, already cooing to Grace as the dog rested her head on her paws.

The sheriff headed toward his office, the tension in his chest easing slightly. Grace was safe for now, and with Shelly watching over her, he could focus on the next steps.

SEVEN

Ethan lounged on the couch, as he flicked through videos on YouTube. He wasn't really paying attention, his thoughts drifting as he absently fiddled with the edge of the blanket draped over his waist. The crunch of tires on gravel pulled him from his haze.

The front door opened, and Lillian stepped inside carrying two grocery bags. She looked at Ethan and smiled. "Hey there! Can you help me with the rest of these? There are a few more bags in the car."

Ethan swung his legs off the couch, setting the blanket aside. "Oh, sure," he said, hurrying to join her at the door.

As they crossed the porch, Lillian spoke again. "Sorry I

didn't leave a note this morning. I didn't mean to make you wonder where I'd gone. I'll remember next time."

Ethan shrugged as they reached her car. "It's fine. I figured you'd be back soon."

"Well, I'll make sure to let you know in the future," Lillian said with a nod. "I don't want you worrying."

Ethan grabbed two bags from the backseat and followed her back into the house.

The two of them worked in comfortable silence, unpacking the groceries, and filling the pantry and fridge.

"I thought it'd be a good idea to mention," Lillian said as she placed a carton of eggs in the refrigerator, "I work at the library three days a week. Normally, anyway. I've taken a little time off while you settle in."

"Library?" Ethan asked, sliding a loaf of bread into the cupboard.

"Yep," Lillian replied. "It's small, but cozy. Lots of books, and the occasional interesting character comes through."

"Do you like it?" Ethan asked, glancing at her.

"I do," Lillian said with a smile. "Books have always been

my thing, I guess. It's nice to work somewhere quiet."

Ethan nodded, unsure of what to say. Lillian seemed at ease now, moving around the kitchen as she put some cookies away. He felt a flicker of gratitude for how she was trying to make him feel at home.

Once the last of the groceries had been put away, Lillian turned to Ethan. "What do you say we head into town for a bit? I can show you around, give you the grand tour. We can grab some lunch while we're at it."

"Into town?" Ethan echoed.

"Yeah," Lillian said with a small laugh. "It's not far, and I think it'll be good for you to get out and see the place. Plus, you'll know where everything is. What do you think?"

Ethan hesitated for a moment before nodding. "Okay, sure."

"Great! I'll just grab my bag, and we'll head out," she said.

A short drive later, they arrived in the heart of town. The main street was lined with small shops and cafes, their signs swinging gently in the morning breeze. The buildings were a mix of brick and pastel-painted facades, giving the street a warm charm.

"This is it," Lillian said as they stepped out of the car. "Not exactly Chicago, huh?"

Ethan gave a small smile. "Definitely not."

As they walked, Lillian pointed out notable spots. "That's the diner," she said, gesturing to a cheerful building with a red-and-white awning. "They make the best milkshakes in town. Chocolate, strawberry, vanilla, you name it."

Ethan chuckled softly as they walked by a bakery with a window display full of cakes and pastries.

Further along, they came upon a small toy store, its window brimming with board games, action figures, and colorful displays. Ethan slowed slightly, his eyes catching on a model kit of a spaceship. Lillian noticed and smiled.

"You like that kind of thing?" she asked, nodding toward the window.

Ethan shrugged, but his eyes lingered on the kit. "Yeah, they're cool. My mom used to get me these sometimes."

Lillian paused for a moment before saying, "Well, let's go inside and take a look."

Ethan blinked. "Really?"

"Really," Lillian said with a grin.

Inside, Ethan wandered the aisles, his fingers brushing over the shelves. Lillian followed, watching as he carefully picked up the spaceship kit he'd seen in the window.

"Alright," she said, reaching for her wallet. "Let's get it."

"You don't have to…" Ethan began, but Lillian cut him off.

"I know I don't have to," she said. "But I want to. Consider it a welcome gift."

Ethan hesitated, then smiled shyly. "Thank you."

"You're welcome," Lillian replied warmly as they walked to the counter.

They ended up at a small cafe with a chalkboard menu propped outside. Lillian ordered a turkey sandwich and tea, while Ethan opted for a cheeseburger and soda. They sat by a window, sunlight streaming in as they ate.

"So, what do you think of the town so far?" Lillian asked between bites.

"It's… nice," Ethan said. "Quieter than I'm used to, but not in a bad way."

"Good," Lillian said with a nod. "I think you'll like it here once you settle in. People are friendly, and there's always something happening, even if it's just a small-town event."

Ethan didn't respond right away, his gaze drifting to the street outside. He watched a group of kids riding bikes and a couple walking hand in hand. It wasn't what he was used to, but maybe that wasn't a bad thing.

Lillian seemed to pick up on his thoughts. "It'll take time," she said gently. "But I think you'll find your rhythm here. And I'm here to help, okay?"

Ethan nodded. "Thanks."

After lunch, they strolled back to the car, pausing to peek into shop windows. By the time they returned home, Ethan was a little more at ease.

As they stepped inside, Lillian set her bag on the counter and turned to Ethan with a smile. "Thanks for coming with me today. I really enjoyed it."

"Yeah," Ethan said, a small smile tugging at the corners of his mouth. "Me too. And thanks again for the kit."

"You're welcome," Lillian said.

EIGHT

Wilbur "Willy" Grant II sat perched on a tree stump, his rifle resting across his knees. A cranky, middle-aged man, Willy didn't care for the government or anyone who tried to tell him what to do. He prided himself on living life on his own terms, far from prying eyes, and that suited him just fine. He'd been out since late afternoon, the November chill seeping into his bones. Tonight, he was after coyotes.

The cooler weather made the coyotes desperate, driving them closer to homes and livestock. Willy didn't have any livestock of his own, but he didn't like animals. To him, they were messy, unpredictable, and a nuisance. He considered himself a master of the craft, his calls designed to fool even the wariest of creatures. He set up his decoys: a battered but effective electronic call and a realistic coyote silhouette. Rifle at the ready, he crouched low, his keen eyes scanning the trees.

The call emitted its first mournful howl, echoing through the woods. Willy adjusted his position, settling into the familiar flow of the hunt.

Minutes passed. Every sound seemed to sharpen, every movement catching his attention. He smiled to himself, imagining the coyote that would inevitably slink into view, drawn by hunger and curiosity.

Another howl erupted from the call, followed by the panicked yips of a distressed animal. Willy tensed, his fingers brushing the trigger. Something moved in the underbrush, just beyond his line of sight. He leaned forward, squinting in the late afternoon light.

A sharp caw cut through the stillness as a crow landed on a branch near him. Its beady eyes fixed on Willy, and it began squawking loudly, its cries almost jarring in the quiet of the woods. Willy scowled, waving a hand at the bird to shoo it away, but the crow stayed, its harsh voice echoing through the trees.

Willy gave up trying to shoo the crow away and looked beyond the decoys, noticing a shape emerging low to the ground. He froze. This wasn't a coyote. It was larger, its movements unnatural. For a moment, he thought it might be a wolf, but no wolf moved like that. The figure paused, its eyes glowing with an unnatural intensity as they caught the light.

"What the hell?" Willy mumbled, his voice barely above a whisper.

He adjusted his aim, his hands steady despite the surge of adrenaline flooding his veins. The creature stood, its form shifting in a way that defied logic. It rose onto two legs, towering over the decoys. Willy gasped. It wasn't a wolf, nor any animal he'd ever encountered. Its muscular frame was covered in coarse, dark fur, and its face was a monstrous, snarling hybrid of beast and nightmare.

The creature's lips curled back, revealing jagged teeth that gleamed in the light. It let out a growl that made Willy grab his chest. Every instinct screamed at him to run, but he was rooted to the spot, his mind grappling with the impossibility of what he was seeing.

"It can't be," Willy mumbled.

Finally, instincts took over. Willy fired, the crack of his .22 rifle splitting the silence. The bullet hit the creature, leaving a small wound that barely seemed to register. It glanced down at the spot with what seemed like annoyance, then fixed its burning amber eyes back on Willy. The seething rage behind its glare was so intense that Willy's bladder betrayed him.

"Oh, shit," Willy breathed, fumbling to reload. The creature dropped to all fours and charged, covering the distance between them in a heartbeat. Willy barely had time to raise his rifle before it was upon him, swiping the weapon aside with a single, powerful blow.

He stumbled back, drawing the hunting knife from his belt. The blade gleamed as he slashed at the creature, landing a shallow cut across its arm. The beast roared, its hot breath washing over him as it bared its teeth. Willy's heart pounded in his chest as he swung again, his knife biting into the creature's side. It howled in pain but didn't retreat.

Before Willy could strike again, the creature's clawed hand shot out, grabbing him by the wrist. Its grip was like iron, unyielding and impossibly strong. With a savage twist, it wrenched the knife from his grasp and flung it into the woods. Willy screamed as the creature's claws dug into his arm, warm blood trickling down his sleeve.

"Let go, you son of a bitch!" he shouted, struggling to free himself. He kicked at its legs, but it was like trying to move a tree trunk. The creature's other hand shot forward, claws slicing through his jacket and into his flesh. Pain erupted in his side, and he gasped, his vision swimming.

The beast lifted him off the ground effortlessly, its fiery eyes boring into his. True fear gripped Willy; a primal, all-consuming terror paralyzed him. The creature's jaws opened wide, and Willy knew this was the end.

With a final, guttural snarl, the beast hurled him to the ground. His body hit the dirt with a sickening thud, pain radiating through every inch of him. His chest heaved as if his heart was straining under the weight of his terror, each beat harder and more frantic than the last. He tried to crawl away, his fingers clawing at the earth, but the creature was faster. It pounced, its weight crushing him as its claws tore into his back.

The creature was in no rush, savoring the fear that radiated from Willy with every panicked breath.

Willy screamed, a raw, agonized sound that echoed through the woods. The creature's jaws closed around the back of his head, its teeth sinking deep. Blood spilled onto the ground, pooling beneath him as his vision blurred.

In his final moments, Willy's thoughts were a chaotic

jumble. He thought of his cabin, his solitary life, the countless hunts that had brought him joy. He thought of the coyotes he had so often outwitted and the irony of his own hubris leading to this.

The Dogman tore into him, feeding until its hunger was satisfied. The snow beneath its paws darkened with blood, steam rising from the torn remains in the cold air. Then, as the predator vanished into the darkness, the coyotes crept in, their yellow eyes gleaming as they circled what was left. They had waited for their turn, just as they always did.

When it was over, nothing remained of Willy Grant but scraps of torn clothing and the blood-soaked earth.

No one would ever know what happened to old Willy.

NINE

The sound of knocking startled Lillian as she stood in the kitchen, stirring a pot of soup for dinner. She wiped her hands on a dish towel and walked to the door, peeking through the side window. Two boys, about Ethan's age, stood on the porch, shifting their weight and glancing around.

She opened the door, smiling warmly. "Hello there. Can I help you?"

The taller one of the two with blonde hair, grinned and spoke up. "Hi, I'm Nick, and this is Ryan. We were wondering if Ethan's home."

Lillian tilted her head, studying them briefly. "You're friends of his?"

"We met him the other day," Nick said quickly. "We were riding bikes, and he seemed cool, so we thought we'd stop by."

Ryan stood slightly behind Nick, his hands shoved deep into his hoodie pockets. He gave Lillian a polite nod but didn't say anything.

Lillian opened the door wider and motioned for them to come inside. "Sure, come on in."

Ethan was in the living room, flipping through channels with a bored expression. Lillian poked her head in. "Ethan, you have visitors."

He looked up, surprised. "Visitors?"

She nodded and Ethan got up, wandering over to see who it was. When he saw Nick and Ryan, his face lit up slightly.

"Hey," he said, shoving his hands into his pockets. "How'd you guys know where I live?"

Nick grinned. "I live just up the street. Small town, you know. Everybody knows everything."

Ryan grinned. "And I'm next door. Not that it matters since I'm always hanging out at Nick's anyway."

Ethan laughed softly, shaking his head. "Figures."

"So," Nick said, glancing around the living room, "you got a PlayStation or something?"

Ethan shook his head. "Nope. Never had one."

Ryan raised an eyebrow. "Seriously? What do you even do for fun, stare at the walls?"

Nick elbowed him. "Ryan! Chill, dude."

Ryan snorted. "What? I'm just saying."

Nick grinned at Ethan. "Don't mind him. He thinks he's funny. Wanna come over to my place? I've got a PlayStation."

Ethan hesitated, glancing toward Lillian. "Is that okay?"

Lillian smiled. "Sure, as long as you're back for dinner."

Ethan turned back to Nick and Ryan. "Alright, let's go."

The three boys walked to Nick's house, just up the street. Nick led the way, his bike rolling beside him, while Ryan trailed behind, occasionally making snarky comments.

When they arrived, Nick pushed open the gate to a modest house with a red door and a basketball hoop over the garage. "Come on in," he said, leading the way.

Inside, the living room was cozy, with a big couch and a large TV mounted on the wall. A PlayStation sat on the stand beneath it, surrounded by stacks of games and a few scattered controllers.

"This is it," Nick said, grabbing a controller and handing another to Ryan.

"Make yourself at home," Nick added, flopping onto the couch and patting the seat next to him. Ethan sat down, taking in the room. "My parents aren't home for another two hours."

Ryan snorted. "You're about to lose, new guy," he said, handing Ethan a controller.

The next couple of hours flew by in a blur of laughs, shouted victories and groans of defeat. Ethan quickly got the hang of the game, surprising Nick with a couple of close wins.

"Okay, one more race," Ryan said, leaning forward with his competitive grin.

"You said that last time," Ethan teased, but he picked up the controller again.

Nick laughed. "He says that every time. Just beat him, and we'll shut it down."

As the sun began to set, Ethan stood up. "I should get back home. Thanks for letting me play."

Ryan raised an eyebrow. "Want us to walk you back? You know, just in case you're scared of the dark or something." He laughed at his own joke.

Ethan rolled his eyes. "No thanks. I think I can manage."

Nick grinned and nudged Ryan. "Come on, leave him alone. You're such a jerk sometimes."

Ryan shrugged, still chuckling. "What? I'm just looking out for him."

Ethan shook his head, smiling slightly. "I'll see you guys later."

"Yeah, we'll stop by again soon," Nick said with a wave.

Ethan waved back as he turned toward Lillian's house, feeling lighter than he had in days.

When he walked through the door, Lillian looked up from the kitchen, where she was setting the table. "Right on time," she said, smiling. "How was it?"

"It was fun," Ethan said, kicking off his shoes. "Ryan's got some great games. I almost beat Nick a couple of times."

"Well, I'm glad you enjoyed yourself," Lillian said. "Dinner's ready."

The table was set with bowls of steaming soup, slices of buttered bread, and a pitcher of water. Ethan sat down, feeling more at ease than he had in days.

"You look like you're in a better mood," Lillian said as she ladled soup into his bowl.

"Yeah," Ethan said, a small smile on his face. "I guess I am."

Dinner was eaten in comfortable silence; afterward, Ethan cleared the table as Lillian washed the dishes.

Later, they settled in the living room, the TV playing softly in the background. Ethan watched for a while, but his eyelids grew heavy as the day's activities caught up with him.

Lillian sat in her favorite chair, crocheting a scarf and glancing at Ethan every now and then. When he yawned and stretched, she smiled.

"Bedtime for you, I think," she said gently.

Ethan nodded, rubbing his eyes as he stood up.

"Don't forget to brush your teeth," Lillian reminded him.

"Got it," Ethan replied with a sleepy nod, heading down the hall and into the bathroom. He turned on the faucet, squeezing toothpaste onto his brush before scrubbing at his teeth, his movements slow with exhaustion.

"Goodnight, Ethan," Lillian called after him.

"Goodnight," he mumbled back around the toothbrush before rinsing his mouth. A moment later, he padded to his room and closed the door behind him.

As the house settled into silence, Lillian leaned back in her chair, her fingers moving idly through the yarn. A small smile touched her lips as life was finally finding its rhythm again.

TEN

Ethan woke with a start. At first, he couldn't pinpoint what had roused him. His bedroom was dark, the faint outline of the curtains glowing softly with moonlight. Half-asleep, he lay still, listening to the quiet hum of the house.

A faint, rhythmic sound then caught his attention.

Footsteps.

He turned onto his side to face the wall, assuming it was Lillian walking around the house. But as the sound grew clearer, his mind sharpened. The steps were too heavy. Each one landed with a faint clicking sound, like nails or claws lightly tapping against the floor.

His chest tightened, his breath quickening as realization

set in. This wasn't Lillian.

The footsteps continued, moving through the house. They started in the living room, shifted to the kitchen, and then looped back again. Ethan lay frozen, his ears straining to follow the sound.

Lillian must have a reason for walking laps around the house, right? Maybe she couldn't sleep? Maybe...

The sound changed direction, heading down the hallway toward his room. Ethan's stomach knotted, and he squeezed his eyes shut. The steps paused just outside his door, and the air in his room seemed to thicken, closing in on him with a suffocating stillness.

For a long moment, there was nothing.

Finally, summoning what little courage he could muster, Ethan sat up. His heart hammered as he swung his legs over the side of the bed, his bare feet brushing against the cool floor.

"It's just Lillian," he whispered to himself, the words thin and unconvincing. Maybe she couldn't sleep. Maybe something startled her. That's all it was.

He crept to the door and opened it slowly.

The hallway stretched out before him, dimly lit by a lamp in the living room. It was empty.

"Lillian?" he whispered, his voice barely audible.

No response.

He stepped into the hallway, glancing toward her room. The door was closed.

"Lillian?" he called again, a little louder this time.

Still nothing.

A chill ran through him. The house seemed strange, as if something unseen was lingering just out of reach. He stood there for a moment longer, debating whether to knock on her door or go back to his bed.

In the end, the unnerving silence won. He turned and hurried back to his room, shutting the door behind him.

Sliding under the covers, he pulled the quilt up to his chin, his pulse still racing. He stared at the ceiling, his ears straining for any hint of sound.

He shut his eyes tightly, willing himself to ignore the creeping unease. Maybe it was his imagination, a trick of his tired mind. The house was old. Old houses creak and settle, right?

But deep down, he knew that wasn't true.

Overtaken by exhaustion, he drifted off to a fitful sleep, the faint echo of footsteps still in his head.

ELEVEN

Snow fell steadily, blanketing the backyard in shimmering white. Thick flakes drifted from the sky, piling on tree branches, and frosting the edges of the window. It muffled the world outside, making everything seem quiet and far away.

Inside, Ethan stirred in his bed, blinking awake. The chill in the air made him pull the blanket tighter around him. For a moment, he forgot where he was, half expecting to hear his mom calling him for breakfast like she always used to. But the memory hit him hard, and the ache in his chest returned.

She wasn't here.

With a sigh, he glanced toward the window. Snow was

coming down hard, covering everything in the backyard. It was kind of cool to watch, but it didn't hold his attention for long.

Sliding out of bed, he grabbed his hoodie from the chair and slipped it on before heading into the hallway. The smell of waffles and maple syrup drifted through the air, pulling him toward the kitchen.

"Good morning, sleepyhead," Lillian greeted him as he walked in. She stood at the stove, flipping waffles onto a plate. A small radio on the counter played an upbeat song, adding a little life to the quiet room.

"Morning," Ethan mumbled, rubbing his eyes.

"Snow's really coming down out there," she said, nodding toward the window. "Thought waffles would be a good start to the day."

Ethan slid into a chair at the table and glanced outside. "It's coming down like crazy," he said, reaching for the syrup. "Guess there's not much else to do, huh?"

"Not really," Lillian said, setting a plate of waffles in front of him. "It's the first significant snowfall, so we might just stay inside and keep warm. People always forget how to drive in the snow and start driving like idiots."

Ethan dug into his food, savoring the warmth and sweetness. For a brief period, everything seemed normal. But as he ate, his mind drifted back to the night before. The sound of footsteps and the weird clicking noise.

"Hey, Lillian?" he asked, hesitantly.

"Hmm?" She sat down across from him, her own plate of waffles in hand.

"Were you walking around the house last night?"

She paused, her fork halfway to her mouth. "No, I wasn't. Why?"

Ethan hesitated again, suddenly feeling silly for asking. "I thought I heard someone. Like… walking around. And then they stopped outside my door."

Lillian frowned a little, setting her fork down. "Walking? Where?"

"Everywhere," Ethan said. "It sounded like they were in the living room, then the kitchen, and then the hall. The steps were really heavy, like an elephant."

For a moment, Lillian didn't say anything. She glanced toward the window, her lips pressed into a thin line. "This house is old," she said after a moment. "It creaks a lot, especially with the snow and cold. Maybe that's all it was."

Ethan nodded, but her answer didn't make him feel better. "Yeah. Maybe."

Lillian reached across the table, giving his hand a reassuring squeeze. "You're safe here, okay? Don't let your imagination run away with you."

"Okay," Ethan said, managing a small smile. He picked up his fork and took another bite, though the uneasy feeling stayed with him.

After finishing breakfast, Ethan helped Lillian wash the dishes and put away the leftovers.

As he glanced out at the backyard, the sound of those footsteps played over in his mind. It hadn't sounded like creaking wood. It had been steady, loud, and clear.

But if it wasn't Lillian, then who, or what, was it?

He shook his head, trying to push the thought out of his mind. Lillian was right. He was safe here. He just had to stop overthinking everything.

"Thanks for helping," Lillian said, giving him a smile as

she dried her hands on a towel.

"No problem," Ethan replied, turning toward the hallway. "I think I'm gonna go work on my spaceship for a bit."

"Alright," she said. "Let me know if you need anything."

"Okay," he said, already heading toward his room. He grabbed the box from the shelf, sat down at his desk, and opened it to reveal the spaceship model. Taking a deep breath, he tried to focus on assembling it, using the tiny pieces as a distraction from the questions swirling in his mind.

TWELVE

The days passed uneventfully. Snow continued to fall in fits and starts, adding layers to the white blanket that covered the town. Lillian stayed busy with errands and household tasks, while Ethan spent his time reading, watching TV, or hanging out with Nick and Ryan. Their days settled into a steady routine, occasionally broken by Lillian's efforts to get Ethan enrolled in the local middle school.

"You'll start after Thanksgiving," Lillian had told him over breakfast one morning, sliding a freshly toasted bagel onto his plate. "I thought it'd be best to let you settle in first."

Ethan nodded, grateful for the extra time. "Yeah, that's probably a good idea. At least Nick and Ryan will be there," he said, a small smile creeping onto his face.

"It'll be nice for you to have some friends already," Lillian agreed, giving him an encouraging look.

Later that day, Lillian came home with a shopping bag and set it on the kitchen table. "I picked up a few things for school," she said with a smile.

Ethan wandered over, curious. Inside the bag was a sleek black backpack, a stack of notebooks, a pack of colorful pens, and some folders with bold designs.

"This is cool," Ethan said, pulling out the backpack and slinging it over his shoulder. He glanced at her with a shy smile. "Thanks, Lillian."

"You're welcome, sweetheart," she said, giving his shoulder a gentle squeeze. "Figured it'd be good to get ahead. I know starting a new school isn't easy, but I think you'll settle in just fine."

"Yeah," Ethan said, inspecting the notebooks. "It's not like I've never done this before."

"You'll do great," Lillian reassured him, smiling warmly.

Ethan spent a few minutes arranging the supplies on his desk. Even though he wasn't looking forward to starting school, having the new gear and knowing Nick and Ryan would be there made it seem a little less intimidating.

Over the next couple of days, Ethan spent more time with Nick and Ryan. The boys had shown him around town, pointing out the local diner, the ice cream shop (closed for the season), and the tiny arcade near the post office. Nick was especially eager to include him in plans, and tonight was no different.

"We're watching movies at Nick's tonight," Ethan had told Lillian at lunch earlier that day. "Ryan's coming too. I'll probably be back tomorrow morning."

"That's fine," Lillian had said. "Just make sure to call if you need anything."

Now, as Ethan finished packing an overnight bag in his room, he heard a soft knock at the door.

"Come in," he called, glancing over his shoulder as Lillian entered. She was carrying a small stack of folded laundry, which she set on the bed.

"I know you won't be home tonight," she began, smoothing the edge of one of his T-shirts, "but I thought I'd let you know a friend of mine is coming over for dinner later."

Ethan turned, curious. "You have a boyfriend?"

Lillian let out a warm laugh. "Yes, child, I'm fifty-eight, not dead."

Ethan snickered, his cheeks flushing slightly. "I didn't mean it like that! You just never said anything."

"I wanted you to feel at home first," she said. "Carter and I have been partners for years now and he usually stays over a few nights a week. He's good company, and he's bringing over a pie for dessert, so I certainly can't complain. He's also the town's sheriff."

"The sheriff? That's kind of awesome," Ethan said, his tone light but intrigued.

Lillian smiled. "He is. Now, do you have everything you need?"

Ethan nodded, zipping up his bag. "Yeah, I'm all set."

"Alright. Be safe, remember to call if you need anything, and don't cause too much trouble," she added with a knowing smile.

"I won't," Ethan promised, grabbing his bag. "Have fun with your sheriff boyfriend."

She shook her head, amused, as she watched him leave the room. "Go on, get out of here," she said affectionately.

THIRTEEN

The air was tinged with the faint smell of woodsmoke as Ethan stepped out onto the porch. He zipped up his coat and adjusted his hoodie, gripping the strap of his overnight bag tightly. Tonight was different. Excitement stirred in him again, something he hadn't experienced in a while. A night of movies and laughter with Nick and Ryan sounded good, and the thought brought a small, genuine smile to his face.

As he walked down the quiet road, he passed a few yards where kids had built snowmen earlier in the day, their lumpy shapes now casting creepy silhouettes. Feeling the cold on his ears, he pulled his hoodie further down.

A crow landed on the roof of a nearby house, its dark shape barely noticeable against the night sky. It sat motionless, its piercing eyes fixed on Ethan as he walked. He didn't notice it at first, but just as he passed, it let out a sudden, sharp squawk.

Ethan flinched and glanced up, spotting the bird watching him. A chill crawled up his spine, not from the cold, but from the sudden awareness of being observed. He tore his gaze away and quickened his pace.

But then, he sensed a shift in the air.

And a presence. A prickling sensation on the back of his neck, like someone's eyes were fixed on him.

He glanced over his shoulder, the feeling of being watched intensifying. Nothing moved. The houses stood silent, their backyards stretching into the dark outline of the forest beyond. He shook his head, telling himself it was just the bird freaking him out.

But as he continued walking, the sensation grew stronger, as though unseen eyes followed his every step.

He stopped abruptly, his boots sinking slightly into the snow. The sensation didn't fade. Slowly, he turned his head, scanning the dimly lit street and the dark spaces between the houses. Still nothing. No one. Just the growing shadows and the faint flicker of porch lights in the distance.

Ethan's heart thudded in his chest. He swallowed hard and forced himself to keep walking, quickening his pace slightly.

"It's nothing," he said under his breath. "Just my imagination."

The feeling didn't fade, and it seemed to emanate from behind the row of houses to his left. He glanced toward the backyards, squinting into the dimness. The forest loomed there, its edges blurred by the dusky light.

The crow landed on a nearby fence, letting out a series of loud squawks. Ethan ignored it and quickened his pace.

The prickle on the back of his neck intensified, and a wave of unease swept over him. Every instinct screamed at him to look back again, but he resisted, keeping his eyes fixed on Nick's house.

As he reached the driveway, he practically jogged up to the porch, his pulse pounding in his ears. He turned, scanning the street and the houses behind him one last time.

Nothing moved.

The crow was gone.

The night was still.

Ethan exhaled deeply and knocked on Nick's door, his knuckles rapping against the wood with more urgency than he intended. He shifted his weight nervously, glancing back over his shoulder again. The prickle on his neck was still there, though he couldn't see anything unusual.

A moment later, the door swung open, and Nick's grinning face appeared. "Hey, you made it!" he said, stepping aside to let Ethan in. The warmth of the house spilled out, wrapping around Ethan like a blanket.

"Yeah," Ethan said. He stepped inside quickly, closing the door behind him. "Thanks."

Nick frowned slightly. "You okay? You look like you've seen a ghost."

Ethan hesitated, then shook his head. "It's nothing. Just the walk over... was kinda weird."

Nick shrugged, already heading toward the living room where the TV was playing. "Well, you're here now. Come on, Ryan's already eating the good snacks."

Ethan followed, determined to put the uneasy feeling behind him and focus on having a fun night.

FOURTEEN

The darkness was its domain, cloaking its massive form as it crouched low among the trees. The house stood at the edge of the woods, a place that had been pulling it closer with each passing night. Although a subtle scent, its undeniable presence triggered an overwhelming, primal reaction impossible to ignore.

Its piercing eyes gleamed faintly, watching as the door creaked open. A young hairless one stepped out, the light from the house spilling briefly across his form before he disappeared into the dim yard. The boy started walking, heading down the narrow path between his house and another nearby.

With slow, steady breaths, the huge Dogman watched, its

chest rising and falling. It did not need to rush. The thrill was not in the kill. It was in the hunt, in the careful, deliberate stalking that stirred the fear in its prey. Fear was a feast all its own, something that made its blood surge with excitement.

The boy wandered farther from the safety of his home, pausing to glance over his shoulder. The Dogman shifted slightly, its claws scraping softly against the bark of a tree. The sound was quiet but enough to stir unease. The boy's head snapped up, his body tense as he glanced into the darkness.

The creature didn't move, content to let the boy's imagination do the work. Fear was like smoke, invisible but filling the air, and the Dogman could almost taste it now.

It crept forward, each step silent, its frame blending seamlessly with the trees. The boy quickened his pace, his shoulders hunching as though he could sense the unseen eyes on him. The Dogman let out a low exhale, more breath than sound. The boy froze briefly before breaking into a hurried walk, his breath quickening.

Hidden from view, the Dogman watched the boy nervously scanned the trees. The boy's steps grew faster, his heart racing now, and a thrill surged through the Dogman.

It loved this part, the delicate balance between terror and confusion. The boy's fear, both intense and alluring, only fueled the predator's patience.

As the boy approached the other house, the Dogman lingered at the edge of the trees, its predatory eyes fixed on him. It didn't need to follow. Not yet.

This was the hunt, the part it craved most of all. The chase would come later, the attack later still. For now, it would let the fear sink deep into its prey, knowing it would stay with him even when the sun returned.

Satisfied, the Dogman turned back toward the woods, its piercing eyes lingering on the houses. The pull was still there, stronger now. It would return soon, but not to kill. Not yet. The boy's fear would be ripest after a few more nights of being watched, of hearing things in the darkness, of knowing something waited just out of sight.

It was patient. Fear was a game it always won.

FIFTEEN

The living room buzzed with laughter and the over-the-top dialogue of a cheesy action movie as Ethan, Nick and Ryan sprawled across the couches. Popcorn bowls and soda cans littered the coffee table, and for the first time since arriving at his grandmother's house, Ethan experienced the feeling of being a regular kid again.

"This movie's garbage," Nick declared, tossing a handful of popcorn into his mouth. "Who even thought it was a good idea to make four sequels to this?"

Ryan snorted. "Your dad's always streaming stuff like this. What does that say about him?"

Nick shot him a look. "It says he's old and stuck in the

past. What's your excuse? You're the one who suggested this one."

Ryan scoffed. "Because it's hilariously bad. You just don't get comedy."

Ethan chuckled softly, shaking his head at their banter.

Ryan suddenly sat up, tossing his empty soda can onto the table. "Okay, this is boring. Let's do something actually fun."

Nick groaned. "Here we go. What now? You wanna TP somebody's house?"

Ryan rolled his eyes. "Nah, that's for babies. I dare you guys to run to the stop sign at the end of the street and touch it."

Ethan frowned, glancing toward the window. The street beyond looked darker than it should, with only a weak halo of light from the porch casting a faint glow. "Why? What's so fun about that?"

Ryan leaned back, a smug grin spreading across his face. "Because it's freezing, it's creepy, and you're too scared to do it."

"I'm not afraid," Ethan retorted, his voice more cutting than he meant. "I just think it's stupid."

Nick laughed. "Same thing, dude. Scared is scared."

Ryan stood and grabbed his coat. "Fine. Prove me wrong. First one to chicken out buys the snacks tomorrow. Come on, let's go."

Ethan hesitated, the uneasy sensation from earlier creeping back. But there was no way he was letting Ryan get the last word. "Alright, fine." He grabbed his coat and gloves, mumbling under his breath, "This is dumb."

Nick groaned, pulling on his boots. "This better not take long. It's freezing out there."

When they stepped outside, the cold cut through Ethan's coat almost immediately. Their boots crunched through the snow, the sound loud in the still night.

"Alright, rules are simple," Ryan said, rubbing his hands together. "You run to the stop sign, touch it, and come back. No stopping, no excuses. Got it?"

"Got it," Ethan said, glancing again toward the woods.

Nick stuffed his hands into his pockets, already shivering.

"Why do I feel like you're gonna turn this into some kind of horror movie setup?"

Ryan grinned, his teeth flashing. "What? You think there's some psycho hiding out there? If you're that scared, you can hold my hand."

Nick huffed. "You're impossible."

They set off, their boots sinking slightly into the soft snow. The surrounding silence seemed unnatural, with every sound amplified by the night. Ethan's chest tightened as his imagination ran wild. Every dark outline of a tree looked like it was leaning toward them, every sound in the distance seemed to grow closer.

"This isn't so bad," Nick said, his voice cutting through the quiet.

They were halfway to the stop sign when Ryan suddenly froze. He stopped so abruptly that Ethan nearly bumped into him.

"Did you hear that?" Ryan whispered, his voice barely above a breath.

Ethan frowned, his pulse quickening. "Hear what?"

Ryan tilted his head toward the woods, his gaze narrowing. "Footsteps."

Nick laughed nervously, the sound out of place in the stillness. "It's probably just a raccoon or something. Keep going."

Ryan didn't move at first, his eyes fixed on the tree line. Then, with a shrug, he started walking again. "You're probably right. Just a raccoon."

Ethan quickened his pace, his eyes glued to the stop sign ahead. The dark shapes of trees seemed to ripple as if something massive shifted among them, but when he looked again, everything was still.

When they finally reached the stop sign, Ryan slapped it triumphantly, his grin returning. "See? Told you it was no big deal."

Nick touched the icy metal next, mumbling under his breath. "This was a stupid dare."

Ethan reached out and tapped the sign, exhaling in relief. "Alright, let's go back. It's freezing."

Ryan turned, scanning the street behind them. "You guys scared of the dark or something?"

"No," Nick said. "Let's just get back already."

As they started back, Ethan couldn't shake the prickling sensation crawling up his neck. It felt like unseen eyes were tracking their every step, hidden somewhere in the darkness beyond the streetlights. He tried to focus on the crunch of their boots, the rhythmic sound keeping him grounded until Ryan suddenly yelled, "Run!"

The panic in Ryan's voice ignited a surge of adrenaline in Ethan. He bolted without looking back, his boots slipping slightly on the snow as his lungs burned from the freezing air. Nick followed close behind, his breath coming fast and uneven.

They didn't stop running until they reached Nick's porch, collapsing against the railing, gasping for air. Ethan's heart hammered in his chest as he rounded on Ryan. "What the hell was that?"

Ryan was doubled over laughing. "Nothing! I just wanted to see if you'd freak out."

Nick glared at him. "Are you kidding me? You're such a jerk!"

Ryan shrugged, still grinning. "It was hilarious. Admit it."

Ethan shook his head, though a faint smile tugged at his lips. "You're insane."

Nick jabbed a finger at him. "Next time, you're buying the snacks."

The warmth of the house was a welcome relief as they stepped inside, kicking off their snow-dusted boots.

Nick's mom walked into the room, her brows raised in suspicion. "Why were you boys outside?"

Nick and Ryan exchanged a glance, scrambling for an answer, but nothing believable came to mind.

"We, uh…" Nick started, but his voice trailed off.

His mom folded her arms. "Uh-huh. Whatever it was, don't do it again. It's too late and too cold to be running around out there."

"Yes, ma'am," Nick said, grateful she didn't press the issue further.

Nick rolled his eyes as she walked away. "That could've been worse."

SIXTEEN

The movie marathon continued late into the night, laughter, and jokes filling Nick's living room. The boys' voices grew louder as they reenacted ridiculous scenes from the movies, throwing popcorn and cracking up at their own antics. The TV blared cheesy dialogue in the background, barely audible over the chaos.

Suddenly, Nick's parents came into the living room, their expressions a mix of amusement and mild irritation.

"Alright, boys, it's late," Nick's dad said, crossing his arms. "Time to settle down."

"And keep it quiet," his mom added, pointing at Nick. "The walls aren't as thick as you think."

The boys exchanged sheepish grins, realizing how loud they'd been. The TV, still blaring, now seemed deafening in the sudden stillness.

"Yes, ma'am," Nick said, giving a mock salute as he grabbed for the remote. His parents rolled their eyes but smiled as they turned to head back into their bedroom. With a chorus of exaggerated groans, the boys began unrolling their sleeping bags and tossing pillows around, their earlier energy fading as the late hour caught up with them.

Huddled in their sleeping bags, the boys watched a quieter TV channel, the dim light a comfort against the darkness. Ryan stretched out on the floor, groaning dramatically. "My back's gonna kill me tomorrow."

"Stop whining," Nick said, tossing a pillow at him. "It's not like your bed's much better."

Ethan chuckled, pulling the edge of his sleeping bag up around his shoulders. He was content, a rare feeling these days. The banter, the cozy house and good company made him feel like an average 12-year-old again.

As the room grew quieter, the boys drifted closer to sleep, their bodies overwhelmed with exhaustion. Ethan was just about to doze off when a howl broke through the silence, long and piercing. It came from somewhere outside, rising above the muffled hum of the television. Ethan shot upright in his sleeping bag, his heart pounding.

"Did you hear that?" he whispered.

Nick and Ryan stirred, sitting up groggily. "What?" Nick asked, rubbing his eyes.

"That," Ethan said, his voice tight. "That howl. You didn't hear it?"

The boys froze as another howl echoed through the night. This one was lower, more guttural, and seemed to stretch out unnaturally long. The sound made Ethan's skin crawl.

"Yeah, I hear it now," Ryan said, his voice quieter than usual.

"It's just a wolf," Nick said quickly. "Wolves howl. It's nothing to be scared of."

"There are wolves here?" Ethan asked, his voice a mix of curiosity and unease.

"Yeah," Ryan replied, shrugging. "We're near the woods. Wolves happen. Relax."

Nick lay back down. "They always sound cool to me," he

said.

Ethan stayed sitting for a moment longer, his ears straining for any other sounds. The howl still lingered in his mind, something about it feeling… wrong. But the house was quiet now, the soft sound of the TV the only thing breaking the stillness.

Eventually, he lay back down, pulling his sleeping bag tighter around him. He forced himself to close his eyes and breathe deeply, willing the tension to leave his body. The comfort of the house, the steady breathing of his friends, and the soft drone of the television finally lulled him into a deep sleep.

SEVENTEEN

A few days had passed since Ethan's night at Nick's house, and the unease from the howl had started to fade. The routine of quiet days at Lillian's house had taken over, and soon Thanksgiving arrived, bringing with it a fresh layer of snow and a sense of anticipation.

Thanksgiving morning dawned bright and cold, the sunlight glinting off the snow-covered rooftops and trees. Ethan woke to the smell of roasted turkey and baking pies wafting through the house. Lillian had been up since early, bustling around the kitchen with a kind of energy he hadn't seen in weeks. She had invited a few close friends and her partner, Carter, over for a late lunch, and the house was filled with the warm scents of holiday cooking.

Ethan wandered into the kitchen, still groggy but drawn by the delicious smells.

"Morning," he said, rubbing his eyes.

Lillian turned from the counter, a wooden spoon in hand and a streak of flour on her cheek. "Morning, sleepyhead. You ready for a busy day?"

Ethan shrugged, smiling faintly. "Yeah, I guess."

"You guess?" she teased. "Go get dressed. People will start arriving soon. And don't think you're getting out of helping set the table."

Ethan laughed softly, heading back to his room to change.

When he returned, Lillian glanced at him as she wiped her hands on a dish towel. Her eyes narrowed slightly, and she stepped closer, tilting her head. "What happened to your neck?"

Ethan frowned. "What do you mean?"

She reached out and gently brushed her fingers near the thin red scratch that ran from his neck up to his ear. "Looks like you scratched yourself in your sleep," she said, her tone casual, though a flicker of concern passed over her face. "Does it hurt?"

Ethan touched the spot gingerly, surprised he hadn't noticed it before. "No. Weird. I don't remember doing that."

"Must've been while you were tossing and turning," Lillian said, smiling as she returned to the stove. "Don't worry, it doesn't look bad."

Ethan shrugged it off, assuming she was right. By the time he finished setting the table, Lillian's friends were starting to arrive, their voices filling the small house with laughter and chatter. Sheriff Carter was among the first, carrying a bottle of wine and a pumpkin pie he claimed to have made himself, though the pristine store packaging hinted otherwise.

"Ethan," the sheriff said warmly, extending a hand. "Good to see you again."

Ethan shook his hand, offering a polite smile. "Hi, Sheriff Carter."

"Just Carter," the sheriff said with a warm grin. "Sheriff Carter makes it sound like I'm about to give you a speeding ticket. Around here, most folks just call me Carter, unless it's something official."

Ethan chuckled softly. "Alright… Carter."

Soon, the dining table was crowded with steaming dishes: turkey, stuffing, mashed potatoes, cranberry sauce, and more. Lillian beamed as she took her seat at the head of the table, motioning for everyone to dig in. Ethan joined in the laughter and conversation, but as the meal went on, he couldn't help but feel a pang of sadness. This was his first Thanksgiving without his mother, and her absence was like a shadow at the table.

"You okay?" Lillian asked quietly, leaning over as the others chatted.

Ethan nodded quickly, forcing a smile. "Yeah. Just thinking."

She gave his hand a squeeze, her eyes soft with understanding. "I'm glad you're here, Ethan."

After the meal, Ethan helped clear the table and wash the dishes. Once everything was cleaned and packed away, he found himself restless. He wandered to the living room window, looking out at the fresh blanket of snow.

"Hey, Lillian?" he called.

"Yes, dear?" Lillian replied, stepping into the room.

"Can I go meet up with Nick and Ryan? They're taking their snowmobiles out and said I could borrow one to ride around."

Lillian hesitated for a moment, then nodded. "As long as you're careful. And don't stay out too late. It gets dark fast this time of year."

"Thanks, I won't." Ethan said, grabbing his coat and gloves.

Nick and Ryan were already waiting when Ethan arrived, bundled up in thick jackets and scarves. The snowmobiles stood ready, their sleek forms gleaming in the sunlight.

"Took you long enough," Ryan called, tossing Ethan a helmet. "You ready to have some fun?"

"Definitely," Ethan said, strapping on the helmet. One of Nick's older brothers had lent him a spare machine, and after a quick tutorial, they were off.

The snowmobiles roared to life, their engines cutting through the cool air as the boys sped across the empty paddocks behind the neighborhood. The wide, open fields were perfect for riding, and Ethan quickly got the hang of steering and managing the throttle. The rush of cold wind against his face and the thrill of speed made him feel alive, his earlier melancholy fading into the background.

Nick led the way, weaving through the snow with ease. Ryan followed close behind, his laughter carried by the wind. Ethan brought up the rear, his confidence growing with each turn and jump over small drifts.

"This is awesome!" Ethan shouted, his voice muffled by the helmet but full of excitement.

The others whooped in agreement, their tracks carving wild patterns into the pristine snow. They raced each other across the fields, skidded around turns, and even stopped briefly to admire a frozen pond that glittered like glass in the fading sunlight.

As dusk began to settle, the boys parked their machines near the edge of the paddock, taking a break to catch their breath.

"Man, this is way better than sitting inside," Nick said, pulling off his helmet and shaking out his hair.

"No kidding," Ryan agreed, grinning. "I can't believe we almost didn't come out here."

"Yeah, this has been awesome," Ethan said.

"We should head back," Nick said, breaking the silence. "Mom'll kill me if I'm late getting back."

The others nodded, pulling their helmets back on and starting their snowmobiles. The machines roared to life, and the boys sped off toward home, their laughter echoing across the snow-covered paddocks.

EIGHTEEN

The snowmobiles roared across the open field, their engines tearing through the stillness of the winter evening. Ethan, Nick and Ryan leaned into their machines, steering them toward the distant row of houses that marked the edge of their development.

The snow crunched and sprayed beneath the tracks as they sped across the frozen ground. The air was cool, but the boys didn't seem to notice as they laughed and shouted above the roar of their engines. Nick led the way, Ryan close behind, and Ethan trailed slightly, his focus split between the glowing lights of the houses ahead and the tree line that bordered the field.

Then, he noticed just ahead, a crow landed in the snow-covered field, its dark shape standing out against the white expanse. It wasn't moving, just watching him. Ethan's grip on the handlebars tightened as an uneasy sensation crept up his spine. The memory of the crow from when he was walking to Nick's house, flashed in his mind. It had watched him then, too.

The crow let out two sharp squawks, the sound cutting through the hum of the snowmobiles. Ethan's pulse spiked. His gaze instinctively snapped toward the woods.

A flicker of motion caught his eye. Initially, he dismissed it as an illusion. A trick of the light or the wind playing through the trees. But then it emerged, unmistakable.

A towering figure moved through the foliage, its nightmarish shape gliding between the trees with an unsettling, otherworldly grace. Ethan's gasped. The thing was huge, its size impossible to miss even in the dim light.

"Nick!" Ethan shouted, his voice cracking as he pointed toward the woods.

Nick slowed his snowmobile and glanced back, his grin fading the instant his gaze followed Ethan's finger. "What the hell?"

Ryan, hearing the panic in their voices, let off the throttle and fell back beside them. "What's going on?"

Ethan could barely get the words out. "There's… something… in the woods!"

Ryan turned to look, confusion etched on his face. "What are you…"

Before he could finish, the creature moved again, weaving between the skeletal trees.

"Is that a… wolf?" Ryan stammered, his voice trembling.

"Wolves don't get that big," Nick snapped, his eyes wide with fear.

"It's following us," Ethan said.

The three boys exchanged a panicked glance before Nick shouted, "Go!"

Their engines roared as they gunned the snowmobiles forward, racing across the field. Snow sprayed up in wide arcs, the machines vibrating beneath them as they pushed for speed. Ethan's heart pounded as he risked a glance back.

The creature was still there, weaving through the trees like a shadow come to life. Its glowing eyes never left them, and its long, powerful strides kept it effortlessly in line with their pace.

"Faster!" Nick yelled, panicking.

Ethan leaned into the handlebars, his engine screaming as he urged the snowmobile to go faster. His breath came in quick bursts, his chest tight with fear.

"It's still there!" Ryan shouted.

Ethan glanced back again and felt his stomach drop. The beast was drawing nearer, its immense size parting the trees with frightening ease.

"What the hell is that thing?" Ryan yelled, panic rising in his tone.

"I don't know!" Nick shouted back. "Just keep going!"

The lights of Nick's house came into view, glowing faintly against the darkening sky. The boys pushed their snowmobiles to the limit, the engines roaring as the machines sped toward the driveway.

Ethan's heart pounded so hard it felt like it might burst. He couldn't stop glancing at the creature. Its powerful limbs churned through the snow, its head low, and its eyes fixed on them. It was relentless, as if nothing could stop it.

Finally, the snowmobiles skidded to a halt in Nick's driveway, sending snow flying in all directions. Ethan jumped off the moment his machine stopped, his boots slipping on the icy ground as he bolted toward the street.

"Ethan, wait!" Nick shouted, but Ethan didn't stop.

Ryan and Nick didn't hesitate either. They ran straight into the house, slamming the door behind them.

Ethan's legs burned as he sprinted toward his grandmother's house, his throat burning from the exertion and frigid air.

By the time he reached Lillian's front door, his chest ached, each breath growing more strained. He burst inside and closed the door behind him, locking it without thinking.

"Ethan?" Lillian's voice called from the living room, tinged with concern.

He didn't respond. He ran straight to his room, shutting the door and collapsing onto the bed. His chest heaved as he tried to calm his racing heart, but the terror refused to fade.

Down the street, Nick, and Ryan stood in Nick's living room as they stared at each other.

"What the hell was that?" Ryan asked, his voice trembling.

Nick didn't answer immediately. His gaze drifted to the back window, where the dark field loomed just beyond the glow of the porch light.

"I don't know," he said quietly. "But I think you should stay here tonight."

NINETEEN

Ethan pushed himself up, his heart hammering in his chest. The image of the massive black wolf burned in his mind, its yellow eyes seared into his memory. He turned toward the window above his bed, grabbing the blind cord with unsteady hands and yanking it down to shut out the snowy yard. His breath came in shallow gasps, his chest tightening as he fought to steady himself.

A knock at the door made him flinch.

"Ethan? It's Carter," the sheriff's calm voice called. "Can I come in?"

Ethan hesitated, staring at the door. Finally, he managed to answer. "Yeah, come in."

The door opened, and Carter stepped inside, his boots quiet on the floor. His eyes immediately landed on Ethan, taking in the sullen face, fidgeting hands, and the tension in his shoulders. "You alright, kid?"

Ethan nodded quickly, though his expression said otherwise. "I'm fine," he said, looking away.

Carter pulled the desk chair out and sat down, resting his elbows on his knees. "You ran in here like you'd seen a ghost. What happened?"

Ethan hesitated, gripping the edge of his hoodie. He didn't want to talk about it, but Carter's steady gaze made it clear he wasn't letting this go. "We were riding the snowmobiles back to Nick's house, and… I saw something in the woods," he said finally.

Carter's expression darkened. "What kind of something? An animal?"

Ethan nodded. "It looked like a wolf. It was huge, with black fur. And its eyes… they were yellow. Bright and uh… like they were glowing."

Carter frowned, his eyes narrowing as the details hit uncomfortably close to the attack he was already investigating. The torn body, the claw marks. It all lined up too well.

Ethan's voice wavered as he continued. "It stayed in the trees, but it kept up with us the whole time. It followed us all the way until we hit the street. I think it was hunting us."

Carter exhaled slowly, processing the description. "You're sure it followed you? Not just running in the same direction?"

Ethan nodded quickly, his voice trembling. "I'm sure. It watched us the whole way back to Nick's."

Carter leaned back slightly, his mind working as he studied Ethan. The boy's fear was real, and the story was too similar to what he already suspected about the creature that killed Adeline Morris. But he didn't want to alarm Ethan more than he already was.

"Alright," Carter said finally. "Thanks for telling me. That's pretty brave of you."

"What do you think it was?" Ethan asked shakily.

Carter offered a reassuring smile, though his thoughts were far from calm. "Could be a big wolf passing through. Sometimes animals act strange when they're on their own. But I'll look into it. For now, how about you come out to the living room? No sense sitting in here alone."

Ethan hesitated, then grabbed his iPad from the bed and stood. "Okay," he said softly, following Carter out.

The living room was warm and inviting, the soft yellow glow of a lamp casting a cozy light over the space. Lillian looked up from her crocheting as they entered, her expression shifting to concern when she saw Ethan.

"Everything alright?" she asked gently.

"Ethan had a bit of a scare earlier," Carter said. "He saw something while he was out with Nick and Ryan."

"What did you see, sweetheart?" Lillian asked, setting her crocheting aside.

Ethan hesitated, glancing at Carter, who gave him a small nod.

"It looked like a wolf," Ethan said quietly. "But it was huge. Way bigger than any wolf I've ever seen. It chased us back to the road."

Lillian's face paled, and she leaned forward slightly. "A wolf? By itself?"

Carter nodded. "That's what he said. Black fur, yellow eyes. It sounds like it's been hanging around the woods."

Lillian pressed her hand to her chest. "Do you think it's dangerous?"

"Hard to say," Carter replied. "Wolves don't usually behave like this, so it's something we need to keep an eye on. For now, make sure Ethan isn't outside alone, and don't let him wander too far."

"Of course," Lillian said quickly. "I'll keep a close eye on him."

Carter's gaze shifted to the window, his thoughts racing. If this was the same creature that killed Adeline, things were worse than he had initially thought.

Ethan curled up on the couch, scrolling through his iPad while Lillian returned to her crocheting, glancing at him occasionally with a concerned expression.

"You're safe here," she said gently, breaking the silence.

"I know," Ethan replied softly, though the image of the glowing eyes replayed endlessly in his mind.

Carter sat in the armchair, his hands resting on his knees as he stared at the window. His instincts told him this was no ordinary wolf, but until he had more information, there wasn't much he could do.

Ethan shifted slightly, pulling the blanket over his lap. He didn't want to think about the creature anymore, so he focused on his iPad, letting the soft sounds of Lillian's crocheting and the warmth of the room calm him.

TWENTY

Later that night, Ethan slipped under the bed covers and pulled the quilt up to his chin. Grabbing his headphones from the nightstand, he slid them over his ears and turned them on. He opened YouTube and started watching a compilation of funny fails, his quiet chuckles breaking the stillness of the room.

He scrolled through a few more videos, landing on a gaming streamer's highlight reel full of over-the-top reactions and chaotic gameplay. The colorful animations and rapid-fire commentary kept him entertained, but as the video played on, his eyelids grew heavier.

His iPad screen dimmed as he yawned, curling deeper into the blanket. The sound of the streamer's voice in his ears began to fade as sleep overtook him, the video continuing to play as he drifted off.

Hours later, around 5 a.m., Ethan was startled awake by a loud, guttural growl.

The sound tore through the stillness, so close and loud that his left ear throbbed in pain. He shot upright, gasping for breath, his heart hammering like a drum.

His headphones had slipped off and lay tangled in the blankets. His iPad screen had gone black, plunging the room into darkness.

For a long moment, Ethan didn't move, his wide eyes scanning the room. The shadows stretched across the floor, faint outlines cast by the dim, gray light creeping through the curtains.

"Lillian?" he whispered, his voice barely audible.

The house was silent.

He swallowed hard, his throat dry. The growl wasn't a dream, it couldn't have been. His ear still hurt from how loud it had been, and the deep, angry sound seemed to echo in his mind, making the hair on the back of his neck stand up.

Ethan scooted back against the headboard, his knees pulled tightly to his chest. His hands gripped the edges of the blanket as his gaze darted toward the window. The curtains were closed, but he had a feeling something was there, watching.

He thought about running to Lillian's room. But what if something was waiting in the hallway? The thought made his stomach twist, and he stayed frozen in place.

Minutes dragged by, feeling like hours. His eyes scanned every corner of the room, every shadow, every darkened shape. His breathing came fast, and his heart pounded so hard it threatened to burst.

The first light of morning finally began to creep into the room, softening the edges of the darkness. Ethan let out a shaky breath, but he didn't move until his alarm buzzed on the nightstand, making him jump.

His hands trembled as he silenced the alarm. Sliding out of bed, he dressed quickly, avoiding the window as much as he could. He refused to look.

The smell of eggs and toast greeted Ethan as he walked into the kitchen.

"Morning, sweetheart," Lillian said, glancing over her

shoulder as she flipped an egg in the pan. "You ready for the first day at your new school?"

"Morning," Ethan mumbled, sliding into a chair at the kitchen table. "I guess."

Lillian turned, setting a plate of eggs and toast in front of him. She studied him for a moment, her brow wrinkling. "You look like you didn't sleep much. You alright?"

Ethan hesitated, picking at his toast. "Yeah, I'm fine. Just... couldn't really get to sleep, I guess."

Lillian raised an eyebrow but didn't push. "Well, try to eat. You'll need your energy."

Ethan took a small bite of toast, chewing slowly. "What if the kids hate me?" he asked suddenly.

Lillian's expression softened. She sat down across from him, her smile reassuring. "They're not going to hate you. Nick and Ryan already like you, don't they?"

"Yeah," Ethan admitted. "But... school's different. What if I say something dumb?"

Lillian reached across the table and gave his hand a gentle squeeze. "You'll be fine, Ethan. Just be yourself. And if anyone gives you a hard time, you let me know, okay? Or the sheriff," she added with a playful grin.

"Okay," Ethan said, managing a small smile.

"Good," Lillian said, patting his hand before standing. "Now finish up. You don't want to miss the bus."

Ethan nodded, focusing on his food. The warm breakfast and Lillian's calm presence helped ease his nerves, but the growl from earlier still haunted his thoughts.

His thoughts wandered. Could the creature in the woods somehow be haunting him in his room at night too? Goosebumps rose on his arms as he shook the thought away, unwilling to dwell on it.

TWENTY-ONE

The car heater worked its magic, warming the air as Lillian pulled out of the driveway. Snow from the previous days had been plowed into neat piles along the edges of the street, but the icy patches glinting in the early light made her drive cautiously.

"You nervous?" Lillian asked, glancing at Ethan in the passenger seat.

He shrugged, staring out the window. "A little, I guess."

Lillian offered him a reassuring smile. "You'll do fine. Nick and Ryan will be there, and I'm sure you'll make plenty of other friends too."

"Yeah," Ethan said, his voice trailing off. He tapped his

fingers against his backpack, trying to focus on anything but the knot in his stomach.

Lillian slowed the car as they approached the bus stop, where Nick and Ryan were already waiting. She parked at the curb and put the car in park, turning to Ethan.

"You've got this, sweetheart," she said. "Just take it one step at a time."

Ethan nodded, grabbing his backpack. "Thanks, Lillian."

As he opened the door, Nick waved at him from the sidewalk. "Hey, Ethan!"

Ethan managed a small smile and climbed out of the car.

Nick grinned as Ethan approached, his breath clouding the air. "Morning! Ready for school?"

Ethan shrugged. "I guess."

Ryan smirked. "You're not ready. Trust me, gym class is going to destroy you. First day back, and I'm calling it. I'm the dodgeball champion."

Nick rolled his eyes. "Ryan, you always lose first."

"Not this time," Ryan said with a grin. "City boy's going

down first!" He laughed, nudging Ethan playfully.

Ethan let out a quiet chuckle, the easy banter easing some of his nerves. He glanced back at Lillian, still parked and watching them with a careful, protective gaze.

Nick nudged him. "Hey, you good?"

"Yeah," Ethan said quickly, brushing it off. "Just tired."

Ryan looked over his shoulder. "Guess we all are. But at least we're not walking in this." He gestured at the snowy street, where faint tire tracks marked the icy surface.

Ethan gave a small nod, silently grateful for the ride, though he wasn't about to say it out loud.

A few moments later, the bus rumbled to a stop, just as a couple of stragglers hurried to join the group. The doors hissed open, and the boys climbed aboard, met with a curt nod from the driver.

Ethan sat near the middle with Nick and Ryan, his gaze drawn to the window as the town blurred past. He could see the edge of the forest in the distance, its bare trees stark against the snow-covered ground.

"So," Ryan said suddenly, leaning toward Ethan. "You

think it was a wolf?"

Ethan blinked. "What?"

Ryan rolled his eyes. "The thing in the woods yesterday. You really think that was just a regular wolf?"

Nick shook his head. "It was huge, man. Easily the size of three wolves."

Ethan hesitated. "I don't know. It looked like a wolf, but it was… I don't know how to explain it. It didn't look normal."

Ryan scoffed. "What else would it be? A werewolf?"

Nick nudged him. "Stop it. You're gonna freak him out."

"I'm fine," Ethan said, though the memory still made his stomach twist. "It's just… weird."

Ryan shrugged. "Whatever it was, it's not gonna mess with us again. It knows we're too fast."

Ethan forced a laugh, though the nervousness still clung to him.

When the bus finally pulled up to the school, Ethan followed Nick and Ryan into the flow of students heading inside. Lillian's words echoed faintly in his mind, take it one step at a time.

TWENTY-TWO

The morning was sunny and clear as Cathy Hensley laced up her running shoes. Her playlist was already queued, featuring *"Sleep to Dream"* by Fiona Apple, a song she'd been leaning on since her divorce. It had become her anthem, reminding her of her strength and independence.

Lockward Trail stretched ahead, its snow-covered path winding through the bare trees of impending winter. Cathy adjusted her headphones and tapped her smartwatch to check the time. She took a deep breath, savoring the quiet and the cold as she set off at a steady pace. Leaving the houses behind, the looping trail took her further into the woods.

This was her first run in weeks. Between court battles and the emotional toll of her divorce, Cathy had avoided the trail.

But today, she was determined to reclaim a piece of her old routine. The cold air filled her lungs as she focused on the path ahead, each step fueling her sense of control.

Her thoughts were clear and focused, a clarity she hadn't experienced in a long time. She thought about how much she had missed this, the stillness, the steady cadence of her steps, the simple act of moving forward. Out here, away from everything, she could finally breathe.

A crow perched on a low branch watched silently as she ran by, its dark eyes tracking her movement. She glanced at it briefly but kept running. A loud squawk broke the quiet behind her.

Two miles into her run, her phone buzzed in her pocket. She slowed, pulling it out and answering the call. "Hey, Beth," she said, her breath visible in the frosty air.

"Hey," Beth replied warmly. "Are you out on your run?"

"Yeah," Cathy said, glancing around. "First time back on the trail in a while. Feels good to get out here again."

"Glad to hear it," Beth said. "Coffee after? You can fill me in on everything."

"Sounds...," Cathy replied, but her words faltered.

Before she could finish, a sudden flurry of squawks erupted nearby. The crow had landed again, its beady black eyes locked onto her as it cawed relentlessly.

Cathy winced and pressed the phone tighter against her ear. "Hang on, Beth, I can't hear you. This damn bird won't shut up." She turned toward the crow, irritation flaring. "Shut up!" she snapped.

The crow flapped its wings but didn't leave.

"Sorry about that. Stupid bird. Anyways, where…"

Before she could continue, a crashing noise erupted from the woods. She froze, her breath catching as the sound grew louder, the underbrush shaking with the movement of something large. It darted through a cluster of eastern hemlock trees, their thick, evergreen branches offering cover even in the starkness of impending winter.

"Cathy? What's wrong?" Beth's voice came through the receiver, distant and concerned.

The creature moved with chilling precision, as if it knew exactly how to remain hidden. Then, the noise stopped abruptly, the dense tangle of trees concealing whatever it was, leaving Cathy rooted in place, her pulse pounding in her ears.

"There's something in the woods," Cathy stammered, her voice trembling. "I can't see it but it's big, whatever it is."

Beth's tone turned firm. "Don't run. Back away slowly. Whatever it is, don't panic."

Cathy's legs refused to move, but she forced herself to step back. Her breath quickened as she scanned the tree line, her ears straining for any hint of movement. "I can hear it moving in the brush," she whispered into the phone.

"Stay calm," Beth urged. "Keep moving, but don't turn your back. It's probably a moose."

The footsteps stopped suddenly, leaving a stark silence. Cathy paused, her heart racing. "I think it's gone. I spook myself so easily," she said shakily, relief creeping into her voice

Beth exhaled audibly. "Good. Just head home and meet me for coffee, okay?"

"Okay," Cathy said, tucking her phone back into her pocket. She jogged away from the area, her music back on within minutes to drown out her lingering unease.

The trail curved abruptly ahead, opening onto a stretch surrounded by spindly, leafless trees. Cathy pushed herself to maintain her pace, eager to leave the woods behind.

Then between the trees, farther down the trail, something large moved. Her legs slowed instinctively, her brow creasing as she squinted to get a better look. The figure blended with the shadows of the forest, but the unmistakable glint of golden eyes pinned her in place.

Cathy froze. Her heart thudded in her chest as the figure shifted slightly, stepping from the deeper woods toward the trail. It was massive, its black fur sleek and catching faint light. Its head tilted, studying her with unnerving focus.

She yanked her headphones out, her breath quickening as fear gripped her.

"Oh my God." she whispered aloud, her voice trembling.

The creature stood on two legs, its fiery eyes giving off a faint glow. It stopped just shy of the tree line, its piercing gaze set on her.

Panic seized her, and she fumbled for her phone. Before she could unlock it, the creature took another step forward. That was all it took for Cathy to turn and run.

With shallow gasps, she struggled forward, sneakers skidding on the ice. Though anxiety consumed her, she couldn't resist looking back.

The creature was following her.

"Oh God," Cathy mumbled.

It stayed in the forest but moved parallel to her, weaving through the trees with horrifying ease. Its size and speed were staggering, and Cathy's stomach twisted with terror as she realized it wasn't breaking pace to catch her. It was stalking her.

She fumbled for her phone again, trying to dial Beth, but her fingers shook too much to hit the buttons. Instead, she shoved the phone back into her pocket and focused on running.

The trail stretched endlessly ahead, and her legs burned as she pushed harder. She cast another glance over her shoulder, only to see the beast closer now, its gleaming eyes watching her. A scream tore from her throat as her foot caught on a root hidden beneath the snow.

Cathy fell hard, her knees slamming against the frozen ground. Pain shot through her, but adrenaline propelled her to scramble back to her feet. The beast had stopped just at the edge of the trail, its head tilted slightly as though enjoying her panic.

Ignoring the agony, she drove herself harder, the icy air a harsh rasp in her lungs. She stumbled again but didn't fall, her feet slipping on the trail's uneven surface.

Cathy's mind raced as she saw a home in the distance. For a brief moment, hope surged through her. She could make it. She just had to keep going.

"Help!" Cathy screamed, though the woods swallowed her cry.

The creature moved suddenly, closing the distance with terrifying speed. Cathy attempted another scream, but it died in her throat as the creature's jaws clamped onto her shoulder. Pain exploded through her body as she was dragged to the ground.

Her cries faded as the world spun, her vision narrowing to the snow beneath her. Its massive jaws clamped down on the back of her neck with a sickening crunch. A searing pain overwhelmed her, then blackness.

The beast dragged her lifeless form off the trail and into the thick underbrush, as the snow bore the marks of a deadly struggle.

In the distance, a crow cawed, its cry the only witness to the horrors that had unfolded on the trail.

TWENTY-THREE

Beth Neale sat at a corner table in the café, her coffee untouched as she stared at her phone. The soft murmur of other customers floated around her, but she barely registered it. Her fingers tightened around the device as she tapped the screen repeatedly, checking for any missed calls or messages from Cathy. Nothing.

Cathy was late, and Cathy was never late.

Beth replayed their earlier phone call, Cathy's voice trembling as she spoke: "There's something in the woods."

Those words haunted her, a growing knot of worry twisting in her chest. Maybe it wasn't a moose?

She dialed Cathy's number again, her hands clammy

against the cold metal of her phone. Straight to voicemail. Her worry transformed into panic, her anxiety rising. Finally, she called 911.

"911, what's your emergency?"

"My friend Cathy," Beth said, her words spilling out quickly. "She's missing. We were supposed to meet for coffee an hour ago, and she hasn't shown up or called. I was on the phone with her earlier, and she said she heard something running at her in the woods on Lockward Trail."

"When was the last time you spoke with her?" the dispatcher asked, their tone steady.

"An hour and a half ago," Beth said, her voice shaking. "She sounded scared, but she hung up after thinking the animal had gone away. I'm afraid something happened to her. She would never just not show up."

Calmly, the dispatcher answered, with the quiet click of keys audible in the background. "We're dispatching deputies to check the area. Do you know where she might have entered the trail?"

"She usually starts at the main trailhead off Lockward Lane," Beth replied.

"Alright, ma'am. Stay where you are, and we'll update you as soon as we can."

Beth didn't stay put.

Within ten minutes, she was pulling into the small gravel lot at the Lockward Trail entrance. The engine hummed softly as she turned it off, glancing nervously at the dark path ahead. Clusters of eastern hemlocks loomed near the trailhead, their dense green needles a stark contrast to the skeletal bare branches of the surrounding trees.

Beth stepped out of her car and walked to the large map posted at the trailhead. Her eyes traced the loop of the main trail and the smaller paths branching off into the woods. The tangled web of routes made her stomach tighten. Cathy could be anywhere.

Flashing lights broke the stillness, and Beth exhaled shakily as a patrol car pulled in. Two deputies stepped out, both tall and broad-shouldered, their faces calm but alert.

"Ma'am, are you the one who called about your friend?" one of them asked as he approached.

Beth nodded quickly. "Yes. I'm Beth Neale. My friend Cathy was supposed to meet me over an hour ago. She said something scared her on the trail, but now she's not answering her phone."

"I'm Deputy Marks," the man said, gesturing to his partner. "This is Deputy Harlan. We'll check it out. Please wait here in your vehicle."

Beth hesitated but nodded, her hands trembling as she stuffed them into her coat pockets. "Just… please find her."

Marks gave her a reassuring nod before he and Harlan moved toward the trailhead.

The trail was quiet as the deputies made their way deeper into the woods. Marks scanned the ground as they walked, his intense gaze noting details easily missed by the untrained eye.

"Tracks," he said, crouching to examine a set of large indentations in the snow. "Look at the size of these. They're too big for a dog or a coyote."

Harlan leaned in for a closer look, his brow creasing. "That's not a wolf either," he said.

"No," Marks said, standing. "Let's keep moving but stay on guard."

The trail wound through the forest, clusters of eastern

hemlocks forming pockets of deep shadow. The woods were unnervingly still, the usual sounds of birds and small animals conspicuously absent.

As they rounded a bend, Marks froze. Red streaks stood out against the white snow, leading off the trail into the dense underbrush.

"Blood," he said grimly.

Harlan instinctively rested his hand on his holster. "Whatever did this might still be close," he said quietly.

Marks nodded and reached for his radio. "Dispatch, this is Deputy Marks. We've got signs of an attack. There's blood and drag marks that go away from the trail. Requesting immediate backup and Fish and Game support."

"Copy that, Deputy," the dispatcher replied.

Harlan glanced nervously at the bushes. "We're not equipped to handle a predator by ourselves. Let's head back."

Marks hesitated, his eyes lingering on the blood trail before nodding. "You're right. Let's go."

Beth sat in her car, her foot tapping anxiously against the floor as she stared at the trailhead. When the deputies reappeared, their somber expressions told her all she needed to know.

"Did you find her?" she asked, her voice trembling.

Marks shook his head. "We found blood and disturbed snow leading into the woods. It looks like there was an attack, but we don't know what we're dealing with yet. Backup is on the way."

Beth's hands flew to her mouth, her eyes filling with tears. "Oh my God," she whispered.

Harlan placed a hand on her shoulder. "We're going to do everything we can to find her. You can wait here, or head home if you prefer. We'll keep you updated."

Beth shook her head quickly. "I'll wait. Please, just find her."

The deputies nodded and returned to their patrol car to wait for reinforcements. Beth stayed in her own vehicle, fidgeting as silent prayers filled her thoughts.

"Please," she whispered, her voice barely audible. "Be okay, Cathy."

TWENTY-FOUR

Sheriff Carter pulled his cruiser into the gravel lot at the trailhead. Deputy Harlan and Deputy Marks were already standing outside, their postures tense. The woman stepping out of the truck behind him, Rebecca Darnell from Fish and Game, adjusted her jacket and approached with a calm but determined expression.

The sheriff stepped out, closing his door as he greeted Darnell. Beth sat in her car, still fidgeting nervously, her hands alternating between gripping the wheel and smoothing the hem of her coat. She offered a weak nod to the sheriff as he glanced her way, then focused on his deputies.

"Alright, Harlan, brief us," Sheriff Carter said as he crossed his arms.

"We found blood on the trail about a mile and a half in," Harlan began. "A lot of it. Drag marks leading off into the bushes. Something big did this going on the tracks we saw when we first hit the trail. We didn't want to risk going further without backup or higher-caliber weapons."

Darnell nodded. "What kind of tracks?"

"Larger than a coyote or even a wolf. Deep. Whatever made them was heavy," Marks added.

Sheriff Carter exhaled deeply. "Alright, let's gear up. Everyone's carrying rifles or shotguns for this. Darnell, you take point with the tracking. We find Cathy, and we'll cordon off the area. Let's move."

The group had only just started along the trail when one of the deputies motioned toward a patch of snow ahead. "Here," he said, crouching to point at the first set of tracks they had found earlier.

The prints were deep and unmistakably large, their shape unlike anything they were accustomed to seeing.

The sheriff and Darnell knelt beside the tracks, studying them closely. "Those are big," Darnell said.

The sheriff nodded. "That's strange. They don't even look

like a bear or a moose.”

They kept moving along the trail, their heads on a swivel looking for any movement amongst the trees or brush until they came upon the scene.

Darnell knelt down, her gloved fingers brushing the crimson stains. “Fresh,” she said. “Whatever did this wasn’t long ago.” “Looks like there was a struggle.” She pointed to the side. “The tracks lead into those bushes.”

“Keep your eyes open,” Sheriff Carter ordered.

They followed the trail of blood, which veered off the main path and into denser underbrush. The snow grew deeper here, muffling their steps. Surrounded by Eastern hemlocks, the forest enveloped them, even in daylight.

Marks halted suddenly, raising a hand. “There,” he whispered, pointing ahead.

Darnell moved closer, her rifle raised. Through the bushes, a shape became visible. It was Cathy’s body, half-hidden under a layer of disturbed snow and torn branches. Blood stained the ground around her, her clothing shredded.

“Oh my God,” Harlan said, as he turned away.

Darnell stepped forward cautiously, scanning the area for any signs of movement. "It's a female," she confirmed, as her eyes narrowed. She crouched near the body, as she took in the scene. "This wasn't just an attack. It fed on her too. Whatever did this dragged her here to eat."

The sheriff sighed heavily. He grabbed his radio. "Dispatch, this is Sheriff Carter. We've located the missing female. Deceased. We need the coroner out here immediately."

The dispatcher's reply crackled through the radio. "Copy that, Sheriff. Requesting the coroner now."

Harlan shifted uneasily. "Do we stay here?"

"We cordon this off and stay alert," the sheriff said firmly. "No one goes off on their own. Whatever's out here is dangerous and might still be close."

Darnell rose from where she'd been examining the body. "If it's still in the area, it won't stray far from a fresh kill. Everybody keep your eyes open."

The group backed away from the body, creating a perimeter while they waited for the coroner. The surrounding forest remained silent. The sense of being watched was intense as each member of the team scanned the tree line with heightened awareness.

TWENTY-FIVE

The yellow school bus hissed to a stop at the corner, and Ethan stepped off, his backpack slung over one shoulder. Nick and Ryan followed close behind, chattering about their math teacher's meltdown earlier that day.

"Man, did you see the look on his face when Tyler asked him if calculators were allowed on the test?" Ryan laughed, nudging Nick.

"Yeah, I thought his head was going to explode," Nick replied, grinning.

Ethan smiled faintly, his mind elsewhere. He adjusted the strap on his backpack and glanced at the rows of houses lining the street. He had a good first day at school but now that he was back, the anxiety in his gut returned.

As they turned down the street toward their houses, a kid from the neighborhood, a wiry kid named Tommy, came sprinting up to them. He skidded to a halt in front of the group, his face flushed with excitement.

"Did you hear?" Tommy asked breathlessly, his eyes wide. "A lady got attacked on the trail behind the houses this morning! They found her all torn up, and there was blood everywhere. My brother said it was a bear, but I think it was, like, a killer wolf or something."

Nick and Ryan exchanged startled glances. "Are you serious?" Nick asked.

Tommy nodded emphatically. "Yeah! My dad said the sheriff and Fish and Game were out there with big guns and everything."

"That's crazy," Ryan said, his voice hushed. "A really big wolf chased us yesterday. I wonder if it got the lady?"

"Probably," Tommy said with a shrug, clearly enjoying the attention. "I'm not scared. If it comes for ya just punch it in the nose." He mimed throwing a punch, grinning as if he were a hero in an action movie.

Nick rolled his eyes. "Yeah, good luck with that."

Tommy smirked, then waved them off. "Anyway, better watch out. See ya." He took off running down the street, leaving the trio standing in uneasy silence.

"Do you think it's true?" Ryan asked, his voice low.

Ethan didn't respond immediately. He glanced toward the woods at the edge of the neighborhood, the bare branches swaying in the wind. The thought of someone being killed so close to home made his anxiety do backflips.

"I'm heading home," Ethan said finally, adjusting his backpack.

Nick frowned. "You okay?"

"Yeah," Ethan said, though his tone lacked conviction. "I just… I need to get home."

His friends didn't argue. "I'm heading to Nick's, so we'll catch you later," Ryan said, parting ways as Ethan turned onto his street.

As he walked, Ethan noticed Lillian's car pull up beside him. Relieved, he climbed into the passenger seat.

"Sorry I'm late," Lillian said, glancing at him as he

buckled his seatbelt. "I got caught up at the store. How was school?"

"It was fine," Ethan mumbled, leaning back against the seat.

"Just fine?" she asked with a soft laugh.

Ethan gave a faint smile but didn't elaborate. His mind was still stuck on Tommy's story and the unsettling thought of the woods being so close.

As Lillian drove them home, Ethan stared out the window, his unease growing with every passing tree.

TWENTY-SIX

The sound of pencils scratching against paper filled Ethan's bedroom as he hunched over his homework, his head propped on one hand. His desk lamp cast a soft glow on the cluttered surface of books, papers, and a half-empty glass of water. From the kitchen, the faint clatter of pots and pans signaled that Lillian was cooking dinner.

Ethan sighed, erasing an equation, and trying again. His thoughts kept drifting back to the conversation he'd overheard earlier. A woman attacked, blood everywhere, the sheriff and Fish and Game involved… it was a lot to process. He glanced toward the window, where the darkening yard reflected his room back at him like a distorted mirror. A shiver ran through him, and he returned to his work.

The front door opened, the sound clear even through his closed door. Ethan paused, listening as heavy boots thudded against the floor.

"Carter," he heard Lillian say warmly, though she didn't sound surprised. "Good, you're here. Dinner will be ready soon."

"Thanks, Lillian," the sheriff replied, his voice carrying easily through the house. "Couldn't miss dinner tonight."

Ethan set his pencil down, curiosity pulling him to his feet. He moved to the door and cracked it open, letting the conversation flow into the room.

"How was your day?" Lillian asked.

"Busy," Carter said, his tone weighted with fatigue. "I'm surprised you haven't heard yet... about the woman on the trail."

"No. What happened?" Lillian asked, her voice edged with urgency.

"This morning. Found a body off Lockward Trail. Looks like another animal attack," Carter said. "It was bad, Lillian. Real bad."

Ethan's stomach knotted as he pressed closer to the door, straining to catch every word.

"Oh, no," Lillian mumbled, followed by the clang of a pot being set down. "That poor woman. Do you know who it was?"

"Yes, but I can't release her name yet," Carter replied. "Fish and Game agree it was an animal. Bear or wolf. Definitely something big. Personally, I think it was that large wolf the boys saw yesterday. Matches the other attack too. And if it was chasing them, well, they're lucky it didn't catch up. We've cordoned off the area, but it's not safe."

Lillian sighed deeply. "That's terrible. Her family must be devastated."

"They are," Carter said. "I'll wash up for dinner, but I won't be staying over tonight. Too much to handle back at the station."

"Alright," Lillian said softly.

Ethan backed away from the door and returned to his desk, his thoughts racing. He stared at the window, the darkness outside seeming deeper and more menacing now.

He tried to focus on his homework, but the numbers and

words blurred together. In Chicago, he'd never worried about wolves. Maybe the occasional coyote or stray dog, but nothing like this. What he'd seen yesterday wasn't normal. It was like something straight out of a nightmare.

Ethan glanced at the window one more time before turning back to his work, his heart still unsettled.

TWENTY-SEVEN

Lillian glanced across the table as she noticed Ethan pushing his soup around with his spoon. He had barely said a word since sitting down.

"You're awfully quiet tonight," she said softly. "Everything alright?"

Ethan looked up, startled by her question. "Yeah, I'm fine," he replied quickly, forcing a small smile before returning his focus to the bowl in front of him.

Lillian didn't look convinced but decided not to push further.

Carter, seated at the kitchen table with them, broke the silence. "Ethan, did you hear about the attack on the trail?" he asked.

Ethan froze mid-spoonful, his gaze flickering between Lillian and Carter. "Yeah. A kid from school was talking about it," he said quietly.

Carter nodded, leaning forward slightly. "Then you know how serious this is. My best guess is that wolf creature that chased you and your friends is responsible for the recent attacks. I need you to promise me something: don't go too far from the house until we figure out how to deal with it."

"I won't," Ethan promised, setting his spoon down.

Lillian watched him closely before turning her attention to Carter. "Are you or Fish and Game going to try and trap it?" she asked, her voice tinged with worry.

Carter sighed, rubbing the back of his neck. "We're waiting on confirmation from Fish and Game about organizing a hunt for this thing. I need to sit down with Rebecca Darnell to figure out the best approach. We've never dealt with anything like this before, and we're not about to rush in blind. This creature is bold enough to attack in broad daylight. Those two women didn't stand a chance."

"I feel so sorry for them," Lillian mumbled, shaking her head. "It's horrifying to think about."

Ethan's stomach tightened. He pushed his bowl slightly away, his appetite gone. "I'll stay close to the house," he said firmly.

Carter gave him a small nod. "Good. That's all I needed to hear."

The rest of the meal passed quietly. After helping Lillian clear the dishes, Carter excused himself. "I need to get back to the station. Still a lot to catch up on."

Lillian walked him to the door, while Ethan retreated to the living room. He turned on the TV, flipping through channels until he settled on an old cartoon.

Lillian joined him for a short while, folding laundry on the couch. "You sure you're okay?" she asked gently.

"Yeah, I'm fine," Ethan replied, glancing briefly at her before focusing back on the screen.

Satisfied for the moment, Lillian eventually said goodnight and headed to her room, leaving Ethan alone in the dimly lit living room. He stayed on the couch for a while longer, letting the cartoons distract him.

Finally, he turned off the TV and grabbed his iPad from the coffee table. After brushing his teeth and changing into his pajamas, he climbed into bed, pulling the quilt up to his chest.

Ethan opened a podcast on his iPad, hoping the soothing voices would help him relax. For a while, it worked. His eyelids grew heavy, and the warmth of the blankets lulled him toward sleep.

Tap. Tap. Tap.

Ethan's eyes snapped open, his chest tightening abrupt, distinct sound. He froze, straining to listen.

Tap. Tap. Tap.

The noise came again, like nails tapping against glass. His heart raced as he turned his head slowly toward the window.

The creature stood just outside, its massive frame partially obscured by the frost-covered glass. Its black fur gleamed faintly in the moonlight, and one sharp claw tapped rhythmically against the window.

Ethan gasped at the sight of the creature, its imposing figure so close. But what struck him wasn't just its presence. It wasn't looking at him. Its glowing eyes were locked on the door to his room.

As though sensing his movement, the creature's head turned. Its piercing eyes locked onto his, and its lips pulled back in a sinister snarl, revealing jagged, glistening teeth.

Panic surged through Ethan as the creature suddenly vanished from view, leaving behind fogged glass where its breath had been.

The room was silent for a moment, except for Ethan's shallow breathing. Then, scratching. The sound was faint at first but grew louder, coming from his bedroom door.

Ethan's gaze darted toward the door. Shadows moved underneath it, and the scratching continued, like claws dragging against the wood.

He wanted to scream, but no sound came. His body trembled as he clutched the quilt tightly, his mind a whirl of fear.

The scratching persisted, relentless and grating. Ethan pressed himself against the wall, unable to move or even think clearly. His imagination ran wild, conjuring images of the creature breaking through the door, its claws reaching for him.

Were there two of them? he wondered.

Eventually, the noise stopped, but Ethan remained frozen in place, too terrified to move. Hours seemed to pass before exhaustion finally overtook him. His sleep was restless and filled with nightmares of glowing eyes and sharp teeth lurking in the dark.

TWENTY-EIGHT

Sheriff Carter leaned back in his chair, the office quiet except for the tv on in the break room. The day had been long, and the grim discovery on the trail wouldn't leave his mind. He rubbed his temples, glancing at the clock: 10:38 p.m. Sleep seemed a distant luxury. The only other person in the building was Maureen, the night dispatcher, who sat a few rooms away.

The phone on his desk rang with a sudden, piercing tone, pulling him from his thoughts. Frowning, he picked it up. "Sheriff Carter."

"Carter, it's Jim Wilkins," came the familiar voice from several counties over. Wilkins sounded weary, his tone carrying an urgency that immediately put Carter on edge.

"Jim," the sheriff said, sitting straighter. "What's going on?"

"Sorry for calling so late but I sensed you might still be up. I'll get straight to it. I heard about the attack on the trail," Wilkins began. "The woman mauled to death. Animal, right?"

"Yeah," the sheriff replied cautiously. "How'd you hear about it?"

"Word travels. You also had that other attack a few weeks ago. Same kind of injuries, same gruesome details. Listen, I'm calling to warn you. This might not be just any animal. It sounds a lot like what we dealt with last fall."

The sheriff's brow creased. "What exactly did you deal with?"

Wilkins sighed heavily. "It started with livestock, cattle, and sheep torn apart. Then it escalated. We lost five townsfolk before it was over, three in one night. This thing was relentless. Bold. It came right up to houses, dragged animals out of barns, and even tried breaking into a home."

"Jesus," the sheriff said, gripping the receiver tighter. "How did you stop it?"

"We didn't stop it. Got lucky," Wilkins admitted. "A semi hit it on a back road late one night. Killed it outright, but not before the driver wrecked his truck. He survived, thankfully. The creature didn't."

"What kind of animal was it?" Sheriff Carter asked.

Wilkins hesitated. "A wolf. But not any wolf I've ever seen. This thing walked on two legs, Carter. Nearly seven feet tall standing upright. Muscles like a bear, but it was no bear. And its eyes…" He trailed off.

"You're serious?" the sheriff asked, leaning forward, his pulse quickening.

"Dead serious," Wilkins replied. "After the second attack, we called in the Feds. That's when it got weird."

"The Feds?" Sheriff Carter asked, his eyebrows lifting. "They got involved?"

"They sent a specialist," Wilkins said. "Some guy in a plain black jacket, no badge, no uniform. He didn't say much, just started tracking it. He'd been on its trail for days when it wandered onto the highway and got hit."

Sheriff Carter blinked. "And it's dead?"

"Yeah. But you probably read about it without realizing," Wilkins said, leaning forward.

"What do you mean?"

"They spun the story," Wilkins said grimly. "Said it was an emaciated bear. Buried it in the local paper, barely a mention. The Feds didn't want a panic, and the mayor agreed to keep it quiet. Said it was for the town's own good."

"A bear?" Sheriff Carter chuckled. "That's the best they could come up with?"

"Most people don't ask questions," Wilkins said. "Slap an official statement on it, and they believe it. But it wasn't a bear, Carter."

"What was it then?" the sheriff pressed.

Wilkins exhaled. "Something that shouldn't exist. It had the body of a wolf, but the way it moved, the way it looked at you… it was like it understood you were prey."

The sheriff leaned back, his mind racing. "Why tell me this now?"

"Because," Wilkins said, "I've seen the photos from your scene. The injuries? Identical to what we dealt with. If I didn't know better, I'd say the damn thing was back."

"That's impossible," the sheriff said quickly.

"I know," Wilkins replied. "I saw it dead with my own eyes. But it's not just a freak of nature, Carter. This thing… whatever it is… didn't come out of nowhere. There has to be others."

Sheriff Carter's stomach churned. "So what do I do?"

"Call the FBI," Wilkins said firmly. "They know what this is, and they've dealt with it before. You don't want to go up against it alone. If you're lucky, they'll take over and keep it out of your jurisdiction."

The sheriff rubbed his face, the gravity of the conversation settling over him. "Alright, Jim. Thanks for the heads-up."

"Don't wait too long," Wilkins warned. "If it's the same kind of thing, you're already on borrowed time."

"I hear you," Sheriff Carter said, hanging up the phone.

A moment later, his phone buzzed with a notification. He opened the message from Wilkins, his breath quickening when he saw the attached dashcam photo.

The creature in the image loomed over the road, its massive frame dominating the scene. Black fur, thick and coarse, gleamed under the harsh glare of the truck's headlights, casting eerie shadows along its muscular form. Standing upright, it bore the unmistakable shape of a wolf, but there was something deeply wrong about it. Its limbs were too long, its clawed hands curled with unnatural dexterity. The glowing eyes burned with intelligence, locked onto the camera with a predator's focus. Its snarling maw parted just enough to reveal jagged, uneven teeth, stained dark with blood, as though it had just finished feasting.

Sheriff Carter stared at the image, his stomach twisting. Whatever this thing was, it was beyond anything he'd ever encountered.

"I need to make a call," he mumbled to himself, already reaching for his notepad to find the FBI's contact information.

TWENTY-NINE

Ethan woke with a start, his body drenched in sweat. His stomach churned uneasily, and his head was foggy. He rolled over, groaning as the light from the half-drawn curtains hit his face. Something wasn't right.

Sitting up, he rubbed his temples and glanced at the clock. It was already past 7:30 a.m., school day. He sighed, swung his legs over the side of the bed, and trudged out to the kitchen where Lillian was already up, humming softly as she buttered some toast.

"Morning, sweetheart," she said with a smile, but her expression quickly shifted to concern when she saw his face. "You don't look so good. Everything alright?"

Ethan shook his head, leaning against the counter. "I don't feel great. My stomach hurts, and my head…" He gestured vaguely. "It hurts too."

Lillian stepped over to him and placed a hand on his forehead. "You're a bit warm," she said, frowning. "Why don't you stay home today? I'll call the school."

Ethan nodded, relieved. "Thanks, Grandma."

Lillian paused, her hand moving to her heart as she heard the word. It was the first time he had called her that, and despite the worry etched on her face, it brought her a small, bittersweet comfort.

As she set the phone down after making the call, she turned back to him, her voice softer. "Is there anything else going on, Ethan? Something bothering you?"

Ethan hesitated. He wanted to keep last night's events to himself, to convince himself it was just a bad dream. But Lillian's gentle tone and concerned eyes made him falter. Finally, he exhaled deeply and said, "Something happened last night."

Lillian pulled out a chair at the kitchen table. "Tell me."

Ethan sat down across from her, fiddling with the edge of

the placemat. His shoulders hunched, and his voice wavered as he began. "I woke up to this tapping on my window." He paused, his fingers gripping the placemat tighter. "When I looked, there was… something outside. It was the wolf that chased us, but it was standing on two legs."

His breath faltered, and his eyes glistened as he looked down. "It was tapping on the glass with its claw, but it wasn't looking at me at first. It was staring at my bedroom door."

Lillian's eyes widened, but she stayed silent, her focus entirely on him.

"Then it turned and looked right at me," Ethan continued, his voice trembling. He gripped the table's edge, his hands trembling slightly. "Its eyes were glowing, and it… it smirked at me, Grandma. Like it knew something I didn't." He swallowed hard, his words unsteady. "And then it was gone. Just disappeared."

He hesitated, his breath uneven as he stared at the table. "After it left, I saw something move under the door. I heard scratching, like claws dragging across the wood. It just kept going, and I didn't know what to do."

Lillian stood and moved around the table, wrapping him in a firm hug. "That must have been terrifying," she said softly, her voice steady and warm. "But you're safe now. We'll figure out what's going on, I promise."

Ethan nodded, grateful for her calm response, though he wasn't sure he believed her.

"Why don't you lay down on the couch?" she suggested. "I'll make you some breakfast."

Ethan agreed and shuffled over to the couch, wrapping himself in a throw blanket. He stared at the TV, though he wasn't paying attention to the morning show flickering on the screen. His mind was stuck on the creature's smirk and the scratching at his door.

Meanwhile, Lillian moved into the next room, her footsteps soft against the hardwood floor. She picked up her phone and dialed Carter's number.

"Lillian?" he answered after the second ring, his voice surprised.

"Carter, something happened last night," she said, keeping her voice low. "Ethan saw the wolf outside his window. He said it was standing on two legs. It tapped on his window and then…" She hesitated, trying to find the right words. "It scared him half to death. But that's not all."

"What do you mean?" Carter asked, concerned.

Lillian gripped the phone tighter. "After it disappeared, he said he heard scratching inside his room. Under the door, like something was in there with him. I don't know what's going on, but it's not just the wolf outside. There's something else, Carter, and it's happening in that room."

There was a long pause on the other end before Carter spoke. "Don't let him leave the house, Lillian. Not for anything. Until I get this animal taken care of, keep him inside. And keep an eye on that room."

"I promise," Lillian said, her voice unsteady. "Just… be careful out there."

"Always," Carter replied before hanging up.

THIRTY

The coffee shop was alive with early morning energy as Special Agent Nicole Beretti leaned against the government-issued SUV, arms crossed, her gaze fixed on her partner through the glass door. *"What the hell are you ordering?"* she mouthed when he glanced her way.

Inside, her partner, Special Agent Noah Jacobi gestured animatedly at the barista in the small town coffee shop, its cozy interior filled with the smell of fresh brews and pastries. The place had a chalkboard menu with handwritten specials and a few locals sitting at scattered tables. A few moments later, he emerged with a cup piled so high with whipped cream it looked ready to topple over. In his other hand, he carried a cappuccino, which he handed to Beretti as he climbed into the SUV.

"What? It's a stressful job," Jacobi said, sliding into the passenger seat. "And look, I even got you a cappuccino. See? I'm thoughtful." He took a triumphant sip, whipped cream sticking to his upper lip.

Beretti rolled her eyes as she got into the driver's seat. "You're going to regret that in about an hour. Hell, *I'm* going to regret that in an hour! Aren't you lactose intolerant? Why are you even eating dairy?"

Jacobi grinned. "Because it tastes good, that's why. And, honestly, it's hit and miss when it bothers me. I'm a betting man. I like to take my chances." He leaned back in his seat, taking another triumphant sip. He buckled his seatbelt and leaned back. "Alright, so, what's the case? Or are you going to make me guess?"

Beretti smiled but kept her eyes on the road. "As usual, not much," she replied. "Couple of attacks, both victims were women. Large animal suspected. Sheriff called it in after the second body was found. Apparently, it's similar to some incidents that happened a few counties over last year."

Jacobi raised an eyebrow. "And by 'similar,' you mean…?"

"I mean, attacks so gruesome the local authorities couldn't handle them," Beretti said, her tone turning serious.

"Same MO: attacks near wooded areas, livestock torn apart, five dead, including three in one night. People reported seeing a werewolf in the area, and tracks were found near the attack sites. The injuries were consistent with a large predator, but nothing matched the behavior or patterns of any local wildlife. After the second incident, they called in the FBI. A specialist was sent to hunt it down."

She paused, glancing at Jacobi. "Apparently, while the agent was closing in, the creature crossed a highway and got hit by a semi. Killed it instantly. The driver wrecked but survived. The Feds swooped in, confiscated all the evidence, and left the locals with a neat little story about an emaciated bear being the culprit."

Jacobi frowned. "Clearly, it wasn't one of our teams sent there."

"Exactly," Beretti said, her brow furrowing. "Whoever they sent, it wasn't anyone we know. The attacks were covered up in the media and here we are."

Jacobi whistled low. "Sounds about right. And now it's happening in… where?"

"Evernight," Beretti said, as she glanced in the rearview mirror. "But you know how it goes. We'll get there, the sheriff will think we're overstepping, and by the time we solve the case, he'll be begging us to stay."

"Ah, the circle of life," Jacobi said with a grin, taking a sip of his coffee. "How do you think this one's gonna end? Me saving you and being the hero?"

Beretti laughed, her tone light but tinged with sarcasm. "Oh, absolutely. That's the dream, isn't it? But let's be real. It's probably going to end with us knee-deep in chaos, wondering why we didn't choose desk jobs."

Jacobi leaned back in his seat, setting the folder on the dashboard. "You know, we could always take a nice, quiet desk job. Less chance of being mauled by a cryptid... or whatever."

Beretti gave him a sideways glance. "You in a desk job? Please. The paperwork alone would kill you. But at least you would always have a restroom nearby."

"Fair point," Jacobi laughed. "Alright, so, two women attacked. Sounds like a Dogman, right?"

Beretti shrugged. "Yes. Dogman, more than likely."

"Aww man. Again? Couldn't we get a Sasquatch or a Sea Serpent?" Jacobi groaned, dragging out the words with exaggerated dismay. "Something new to spice things up?"

"Unfortunately, we don't get to choose," Beretti said. She reached over and turned up the heat, the car's vents blowing warm air over their hands. "This is my third Dogman case in a row. Seems like they're getting bolder across the nation. At this rate, we're going to need a dedicated Dogman task force."

Jacobi let out a mock sigh. "At least a Sea Serpent wouldn't follow you home. I'd take water-based nightmares over this any day."

"Be careful what you wish for," Beretti quipped. "You know how these things go."

That left them quiet for a moment, their thoughts filling the space as they drove past snow-covered fields and sparse patches of forest. The sheriff's department was only a few miles away, and both of them were mentally bracing for what lay ahead. For now, though, the familiarity of their banter kept the chill at bay.

THIRTY-ONE

Sheriff Carter pushed open the morgue door, finishing a conversation on his radio. "Just keep me updated," he said, his voice firm. He clipped the radio back to his belt and stepped inside. No matter how often he entered the sterile room, the unsettling atmosphere never diminished.

Dr. Evelyn Harker stood at the steel table, focused on her iPad.

"Sheriff," she greeted without looking up. "I was wondering when you'd get here."

"Been a busy morning," Sheriff Carter replied, his tone steady as he approached. "What do you have for me?"

Dr. Harker gestured toward the sheet-covered body on

the table. "Cathy Hensley," she said, pulling the sheet back to reveal her shoulders upward. Jagged wounds marred the pale skin, and Sheriff Carter's expression tightened as he took in the sight.

"I've completed the initial examination," Harker began. "The injuries are highly unusual."

"How unusual?" the sheriff asked, though he already suspected the answer.

Harker pointed to the deep puncture wounds along Cathy's shoulder and neck. "These bite marks are consistent with a large canine, but the spacing and depth suggest something much bigger than a wolf or dog. And the claw marks..." She gestured to the raking wounds down Cathy's torso. "They're sharp, precise, and deep. Whatever did this had immense strength."

The sheriff studied the injuries silently, his thoughts racing.

"The pattern indicates the predator dragged her after the attack," Harker continued, flipping through her notes. "And these aren't the first injuries like this. Adeline Morris had nearly identical wounds. The bite radius alone is nearly double that of a timber wolf."

She paused, glancing at the sheriff. "The size, the strength, the precision… it's unlike anything I've seen in local wildlife. This wasn't a typical predator."

Sheriff Carter nodded, his expression hardening. "What else did you find?"

"The dental impressions are strange," Harker said. "There are signs of wear, like an older animal, but the sheer power behind these attacks suggests it's still incredibly capable. And based on the injuries, I don't believe it's hunting for food. The pattern, the brutality… it seems more like sport or dominance than survival."

Sheriff Carter clenched his jaw. "So we're dealing with something that's experienced, deadly, and not afraid of people."

Harker nodded grimly. "That sums it up."

The sheriff exhaled slowly, his gaze lingering on Cathy's lifeless form. "Alright, Evelyn. Thanks for your work on this. Let me know if anything new comes up."

"Will do," she replied, covering Cathy's body again. "And Sheriff? Be careful out there. Whatever did this isn't afraid of humans."

Sheriff Carter gave a curt nod before turning and heading down the corridor to the foyer. His mind churned with the implications of what Harker had just told him. He knew this wasn't just an ordinary predator. It was the same wolf-like creature Ethan had described, and it wasn't going to stop until someone put an end to it.

THIRTY-TWO

Rubbing at his temples, Sheriff Carter pushed through the doors of the office, the ache in his head refusing to let up. He waved to a deputy near the front desk before making his way to the dispatcher's counter. The fluorescent lights overhead made him squint as he leaned lightly against the counter.

"Have you got any ibuprofen handy, Shelly?" he asked, his tone edged with fatigue.

Shelly glanced up from her computer. "Rough day?"

"Rough week," Sheriff Carter said with a tired smile.

Shelly reached into a drawer, pulling out a small bottle and handing it to him. "Careful, or I'm going to start charging you for these."

He shook out two pills, swallowing them dry. "Thanks. You're a lifesaver."

Shelly tilted her head slightly, her tone brightening. "Speaking of saving lives, Grace is doing great. She's with my sister today, having a playdate with her dog, Max."

The sheriff smiled faintly. "Good to hear. After all she's been through, and the family not wanting her, it's nice to know she's settling in."

"She really is," Shelly said. "Sweet as ever. Max is going to sleep well tonight after trying to keep up with her energy."

Sheriff Carter smiled. "Glad to hear it. You're doing good work there, Shelly."

The sound of the station's front doors opening drew his attention. Turning, Sheriff Carter spotted two figures striding in, their presence immediately commanding the room.

They were dressed in black tactical cargo pants and fitted black shirts that suggested practicality over anything else. The man, with neatly styled brown hair, surveyed the room with an air of confidence that bordered on arrogance, his focused gaze taking in every detail.

Beside him, the woman was striking, her piercing blue eyes scanning the space with the precision of someone who missed nothing. She was taller than average, her athletic frame, and the way she carried herself making it clear she was more than capable of handling herself. Her long blonde hair was pulled back into a ponytail, emphasizing her angled features and no-nonsense demeanor.

The sheriff stepped forward, eyeing the pair. "Agents?"

The woman nodded, her gaze locking with his. "Sheriff Carter?"

"That's me," he replied, extending a hand.

She took it, her grip firm. "Special Agent Nicole Beretti. This is my partner, Special Agent Noah Jacobi."

Jacobi offered his own handshake, "Appreciate you having us, Sheriff. We're ready to help where we can."

The sheriff motioned toward his office. "Let's get started. There's a lot to cover."

The agents settled in as Sheriff Carter returned to his chair, leaning forward with his elbows on the desk. "So," he said, "here's what we know so far. Two women attacked, Cathy Hensley and Adeline Morris. Both cases are gruesome. Large animal suspected, but the details don't match anything local wildlife should be capable of."

He opened a folder on his desk and slid it toward Beretti and Jacobi. "Here's everything we have so far. Photos from the scenes, coroner's reports, and witness statements. Not much to go on, but maybe it'll give you a clearer picture."

Jacobi took the folder and began flipping through it while Beretti leaned in to glance at the pages. "Tracks too big for a wolf," Jacobi said, pointing to one of the photos. "And those claw marks... they look familiar."

Beretti nodded. "It fits the pattern we've seen before. These kinds of predators aren't typical, they're something else entirely."

Sheriff Carter leaned forward, his brow creasing. "What do you think it is?"

Beretti exchanged a glance with Jacobi before answering. "We believe it's a cryptid called a Dogman. It's a creature that resembles a large wolf but stands upright like a human. Dogman attacks seem to be increasing, given this is the 3rd case in a row for me dealing with them. They're vicious and highly intelligent."

Sheriff Carter leaned back in his chair and exhaled slowly. "So, this thing really exists?" he said, his tone disbelieving but edged with resignation. "Because what you just described sounds almost impossible, but... it fits what we've seen so far."

Jacobi nodded. "It exists, Sheriff. And it's dangerous. That's why we're here."

"So," Sheriff Carter began, "what's your experience with cases like this? If you don't mind me asking."

Beretti exchanged a glance with Jacobi, a small smile playing at the corners of her mouth. "More than you can imagine," she said simply.

He nodded, the impact of her words settling upon him. "Alright then. I assume you'll be taking the lead here?"

"That's typically how this works," Jacobi said, his tone light but respectful. "We'll keep you in the loop and call on your department as needed. Teamwork makes the dream work, right?"

The sheriff chuckled despite himself. "Fair enough. What do you suggest I do in the meantime? Should I warn the townsfolk?"

Beretti tilted her head thoughtfully. "How do you normally communicate with your town?"

"We've got a couple of options," Sheriff Carter replied. "I could hold a meeting or send out an SMS alert to everyone. Cathy's attack is already front-page news, so people are talking."

"A meeting might cause unnecessary panic at this stage," Beretti said. "An SMS could work, though. Keep it simple by warning them about a wild animal, advise them to avoid walking or jogging alone."

"I'll also talk to the local paper," Sheriff Carter added. "Ask them to print a warning in tomorrow's edition. Something official but not alarming."

Jacobi nodded. "That sounds like a solid plan. Just keep the tone calm. No need to start a stampede."

"Got it," the sheriff said. He hesitated, then added, "There's one other thing. My partner's grandson, Ethan, has been seeing this… thing. It chased him and his friends and was at his window last night. He's also been experiencing strange things in his room at night. It's got Lillian and me both spooked and worried sick."

Beretti exchanged a glance with Jacobi before replying. "We'll make a point to talk to him at some stage. Thanks for letting us know."

"Anything else you need from me right now?" Sheriff Carter asked, shifting back to business.

"Not at the moment," Beretti replied, glancing at her phone to confirm the location of their accommodations. "We'll be staying at the Lucky Bear Inn. If anything urgent comes up, we'll be in touch."

"Thank you, Agents," Sheriff Carter said. "I appreciate you coming and assisting. We will work with you wherever needed."

As the agents stood to leave, the sheriff offered one last piece of advice. "If you're looking for dinner, try the Pines Diner on Main Street. Best burgers and pie in town."

"Noted," Jacobi said with a grin. "Thanks, Sheriff."

Beretti and Jacobi stepped out into the cold, snowflakes lazily drifting down as the icy air nipped at their cheeks. Pulling her coat closer, Beretti glanced at Jacobi as they headed towards their car.

"Well, that was a pleasant surprise," Jacobi said, his

breath visible in the icy air. "A sheriff who's actually on board and willing to help. Mark it on the calendar."

Beretti smiled faintly. "Don't get too used to it. It's probably the exception, not the rule." Still, she couldn't help but note the sheriff's reaction during their meeting. He hadn't flinched or dismissed their explanation of the Dogman like most did. Instead, he had taken it in stride, almost as if he'd been expecting something extraordinary. "He's more open-minded than most," she added thoughtfully.

They climbed into the car, the engine rumbling to life as Beretti cranked the heat to full blast. As they pulled onto the road toward the Lucky Bear Inn, the details of the case lingered in their minds. They had only just begun piecing together the facts, but even in these early stages, one thing was clear: this was no ordinary investigation.

THIRTY-THREE

The knock at the front door startled Ethan from his half-hearted attempt at reading. He glanced at the clock, school was out. Swinging his legs off the couch, he shuffled to the door, pulling it open to reveal Nick and Ryan standing on the porch, bundled up in their winter coats and grinning at him.

"Hey, man," Nick said, giving a small wave. "We heard you were sick. You ok?"

Ethan shrugged. "Yeah," he said, leaning against the doorframe.

"Good," Ryan chimed in. "We were gonna see if you wanted to come over and play some games."

Ethan hesitated, his stomach twisting. The thought of leaving the house made him uneasy. "I think I'll pass," he said. "But, uh, I've got to tell you something."

Nick and Ryan exchanged curious looks. "What's up?" Nick asked.

Ethan glanced around, as though checking to make sure no one else was listening. "You... you know the woman who got attacked on the trail, right?"

Nick nodded, his grin fading. "Yeah. My mom was talking about it this morning."

"It wasn't just some wild animal," Ethan said, his voice dropping to a whisper. "I think it was that wolf that chased us the other day. You guys shouldn't play outside. Not until they figure out how to get rid of it."

Ryan suddenly broke into a grin. "You're just trying to scare us, aren't you? Maybe we should go check out the woods, see if we can find it ourselves."

Nick turned to him, frowning. "Nah, man, that's a stupid idea. You really want to end up like that lady?"

Ryan shrugged, still grinning. "I'm just saying, it'd be kind of cool. Like an adventure or something."

"Yeah, an adventure that gets us killed," Nick shot back. "Ethan's right. We should stay out of the woods. At least for now."

Ethan nodded, grateful for Nick's level-headedness. "Seriously, guys. Just be careful, okay?"

Ryan sighed dramatically. "Fine. We'll stay out of the woods. For now."

"Thanks," Ethan said, offering a small smile. "I'll catch up with you later."

"Sure thing," Nick said, nudging Ryan. "Come on, let's head back."

"See ya, scaredy city boy," Ryan teased, laughing as Nick turned to glare at him.

"Knock it off, Ryan," Nick mumbled, shoving his hands into his pockets as they headed down the driveway. Their voices drifted away, Ryan's laughter mixing with Nick's annoyed retorts.

Ethan shut the door and leaned his forehead against it, a knot of unease forming in his chest. He could only hope they'd take his warning seriously.

THIRTY-FOUR

The Pines Diner was a classic small town spot, its bright neon sign buzzing faintly against the darkened sky. Inside, the lively chatter of locals and the inviting warmth of the room created a welcoming atmosphere.

Beretti and Jacobi slid into a booth near the back, their appetites growing as they scanned the menus. A cheerful waitress introduced herself, set down two glasses of water, and quickly moved on to another table. Jacobi wasted no time, his eyes skimming the menu for something hearty enough to satisfy his growing hunger.

Beretti raised a brow, taking the file from her bag, and placing it on the table. "Try not to order anything with dairy this time, Jacobi. I'm not pulling over halfway back to the inn."

Jacobi glanced up with a sheepish grin. "Yeah, lesson learned. I shouldn't have gambled on that macchiato earlier." He closed the menu dramatically. "Fine, no dairy. But I'm getting the burger."

Beretti glanced at the menu, tapping her finger thoughtfully. "I'll go with the stuffed bell peppers. They're filled with quinoa, black beans, and diced vegetables, topped with a light tomato sauce. Sounds good."

"Yeah, that does," Jacobi replied, leaning back in his chair.

Beretti set the menu aside and flipped open the folder in front of her. "Alright, let's get to work."

Jacobi leaned forward, peering over the edge of the folder as she spread the papers across the table. Notes from Sheriff Carter detailed the injuries sustained by Cathy Hensley and Adeline Morris, along with summaries of the coroner's findings. Beretti had deliberately left out any graphic photos, mindful of the public setting.

"This is a mess," Jacobi said, picking up one of the coroner's reports. "Two women, killed weeks apart, but almost identical injuries. And look at this..." He pointed to the mention of the attack in Livingston. "Five people dead last year, similar bite patterns, and claw marks."

"Both Dogmen, no doubt," Beretti said, her voice low.

The waitress returned with their drinks, setting down two sodas and scribbling their dinner orders onto her notepad. She lingered for a moment, her eyes drifting to Jacobi. "Anything else I can get *you*?" she asked with a playful smile.

Jacobi grinned back. "I think we're good for now, but I'll let you know if I change my mind."

The waitress chuckled softly and gave him a little wink before heading off to another table. Beretti, watching the exchange, raised an eyebrow. "Well, aren't you popular?"

Jacobi leaned back in his seat, looking thoroughly pleased. "What can I say? Some of us have a way with the ladies."

Beretti let out a dry laugh, shaking her head. "Yeah, it's obvious."

"So, what's our plan of attack?" Jacobi asked, taking a sip of his soda.

Beretti tapped one of the maps included in the file. "We

start by heading to the scene of the last attack on the trail," Beretti said. "We'll retrace its movements from there and try to figure out where it's been and why it's targeting this area. Could be to do with the boy Sheriff Carter mentioned, but worth checking the scene out."

"Agreed," Jacobi replied.

Beretti glanced up at a television mounted above the counter. The local news was playing, the headline scrolling across the bottom of the screen: "HEAVY SNOWSTORM EXPECTED TO HIT REGION TOMORROW NIGHT."

"Of course," she said. "That's going to make it even more challenging."

Jacobi followed her gaze and groaned. "Snow's going to make tracking it a nightmare. And if it's already hard to find, we're in for a long couple of days."

Beretti nodded. "We'll need to move fast tomorrow. Cover as much ground as we can before the storm hits. And," she added, glancing at Jacobi, "We should also talk to the friend who was on the phone with Cathy when it happened. She might have heard something that could help us."

Jacobi nodded. "Good call. That might give us more context on the attack itself."

Their food arrived, the comforting aroma of burgers and fries mixing with the savory scent of roasted peppers and tomato sauce. Jacobi immediately picked up his burger, taking a big bite. "Oh yeah," he said, his voice muffled by the mouthful of food. "This is exactly what I needed."

Beretti curled her lips in amusement as she cut into one of her stuffed peppers. "Glad you're enjoying yourself."

The rest of the meal passed in relative ease, with Beretti finishing her food and Jacobi occasionally tossing in a light-hearted comment. The reports stayed untouched on the table, and for a little while, the two agents managed to shift their focus from the case to something as simple as a good meal.

Twenty minutes later they stepped back into the cold night air. Beretti pulled her coat tighter, glancing at Jacobi.

"You ready for another Dogman?" she asked.

Jacobi grinned, shoving his hands into his pockets. "Not even a little. But let's do it anyway."

THIRTY-FIVE

The aroma of roasted chicken and vegetables filled the cozy kitchen as Ethan pushed a piece of broccoli around his plate with his fork. He wasn't particularly hungry, and his mind was elsewhere. Across the table, Lillian watched him with a mix of concern and quiet patience.

"You feeling any better, sweetheart?" she asked gently, breaking the silence.

"Yeah, a little," Ethan mumbled, though his tone lacked conviction.

A knock at the door interrupted the moment, and before Lillian could rise, the door creaked open. Carter stepped inside, brushing snow off his shoulders as he entered.

"Evening, Lillian. Hope I'm not intruding," he said with a warm smile, closing the door behind him.

"Not at all, Carter," Lillian replied, gesturing toward the kitchen. "We were just having dinner. Sit down, join us."

Carter nodded and took a seat at the table, his gaze settling on Ethan. "How's the patient? Feeling any better?"

Ethan shrugged, still poking at his food. "A little."

Carter studied the boy for a moment, noting the tension in his shoulders and the tired look in his eyes. He glanced at Lillian, then back at Ethan. "Let me guess," he said, leaning forward slightly. "You're nervous about sleeping in your room tonight."

Ethan's fork paused mid-push, and his wide eyes darted to Carter. He didn't need to answer. His expression said it all.

Carter smiled reassuringly. "How about this? I'll stay over tonight. You can take the couch, and I'll sleep in your room. If anything happens, I'll be right there to deal with it. That is, if it's okay with your grandma. How's that sound?"

Ethan's face lit up, the first genuine smile Lillian had seen all day. "Really? You'd do that?"

"Of course," Carter replied.

Lillian glanced between them, her lips curving into a soft smile. "I think that's a great idea," she said. "Thank you, Carter."

The pressure in the room lifted slightly, and Ethan seemed to relax, taking a few bites of his dinner. He looked up at Carter, curiosity sparking in his eyes. "Do you have any kids?" he asked.

Carter nodded, leaning back in his chair. "I do. I have a son, Ben. He's grown now, lives in New Hampshire with his family. I don't get to see him as much as I'd like, but we stay in touch."

Ethan's brow furrowed. "What's he like?"

"Ben's a good man," Carter said, his voice tinged with pride. "Hardworking, kind. He's got a little boy of his own now, Hunter. My grandson. Keeps me on my toes whenever I visit."

Ethan's eyes lit up. "That's cool. I bet he's fun."

Carter chuckled. "Oh, he's a handful, that's for sure. Always full of questions, always running around. Kind of like someone else I know," he said, giving Ethan a pointed look.

Ethan grinned, finishing the last bite of his chicken. A hint of relief washed over him, as if a burden had loosened, even if only slightly.

As the meal wound down, Lillian cleared the table while Ethan helped with the dishes. Carter leaned against the counter, watching them with a thoughtful expression.

"Thank you for dinner, Lillian," he said after a moment. "And Ethan, don't worry. We'll figure out what's going on. You just focus on getting some rest tonight."

Ethan nodded, his gratitude evident in his small smile. Tonight, at least, he felt a little less alone.

THIRTY-SIX

The room was still and quiet as Carter sat on the edge of Ethan's bed, rubbing the back of his neck. He glanced around the small room, reflecting on the responsibility of keeping Ethan safe and the trust Lillian had placed in him. He didn't understand what was going on, but he felt protective of the vulnerable boy.

He laid down on the bed, pulling the covers over himself as he tried to relax. The pillow smelled faintly of detergent, a subtle reminder of the homey environment he was a part of. Yet, despite the warmth of the room, a chill prickled at his skin, and his thoughts kept drifting back to the strange and gruesome details of the recent attacks. He closed his eyes, forcing himself to think of something else, and eventually drifted into a light, uneasy sleep.

Carter woke with a start, his heart racing. For a moment, he couldn't remember where he was. The dim room came into focus, the shadows cast by the moonlight playing tricks on his eyes. He exhaled slowly, but then his gaze landed on the mirror across the room.

Carter froze when something moved.

In the reflection, a dark shape lingered near the window, tall and unnaturally still. His pulse quickened as he turned his head toward the window itself. Nothing. When he looked back at the mirror, the figure was gone. The air in the room was unmistakenly thick, making it difficult to breathe.

He sat up and looked around the room. "Get it together," he said under his breath. It had to be his imagination, his nerves getting the better of him. He lay back down, staring at the ceiling until his breathing evened out again.

THIRTY-SEVEN

Eddie Shetfield adjusted his knit cap as he walked through the dark alley behind the row of houses. A biting wind whipped at his face as the snow crunched under his boots. No matter how frigid the weather, Eddie was always out looking for a quick buck. It was what he did best. In and out of jail since he was a teenager, robbery was his bread and butter. Tonight was just another job.

Joe "Four Fingers" Malley walked beside him, pulling his coat tighter. "I dunno about this, Eddie," Joe said, his breath visible in the freezing air. "This place gives me the creeps."

"You always got the creeps," Eddie shot back, his voice low. "We've been watching this guy for a week. Lives alone. No dog, no alarm system. He's probably fast asleep right now."

Joe glanced over his shoulder, scanning the darkness. "Yeah, but it's too quiet. You notice that? It's just… dead."

Eddie waved him off. "You're paranoid. Come on, let's get this done."

As they neared the house, a crow landed on a low branch above them and let out two sharp squawks, the sound cutting through the silence. Joe jumped, his heart pounding as he looked up at the bird.

"What the hell?" he said, staring at it like it might swoop down on him.

"It's just a bird, you idiot," Eddie said, shaking his head as he kept walking. "Focus."

Joe lingered for a moment, his gaze locked on the crow as it tilted its head and watched them. With a nervous glance back at the woods, he reluctantly followed Eddie to the house.

Eddie pulled a crowbar from his backpack, testing the window. It popped open with minimal effort.

Joe stopped suddenly, his head jerking back towards the woods. "Did you hear that?" he whispered.

Eddie didn't even look up. "Hear what? Stop stalling and

keep watch."

"I'm serious, Eddie," Joe insisted, stepping back from the house. "It sounded like growling. From over there." He pointed toward the dark line of trees.

Eddie turned and glared at him. "You're such a wimp, dude. Shut up and let me do my job."

"Fine, but you'll need a boost," Joe said reluctantly, crouching down. Eddie stepped onto Joe's hands, using the leverage to push himself up toward the window.

Gripping the windowsill, Eddie began to hoist himself up when Joe froze, his head snapping toward the woods. A low growl echoed through the stillness, closer this time, reverberating in his chest.

"There it is again," Joe whispered, his voice trembling.

Eddie gritted his teeth, his weight balanced awkwardly as Joe held his foot. "Stop stalling and hold steady," he snapped, his irritation mounting.

Before Joe could reply, the crow squawked again, loud and jarring in the silence. The sound sent a jolt through Joe, his nerves snapping entirely. Without warning, he released Eddie's foot and bolted, sprinting back toward the car.

"Joe! What the hell?" Eddie said, his frustration boiling over.

Joe didn't answer, his footsteps growing fainter as he disappeared into the snow.

Eddie clung to the windowsill, his footing suddenly gone. Dangling awkwardly, he strained to pull himself upward, his muscles burning with the effort. Gritting his teeth, he managed to haul himself partially onto the ledge, his head, and shoulders now inside the house while his legs dangled outside.

Eddie cursed under his breath as he wriggled further through the window. "Useless fool," he mumbled. "Always jumps at his own shadow."

But then, a chill crept over Eddie, unrelated to the cold night air. The hair on the back of his neck stood on end, and a primal instinct screamed at him to get out of there. Stupidly he shook it off, determined to grab whatever valuables he could and be done with it.

As he started to pull himself through the window, a sound broke through the stillness: footsteps approaching from behind the house. Eddie froze, unable to turn and see what was coming. His grip on the windowsill tightened, and his pulse quickened.

"Joe?" Eddie called softly, his voice shaky but quiet enough not to draw attention from inside the house. "If that's you, quit messing around and give me a hand."

The footsteps grew louder, steady and unnerving, each one adding to the tension in the air. Eddie stopped, gripping the windowsill tighter. For a fleeting moment, he thought the homeowner might have heard him breaking in and was coming to confront him. His chest tightened at the thought, but something about the way the steps moved seemed unnatural.

As he strained to listen, a pungent, overwhelming smell hit him. Wet dog, acrid and foul, filled his nostrils, making his stomach churn and a new wave of panic set in.

"Joe?" he called again, his voice barely above a whisper. "Come on, man. This isn't funny."

The steps stopped directly behind him. Eddie inhaled sharply as dread surged through him. Whatever was behind him, it wasn't Joe, and it sure as hell wasn't the homeowner.

His instincts screamed at him to pull himself through the window, and he strained against the sill, trying to haul himself inside.

But it was too late.

The Dogman lunged.

Pain exploded through Eddie's body as claws raked down his back, tearing through flesh like paper. He screamed, the sound echoing through the still night. Blood-soaked his coat as he thrashed, his legs kicking uselessly.

The Dogman lunged again, its massive weight crashing into Eddie and shattering the window above him. Shards of glass rained down, slicing his exposed skin as he struggled in vain to free himself.

The creature's jaws clamped down on his thigh, the pressure so intense it threatened to shatter his bones. Eddie's screams turned to guttural cries as the Dogman bit down harder, severing his leg with terrifying efficiency. Blood spurted from the wound as the creature yanked the limb free, leaving Eddie half-stuck in the broken window.

His body slumped forward as shock overtook him, the world spinning into darkness. Blood dripped from the Dogman's jaws as it let out a chilling howl, a sound that echoed through the empty streets and into the frozen woods beyond. The Dogman snarled, gripping the severed leg in its jaws before retreating into the woods, its silhouette vanishing into the night.

****

Joe nervously chewed his nails while sitting in the car, his gaze locked on the alley. He willed Eddie to appear, his fingers drumming anxiously against the steering wheel. Minutes stretched into what felt like hours. He debated starting the car and leaving but couldn't bring himself to abandon his friend completely.

Then a howl shattered the silence, long and mournful, cutting through the night like a warning. Joe's breath caught in his chest as icy dread crept over him. He gripped the steering wheel tightly, his heart racing.

"To hell with this," he mumbled under his breath. With shaking hands, he threw the car into gear and sped away, the tires skidding on the icy road.

Across the street, a neighbor peered out their window, watching the car vanish into the night. Frowning, they pulled the blinds shut and retreated back into the safety of their home, leaving the quiet street undisturbed once more.

THIRTY-EIGHT

It was around 4 a.m. when Carter woke again, his senses on high alert. Something wasn't right, tugging at his instincts and refusing to let go. He sat up slowly, his eyes scanning the room. The stillness seemed unnatural, every sound in the house amplified by the quiet.

The feeling of being watched crept over him like ice water running down his spine. His gaze shifted to the window, drawn by an inexplicable pull. The sheer curtain was pulled aside slightly, revealing the snow-covered landscape outside.

A shiver ran through him as he saw the silhouette of the Dogman perched on the neighbor's barn roof, like a predator surveying its territory. Carter was overwhelmed by dread, unable to avert his gaze. It shifted slightly, and the faint moonlight caught its glowing fiery eyes. They burned like embers, unblinking and filled with an intelligence that made Carter's stomach churn.

The creature turned its head slowly, as though sensing his gaze. When their eyes met, a jolt of terror so visceral that Carter could barely breathe seized him. The creature's lips pulled back in a faint snarl, revealing jagged, glinting teeth.

Then, without warning, it leapt from the barn, landing soundlessly in the snow below. Carter scrambled to the window, his hands braced on the sill as he watched it dart behind the house, disappearing into the darkness.

He remained rooted to the spot, his eyes fixed on the empty darkness where the creature had disappeared. Hearing Ethan describe the Dogman had been unsettling enough, but seeing it with his own eyes was something else entirely.

Sleep evaded him for the rest of the night. By the time dawn began to break, he was still wide awake, his thoughts consumed by the encounter.

When Ethan knocked on the bedroom door that morning, rubbing his eyes sleepily, Carter forced a smile. "Hey, kiddo. Sleep okay?"

Ethan nodded, climbing onto the bed. "Yeah. Did you?"

Carter hesitated, then ruffled Ethan's hair. "Sure," he said. "Nothing to worry about."

THIRTY-NINE

The GPS chimed, directing them to turn left into the small parking lot at Lockward Trailhead. Nicole Beretti guided the black SUV off the road, the tires crunching softly over the snow-dusted ground. Beside her, Jacobi was focused on his phone, typing out a quick update to their boss, ASAC Ward.

As Beretti brought the vehicle to a stop, Jacobi hit send and tucked his phone into his jacket. "Trailhead looks quiet," he said, glancing out the window at the untouched snow.

Beretti scanned the empty lot as she stepped out, her boots sinking into the soft snow. The trailhead stood silent, a stark reminder of the warnings issued after the attacks. People had been told to stay indoors, to avoid the woods at all costs.

Jacobi joined her, shrugging his pack into place. "Not exactly the kind of scene you want to hike into, is it?"

"Definitely not," Beretti replied, opening the back of the SUV. She pulled out a folder of notes and a GPS device, her eyes scanning the map she'd marked earlier. "The attack site is just over a mile in."

Jacobi nodded, grabbing two high-powered rifles from the back and handing one to Beretti. Both agents also checked their holstered firearms on their hips.

"All set?" Jacobi asked.

"Let's go," Beretti replied, slinging the rifle over her shoulder.

Despite the serene surroundings, both agents were on edge, their senses tuned to every sound.

After a short while on the trail, they came across an older man in a bright yellow windbreaker who was jogging toward them. He slowed as he approached, giving them a curious glance.

"Morning," Jacobi greeted.

"Morning," the man replied, as he jogged on the spot.

"Something going on here? You two look serious."

"We are," Beretti said. "There was an attack here the other day. A woman was killed. We strongly advise against jogging alone on this trail."

The man waved a dismissive hand. "I've been running these trails for years. Probably just a bear or a coyote. I'm not worried."

"This isn't something to take lightly," Jacobi added, stepping forward. "It's not safe."

The jogger chuckled, shaking his head. "You folks do your thing. I'll be fine." He jogged off, his footsteps quickly fading down the trail.

Beretti sighed, exchanging a look with Jacobi. "Arrogance is a dangerous thing."

"Let's just hope he's lucky today," Jacobi replied.

They continued along the trail, their heads on a swivel as they scanned the woods for any signs of movement.

The GPS beeped softly, signaling they had reached the marked coordinates. The trail widened slightly, revealing a patch of disturbed snow partially hidden by a thin layer of fresh snowfall.

Beretti and Jacobi stopped, their eyes sweeping the scene.

"This is where Cathy was attacked," Beretti said, pointing to the edge of the trail where the snow was scuffed and scattered. She turned, gesturing toward a cluster of eastern hemlock trees off the trail. Their dense green needles stood out starkly against the barren winter landscape. "And that's where she was dragged."

Jacobi knelt near the disturbed snow, brushing away the fresh layer to expose faint patterns underneath. "It's hard to make out anything distinct," he said. "The snow's covered most of it."

Approaching the trees, Beretti's concentration intensified as her eyes searched the surroundings. Near the hemlocks, she spotted faint indentations in the snow leading deeper into the woods. She crouched, studying them closely.

"Tracks," she said, her voice low but certain. She glanced back at Jacobi. "Faint, but they're still visible. Definitely the size of Dogman tracks."

As Beretti stood, brushing snow off her gloves, her gaze drifted upward. A crow perched silently on a branch above them, its dark eyes fixed on the scene below. It didn't move, watching them with an almost curious stillness.

"Let's head back," she said, turning away from the bird. "We've seen enough for now. We weren't expecting much under the snow, but it's good to get an idea of the area. Looks like it ambushed her right at the trail and dragged her quickly into the woods."

Jacobi nodded. "Yeah, classic ambush."

They both exchanged uneasy looks, their minds already planning their next steps before they turned back toward the SUV.

As they continued back, Beretti's phone buzzed in her pocket. She pulled it out, glancing at the screen. "It's the sheriff."

She answered, putting the phone on speakerphone. "Sheriff Carter. What's up?"

"I'd like to meet with you both," Sheriff Carter said. "Diner on Main Street, when you're free."

Beretti nodded. "Understood. We're planning to talk with Cathy's friend first, the one who was on the phone with her during the attack. After that, we'll head your way."

"Sounds good," Carter replied. "See you soon."

Beretti ended the call and slid her phone back into her pocket as they came to the parking lot. "Let's roll. We've got a long day ahead."

Jacobi climbed into the driver's seat as Beretti took the passenger side, the SUV rumbling to life as they pulled out of the lot and onto the snowy road.

FORTY

Beth Neale's workplace was a small, bustling bakery on the corner of Main Street. She had been expecting the special agents after their earlier call to arrange the meeting. The scent of fresh bread and pastries wafted through the air as customers came and went, their boots leaving faint snowy trails on the wooden floors. Beretti glanced at her watch as they stepped inside, the warmth of the shop a welcome contrast to the chill outside.

Beth stood behind the counter, arranging a tray of croissants. She was in her late thirties, with a friendly face that now bore an unmistakable strain. The dark circles under her eyes spoke of sleepless nights and grief.

"Beth Neale?" Beretti asked, stepping forward.

Beth looked up, startled. "Yes? Can I help you?"

Beretti flashed her badge. "Special Agent Nicole Beretti. This is my partner, Special Agent Noah Jacobi. First, let me say we're deeply sorry for your loss. We'd like to ask you a few questions about the phone call you had with Cathy Hensley."

Beth's face dropped, and she glanced at the customers still milling about. "Can we… do this somewhere private?"

"Of course," Jacobi said, his tone gentle. "Wherever you're comfortable."

Beth told her coworker she was taking a break and showed them to a small back office in the bakery, closing the door. She motioned for them to sit as she sank into a chair, wringing her hands nervously.

"I… I still can't believe what happened," Beth began, her voice trembling. "We were supposed to meet for coffee that morning. I just…" She trailed off, shaking her head.

"Take your time," Beretti said. "We just need to understand what you heard during that call. Anything you can remember could help."

Beth took a deep breath, composing herself. "We were talking about nothing important," she said. "Just catching up, you know? Cathy mentioned she was on the trail. Then, all of a sudden, she stopped talking."

Jacobi leaned forward slightly. "What do you mean, she stopped talking?"

"She just… went to continue talking and stopped. Like the words got stuck in her mouth," Beth said. "I heard this crashing sound, like something big was moving through the woods. Cathy whispered something about hearing it too. I told her not to run, to back away slowly."

"And did she?" Beretti asked.

Beth nodded quickly. "She said she was, but I could hear the fear in her voice. She told me it was following her, staying in the trees. I kept telling her to stay calm, to keep moving slowly."

"What happened next?" Jacobi prompted.

Beth's hands tightened into fists. "It was quiet for a moment. Then Cathy said she couldn't hear anything anymore and thought it was gone. We agreed to meet for the coffee then we hung up. When she didn't turn up, I started to worry that the thing had come back."

"What did you hear, Beth?" Beretti asked gently.

Beth swallowed hard. "Other than something heavy running, I didn't hear anything else."

"Did Cathy mention seeing anything specific?" Beretti asked after a moment.

Beth shook her head. "No. She only said she heard something. But whatever it was, it was big."

A crease formed between Beretti's brows. "Anything else?"

Beth hesitated, her gaze flickering downward in thought. "Well… she did say she kept hearing this bird, squawking over and over. Like a crow or a raven. It was so loud she could barely hear me on the phone." She let out a shaky breath. "That was right before she heard the ruckus in the woods."

Beretti and Jacobi exchanged a glance.

"You did the right thing calling for help. It's not your fault, Beth," Jacobi assured her.

Beth nodded, but her face crumpled, tears welling in her eyes. "I just wish I could have done more."

"You gave us more than enough," Beretti said, standing. "Thank you for talking with us. If you think of anything else, no matter how small, please call us." She handed Beth a card.

Beth took it with a shaky hand. "Will you catch whatever did this?"

Beretti's expression hardened. "That's the plan."

As they stepped out of the bakery and into the street, Jacobi let out a low whistle. "Poor woman feels guilty."

"Yeah, but there was nothing she could have done," Beretti agreed. "Let's get to the sheriff and compare notes."

Jacobi nodded, as they walked down the street toward the diner.

FORTY-ONE

Abdul Shire woke slowly, his body sluggish from the lingering effects of the flu that had kept him bedridden for days. His head throbbed faintly, and his mouth was dry as sandpaper. Reaching for the small nightstand beside his bed, his fingers fumbled for the half-empty bottle of cold medicine and the glass of water he'd left there the night before.

He downed the last of the water, the cool liquid soothing his throat. The medicine left a faintly bitter aftertaste, but the slight relief it offered was worth it.

At sixty-one years old, he no longer bounced back from illness the way he used to. Still, he prided himself on his independence. He had no wife, no children, and he liked it that way. Born in Somalia, Abdul had immigrated to the United States in the 1990s, building a life as a long-haul truck driver before retiring two years ago.

Most of Abdul's days were now spent reading novels or making the drive to a nearby town to visit his girlfriend, Margaret. They weren't serious, just a comfortable companionship that suited them both. Twice a week was all he needed.

Glancing at the clock, he noted it was 9.30 a.m. Later than he'd like, but the flu demanded its due.

Dragging himself out of bed, Abdul immediately noticed the house was cooler than usual. A brief frown crossed his face as he wondered if something was wrong with the thermostat. Shuffling to the kitchen, he tied his robe loosely around his waist. He filled the kettle, set it on the stove, and turned on the burner. A hot cup of tea would help clear his head.

He stood leaning on the counter, watching the snow drift lazily past the window. The soft white light brightened the otherwise somber morning. Abdul's home was modest but comfortable, a single-story structure with a cozy sunroom just off the kitchen. He rarely used the sunroom in the winter, as it was drafty and cold, but he enjoyed sitting there in the spring to watch the birds.

A sudden chill swept through the kitchen, raising goosebumps on his arms. Abdul frowned, rubbing his hands together. The cold was sharper than usual, as though someone had left a door open. He turned toward the sunroom, his brow wrinkled.

The door leading to the sunroom was ajar, swaying slightly as another icy draft slipped through. "What on earth…" Abdul mumbled, as he walked toward the room.

As he stepped into the sunroom, his mouth dropped as he struggled to process what he was seeing. There, halfway through the shattered window, was the body of a man. Snow and shards of glass littered the floor around him, the icy draft making Abdul's skin prickle. Abdul staggered back, his heart pounding in his chest.

The man's torso was inside the room, his back facing up, and the rest of his body remained obscured outside the shattered window. The back of his shirt was shredded, exposing deep gashes that oozed blood onto the floorboards. Abdul couldn't tell if the man was alive or dead. The sight was so surreal, so horrifying, that for a moment, he wondered if he was still feverish and dreaming.

Snapping out of his stupor, Abdul backed away, his hand reaching instinctively for the wall to steady himself. He stumbled slightly, nearly losing his footing.

"This can't be happening," he whispered, his voice trembling.

He turned and hurried back through the kitchen, his bare feet slipping slightly on the tile. Reaching his bedroom, Abdul grabbed his cellphone from the nightstand. His hands shook as he dialed the number for the sheriff's office. Each ring seemed to stretch on forever until a calm voice finally answered.

"Sheriff's Department, this is Shelly."

"This is Abdul Shire at 12 Seabury Lane," he said, his voice hoarse. "You need to send someone to my house. There... there's a body. A man. In my sunroom."

There was a pause on the line before Shelly's tone grew more urgent. "A body? Are you saying there's someone injured in your home?"

"I don't know if he's injured or dead," Abdul admitted, his words tumbling out in a rush. "But he's halfway through my window, and there's blood everywhere. Please, send someone quickly."

"We're dispatching deputies right now," Shelly assured him. "They should be there shortly."

Abdul nodded, even though she couldn't see him. "All right. I… I'll wait in the kitchen."

He sat down at the small table, his hands gripping the edge tightly. The kettle on the stove began to whistle, the shrill sound cutting through the silence. Abdul startled, almost knocking over the chair as he stood to turn off the burner. The mundane act of removing the kettle seemed absurd in the face of what was happening.

Minutes later, the sound of approaching sirens reached his ears. Abdul's breath came in shallow bursts as he heard car doors slam and hurried footsteps crunching through the snow. He unlocked the front door and opened it to find two deputies standing on his porch, their expressions grave.

"Mr. Shire?" one of them asked.

Abdul nodded, stepping aside to let them in. "The sunroom," he said simply, pointing toward the kitchen.

The deputies moved quickly, heading toward the back of the house. Abdul stayed in the living room, clutching his phone, and listening as they entered the sunroom. He heard their voices, followed by the crackle of their radios as they called it in.

Abdul sat heavily on the couch, his head in his hands. He had always liked to keep to himself, to avoid unnecessary entanglements. But now, his home had become the scene of something horrific.

From the sunroom, one of the deputies called out. "Mr. Shire, we're going to need you to answer some questions."

Abdul lifted his head, his eyes weary. "Of course," he said softly, though he doubted he would have any answers. He only knew one thing for certain: life in this quiet neighborhood would never feel the same again.

FORTY-TWO

Beretti and Jacobi stepped into the bustling diner on Main Street, their boots leaving trails of melted snow on the tiled floor. The smell of fried food and fresh coffee greeted them as they scanned the room. Sheriff Carter was seated in a corner booth, his beanie resting on the table and his expression as grim as ever.

Beretti approached first, offering a polite nod. "Sheriff."

"Agents," Sheriff Carter replied, motioning for them to sit. Jacobi and Beretti slid into the booth opposite the sheriff. A waitress approached, and Jacobi ordered a black coffee while Beretti opted for a cappuccino. The sheriff already had a mug of coffee in front of him.

"What do you have for us sheriff?" Beretti asked and she pulled a small notepad from her coat pocket.

Sheriff Carter sighed, his shoulders slumping slightly. "Ethan. He's twelve. Been staying with Lillian, my partner since his mom passed away about a month ago. Poor kid's been through hell. I mentioned him to you yesterday, about how he's been seeing this thing.

Beretti leaned forward. "Start from the beginning. What's been going on?"

The sheriff rubbed his hands together, his brow creasing as he spoke. "It started with Ethan hearing things. Growling in his ear at night, footsteps pacing the house… and claws. He'd hear them scratching on the floors and walls. At first, we thought it might be his imagination, you know? A kid's mind running wild after everything he's been through."

"But it wasn't just that," Jacobi said, already sensing where this was going.

"No," Sheriff Carter confirmed. "Ethan and a few friends went snowmobiling and he came running into the house scared. Says a large wolf chased them but stayed in the wood line."

"Then, things escalated. Ethan said he saw the same big

wolf standing on two legs outside his window. It was tapping on his window, but… it wasn't looking at him."

Beretti raised an eyebrow. "Not at him? Then what?"

"The door," Sheriff Carter said simply. "Ethan said it was looking at his bedroom door. Then later, he heard scratching coming from the other side of it. Movement too. Whatever this creature is you're after… it's fixated on more than just the boy."

Jacobi leaned back in his seat. "Sheriff, have you or Lillian seen or heard anything yourselves?"

Sheriff Carter nodded, his expression darkening. "I stayed in Ethan's room last night, just to give the kid a break. I had been asleep for a while when I woke up suddenly. Not sure why but I looked around the room and caught a glimpse of something in the mirror. A tall shadow, dark and transparent, that moved just out of sight. It froze me for a second, gave me the chills. Then, around four in the morning, I woke up… and I felt it. This… heaviness. Like the air in the room had changed, thick and stifling. Also this sense of dread I have never had before and like something was watching me. I looked out the window and… uh the creature was sitting on the neighbor's barn roof. It was sitting there eating something, then it turned its head towards me, with these glowing orange or amber eyes. When it looked directly at me, it seemed like it was on purpose. It jumped down and disappeared behind the house in a blink. I couldn't get back to sleep after that."

Beretti's brown crinkled as she jotted down notes. "I agree; its interest in that room is evident, despite the other attacks."

"Sounds like it," Jacobi said. "It may be killing for fun while it hangs around. Dogmen are opportunists and vengeful."

"I'm worried about Ethan," Sheriff Carter said, his tone laced with concern. "He's been through so much already, and now this. He can't sleep, doesn't want to eat. I think we're dealing with more than one threat here."

Beretti leaned back, her pen tapping against the notepad. "Sounds like the Dogman is interested in the boy, but whatever's in that bedroom might be drawing it there. The scratching, the sounds... it's as if the Dogman can see whatever's in there."

Jacobi frowned. "That's a terrifying thought. Two entities converging on one place for different reasons."

"Which means we need to talk to Ethan," Beretti said

firmly. "The kid's seen and heard more than anyone else. He might have details that could help us."

The sheriff hesitated, his protective instincts kicking in. "I'll have to clear it with Lillian first. She's been through a lot too, and I don't want to push Ethan too hard. But I'll talk to her and let you know."

"Sounds good," Beretti said. "In the meantime, we'll start piecing together what we know so far. Keep us updated."

Sheriff Carter nodded, his gaze steady. "Sounds good. And agents… thank you for taking this seriously. Most people would've laughed us out of the room by now."

Jacobi replied. "This isn't our first rodeo, Sheriff. We're here to help."

The three of them exited the diner into the cold late morning air. Snowflakes were swirling lazily in the wind. Jacobi glanced at Beretti. "Two threats, one house. What do you think?"

Beretti glanced at the cars driving by before looking back at Jacobi. "I think we're in for one hell of a fight."

FORTY-THREE

Sheriff Carter had been standing outside the diner with Nicole Beretti and Noah Jacobi, discussing plans to regroup later that evening, when his phone buzzed in his pocket. He pulled it out, glancing at the screen.

"Sheriff Carter," he answered. He listened for a few moments, as he held up his hand to the agents.

"We're on our way," he said, hanging up quickly. He turned to the agents, his expression grim. "We might have another victim. Follow me."

Beretti and Jacobi exchanged a look, both immediately alert. They hurried to their SUV, following the sheriff's cruiser as it drove through the snow-covered streets. The sky was overcast, the beginnings of a heavy snowfall threatening to blanket the town.

Soon, they arrived at a modest single-story home, its yard bordered by a low wooden fence. A patrol car was already parked out front, its lights flashing. Carter parked on the curb, and the agents pulled up behind him.

As they stepped out, a deputy approached, the color drained from his face. "Sheriff, the homeowner found the body about an hour ago. He called it in immediately. It's... pretty gruesome."

Carter's jaw tightened. "Anyone see or hear anything?"

The deputy shook his head. "I already checked with the neighbors. Nobody saw or heard a thing."

"Stay here and keep the area secure," Sheriff Carter instructed, striding toward the house. Beretti and Jacobi followed, anxious to see what they were dealing with.

They entered through the side gate, which creaked slightly as it swung open. The house backed onto a wooded area, and the broken window into the sunroom was immediately visible. Jagged glass framed the opening, and the torso of a man hung half inside and half outside. From where they stood, they could see everything: the deep claw marks running the length of his shredded back, the blood pooling beneath him, and the jagged, bloodied stump where his leg should have been.

"Well, you don't see that every day," Jacobi said, his voice low.

Beretti shook her head, her gaze fixed on the scene. "Thankfully, we don't."

They approached cautiously, the snow beneath their feet crunching softly. The closer they got, the more the grim details stood out: the torn clothing, the streaks of blood across the window frame, and the dark stain in the snow spreading outward like a morbid halo.

Sheriff Carter's eyes darkened as he studied the scene. The memory from the previous night flashed vividly in his mind: the Dogman sitting on the barn roof, something clutched in its hands. He shivered despite himself. Could it have been the man's leg? The thought made his stomach churn.

"Sheriff," Beretti said, drawing his attention. "What are you thinking?"

He hesitated before answering. "Like I told you guys, I saw the Dogman creature last night. It had something in its hands. I didn't get a good look, but now..." He trailed off, gesturing to the mutilated body. "Now I'm wondering if it was this."

Beretti and Jacobi exchanged a glance. Jacobi knelt near the body, careful not to disturb anything. "Looks like the dogman's claw marks," he said. "And the missing leg…" He shook his head. "This wasn't just a kill. It's like it's toying with its victims."

As Jacobi stood, Beretti's gaze drifted upward. A crow perched silently on a low branch nearby, its dark eyes fixed on the scene below. It didn't move, didn't make a sound, but its presence seemed deliberate, as though it were studying them. Beretti watched it for a moment before turning her attention back to Sheriff Carter.

The sheriff sighed. "The homeowner called it in. He's inside, probably scared out of his mind. I'll need to talk to him after this."

"We'll come with you," Beretti offered.

The sheriff didn't reply, his gaze fixed on the mangled body. The memory of those glowing eyes burned in his mind.

For a moment, the three were silent, enveloped by the cold wind. Then Beretti spoke, her voice resolute. "Let's finish up here. We'll need to talk to the homeowner and regroup."

FORTY-FOUR

The trio stepped out of Abdul's house into the biting cold of the afternoon. The wind carried a sharp edge that cut through their layers, making Sheriff Carter zip up his coat as he glanced at the agents.

"Storm's coming," he said, his breath visible as he spoke. "We're supposed to get at least a foot of snow by tonight. Roads are going to get dicey, so we should move fast."

Beretti nodded, pulling on her gloves. "Good idea. What's next?"

Sheriff Carter motioned toward his cruiser. "Let's head over to see Joe Malley. He's Eddie Shetfield's usual partner in crime. If anyone knows what Eddie was up to last night, it'll be him."

Jacobi adjusted his beanie against the chill. "You think Joe's going to tell us the truth?"

"Not likely," Sheriff Carter admitted. "But I've dealt with him before. He'll talk if you push the right buttons."

Beretti exchanged a glance with Jacobi before turning back to the sheriff. "We'll follow you. It's worth a shot. From what we've seen, it looks like Eddie was trying to break into Abdul's house when the Dogman attacked him. What do you think?"

The sheriff paused, pulling his collar tighter against the cold. "Sounds about right. I think Eddie didn't stand a chance. Maybe Joe can fill in the blanks."

"Or deny it," Jacobi added with a smirk. "Either way, we'll get something."

The sheriff chuckled dryly. "Exactly. Let's get moving."

Sheriff Carter climbed into his cruiser, as Beretti and Jacobi got into their SUV. The vehicles pulled out onto the snow-covered street, their tires crunching over the fresh layer of snow as thick flakes continued to fall steadily. The sky had darkened further, gloomy clouds threatening an even fiercer storm.

The drive to Joe's house took them to a rundown neighborhood on the outskirts of town. The houses were older, many of them in varying states of disrepair. Joe's place was no exception. The small, single-story home had peeling paint, a sagging porch, and a yard cluttered with junk.

Sheriff Carter parked out front, and the agents pulled in behind him. The three bundled up against the cold as they walked through the snow towards the house. The sheriff knocked on the door firmly, the sound echoing in the quiet street.

For a moment, there was no response. Then, shuffling footsteps approached, and the door creaked open a few inches. Joe Malley's face appeared in the gap, his eyes narrowing as he recognized the sheriff.

"What do you want, sheriff?" Joe grumbled, his voice rough.

"We need to talk," Sheriff Carter said. "Mind if we come in?"

Joe hesitated, his gaze flicking to Beretti and Jacobi. "Who's the pretty lady and her sidekick?"

"FBI," Beretti said, flashing her badge. "We have a few questions about Eddie Shetfield."

Joe's eyes widened slightly, but he quickly masked his surprise. "Eddie? What about him?"

"Can we come in?" Sheriff Carter repeated, his tone firm.

Joe grunted but opened the door wider, stepping aside. "Fine. But make it quick."

The three of them entered the small living room, which was cluttered with mismatched furniture and smelled faintly of stale beer. Joe motioned for them to sit, but the agents and the sheriff remained standing.

"What happened to Eddie?" Joe asked, crossing his arms defensively.

Sheriff Carter didn't mince words. "He's dead. We found his body this morning."

Joe paled, his bravado faltering. "Dead? What... what happened?"

"We were hoping you could tell us," Beretti said. "Was Eddie planning to break into a house on Seabury Lane last night?"

Joe's mouth opened and closed like a fish out of water. Finally, he shook his head. "I don't know what you're talking about."

Jacobi stepped closer, his imposing frame towering over Joe. "Come on, Joe. We know you and Eddie were thick as thieves. Literally."

Joe shifted uncomfortably, avoiding Jacobi's stare.

Jacobi's eyes narrowed. "Hell, you already knew something happened to him."

Joe's eyes darted between the three of them, his hands fidgeting nervously. The storm outside picked up, the wind rattling the windows. Finally, he sighed and sank into an armchair.

"Yeah, okay. Eddie… he had this plan," Joe admitted. "Said he'd been watching the house for a while. Thought the old guy would be an easy mark. He wanted me to go with him last night, but I… I bailed."

"Why?" Sheriff Carter asked, his eyes narrowing.

Joe hesitated. "I… I heard something. While we were outside. A growl. Like something out of a horror movie. It freaked me out. I told Eddie I was out, and I left. Didn't see him after that."

Beretti and Jacobi exchanged a glance. "A growl?" Beretti repeated. "Did you see anything?"

Joe shook his head. "No, but it felt all kinds of... wrong. Like something was watching us. I didn't stick around to find out what it was."

Sheriff Carter crossed his arms. "So, you left Eddie to handle it alone."

Joe shrugged, guilt flickering across his face. "Look, I didn't know he'd end up dead, okay? I just... I couldn't stay. It gave me the creeps, man."

He hesitated, then mumbled, "The damn bird did too."

"What bird?" Jacobi asked.

Joe shifted his weight, still staring at the ground. "A crow or whatever. The damn thing screeched and scared the crap out of me."

Sheriff Carter nodded slowly. "All right, Joe. That's all for now. But don't leave town. We might have more questions for you."

Joe exhaled. "You gonna tell me how Eddie died?"

Beretti turned to face him as they were walking out the door. "Alone and in a lot of pain," he said. "That's how."

The trio stepped back out into the snow, the wind whipping around them. Sheriff Carter glanced at the agents. "Well, that confirms it. Eddie was trying to break in when the Dogman got him."

Jacobi sighed. "At least we're starting to piece this together."

The sheriff checked his watch, his brow creasing. "Ethan will be home from school soon," he said. "We should head there. I'll call Lillian on the way and run it by her."

Beretti nodded, pulling her coat tighter against the cold. "Sounds good. Let's get moving. This storm isn't going to make things any easier."

FORTY-FIVE

The snow fell in thick, relentless sheets, blanketing the roads and reducing visibility to a mere thirty feet. Jacobi shook his head, gripping the wheel as he kept the SUV steady behind Sheriff Carter's cruiser. "These idiots drive like it's a sunny day," he mumbled, his eyes flicking to a car speeding past in the opposite direction. "Way too fast for the conditions."

Beretti didn't respond, her focus on the faint glow of the sheriff's taillights ahead. The windshield wipers struggled to keep the glass clear as the storm worsened. The streets of Evernight, usually calm and picturesque, now carried an unsettling edge under the storm's relentless grip, every turn and stop treacherous.

Jacobi peered through the windshield, squinting against the swirling snow. "This storm's turning into a mess. How much farther to Lillian's place?"

Beretti glanced at the GPS. "A few miles. But at this pace, it's going to take a while."

By the time they reached Lillian's neighborhood, the world was a blur of white.

Sheriff Carter parked at the curb near the bus stop, staying in his cruiser as the snow continued to fall heavily. The streetlights cast a dim glow over the swirling flakes, creating a surreal, almost otherworldly atmosphere. He checked his watch, glancing in the rearview mirror at Beretti and Jacobi waiting in their SUV behind him.

Sheriff Carter pulled out his phone and hit a button on the dash to call Beretti. She answered on speakerphone quickly.

"Sheriff?"

"Hey, just a heads-up," Carter said. "You and Jacobi might want to swing by your hotel and grab a change of clothes. Storms around here have a habit of rolling in fast and fierce. If it gets bad, you could be stuck inside at Lillian's for a few days."

"Got it," Beretti replied. "Thanks for the tip. We'll take care of it."

"Good. Lillian's house is just down this road, number 12. See you soon," Carter said, hanging up and sliding the phone back into place.

As Jacobi put the SUV into gear and did a three-point-turn, he glanced at Beretti. "I can't imagine being twelve these days, especially with social media everywhere," he said, shaking his head.

Beretti scoffed. "I don't even want to imagine what a terror *you* would've been at twelve. Let me guess, you probably spent thirty minutes in front of the mirror every morning, perfecting your hair."

Jacobi chuckled. "How'd you know?"

The humor faded as Jacobi's expression grew more serious. "But really, I feel for this kid. Losing his mom, and now he's thrown into a world where he knows things like the Dogman exist."

Beretti nodded, her tone softening. "He's probably scared out of his mind. We'll have to tread carefully."

****

The yellow school bus appeared through the storm, its headlights cutting through the snow. It came to a slow stop, and the door creaked open. Carter stepped out of his cruiser and walked across the street to meet Ethan as he descended the steps, his small frame bundled tightly against the cold.

"Hey, kid," Carter said, his voice gentle. "Let's get you in the car. It's freezing out here."

Ethan nodded silently, his cheeks flushed from the cold. He climbed into the cruiser, and Carter shut the door behind him, giving a brief wave to the bus driver before heading back to the driver's seat.

As the bus pulled away, Carter glanced over at Ethan in the passenger seat. "You good?" he asked, keeping his tone light.

Ethan nodded again. "Yeah. School was good. It was a good day."

Carter gave a small smile, steering the cruiser onto the snowy road. After a beat, he spoke again, his tone cautious. "Ethan, would it be okay if some FBI special agent friends of mine ask you a few questions? About what's been happening. They're here to help figure this thing out."

Ethan's eyes widened slightly. "The FBI?" His voice carried a mix of intrigue and skepticism, as if he wasn't sure whether to be impressed or wary. After a moment, he shrugged. "Yeah, I guess. If they can help get rid of… whatever's going on."

"They'll do their best," Carter said, his voice steady.

FORTY-SIX

Lillian moved about the kitchen, the comforting clatter of cups and saucers filling the air as the scent of freshly brewed coffee mingled with the faint sweetness of cookies. The warm glow of the fire in the living room radiated through the house, offering a cozy contrast to the bitter cold outside. Inside, the house appeared a sanctuary, a small refuge from the chaos.

It was late afternoon when Beretti and Jacobi arrived at Lillian's house. They pulled their SUV into the driveway, grabbed their bags, and knocked at the door. Carter opened it, stepping aside to let them in.

"Lillian, this is Special Agent Nicole Beretti and Special Agent Noah Jacobi," Carter said, gesturing to each of them in turn.

Lillian gave them a polite smile, wiping her hands on a dish towel. "Nice to meet you both. Come in, get warm."

Ethan peeked out from the kitchen, his eyes widening slightly at the sight of the newcomers.

"And this," Carter added, "is Ethan."

Beretti offered Ethan a small, reassuring smile. "Hey there."

Jacobi grinned and gave a small wave. "What's up, kid?"

Ethan nodded hesitantly, his gaze darting between the two agents.

With introductions made, the group settled at the kitchen table. Ethan sat quietly, his small hands wrapped around a glass of water.

Carter and the agents took their seats nearby, their postures relaxed but their eyes sharp. Jacobi glanced at Ethan again, his usual easy-going demeanor softened by genuine concern.

"So, Ethan," Jacobi began, his voice light, "what's been going on around here? Anything unusual?"

Ethan shrugged, avoiding eye contact. "Yeah."

Jacobi exchanged a glance with Beretti. She leaned forward slightly, her expression kind but firm. "Ethan, I know this isn't easy to talk about. But the more we know, the more we can help. Did you hear or see anything strange?"

The boy's fingers tightened around his glass. "Just… stuff. Noises and… things."

From the kitchen, Lillian glanced over her shoulder, worry etched across her face. She carried a tray of steaming mugs to the table, setting them down with a soft smile. "Here you go, coffee for the adults and cocoa for Ethan."

Ethan mumbled a quiet thanks, his gaze fixed on the tabletop.

Jacobi took a sip of his coffee, then leaned back in his chair. "You know, Ethan, when I was your age, I used to think I could handle everything by myself. But sometimes, letting someone else in helps. We're here to listen, not to judge."

Ethan didn't respond, but his shoulders seemed to relax just a fraction.

Beretti studied the boy for a moment before speaking. "I understand how hard it is, Ethan. When I was just a little older than you, I lost both my parents. It was sudden, and I felt like my whole world had been turned upside down. I went to live with my Uncle."

Ethan looked up at her, his eyes wide. "Your parents died?"

She nodded, her expression soft. "They did. And I know how hard it can be to trust someone when everything feels so wrong. I want to know what's been happening here. What have you seen or heard?"

Ethan hesitated, his gaze shifting to Carter before settling back on Beretti. "It started the second night. I started hearing footsteps. Like someone was walking around the house. But it wasn't Grandma."

Beretti nodded encouragingly. "Go on."

"It kept happening," Ethan said, his voice trembling slightly. "Footsteps at night. Scratching sounds at my door. One time, I even heard something growling in my ear while I was trying to sleep." He paused, his hands gripping the edge of the table. "When Nick and Ryan and I were snowmobiling, this... huge wolf chased us. I thought it was going to catch us."

He swallowed hard before continuing, his words

tumbling out in a rush. "That night, I saw it. It was outside my window, tapping on the glass. But it wasn't looking at me, it was staring at the bedroom door. Then it turned, looked right at me, and… it smiled. And then it just disappeared."

Beretti's stomach clenched, but her face remained calm, her voice steady. "That must have been terrifying. Did anything else happen after that?"

Ethan nodded, his eyes darting to the floor. "Right after it left, I heard scratching at my door. I thought it could be just the wind, but then I saw movement under the door. Like… like something was standing in the hallway."

"You've been really brave," Beretti said, her voice filled with genuine admiration. "But we're here now, and we're going to figure this out. You're not alone in this, Ethan."

Ethan's gaze flickered to hers, and for the first time, a small smile tugged at the corners of his mouth. "Thanks," he said quietly.

Jacobi leaned forward slightly, his tone light and reassuring. "And don't worry, kid. We're pretty good at handling things like this. The sheriff called us because he knew we could help."

Ethan looked at him, his shoulders relaxing slightly. "You

think you can stop it?"

Jacobi smiled. "That's the plan. And we don't plan on failing."

Beretti gave Ethan a small nod. "We're here to help. If you remember anything else, no matter how small, you let us know, okay?"

"Okay," Ethan said, his voice steadying a little more.

The conversation shifted to lighter topics as they finished their drinks. There was a sense in the air that maybe, just maybe, they were starting to piece together the puzzle of the horrors that had plagued not only Ethan, but this small town.

FORTY-SEVEN

As Carter was washing the coffee mugs, his phone buzzed on the table, breaking the quiet lull that had settled over the room. He reached for it, squinting at the screen as he answered. "Sheriff Carter."

The voice of dispatcher Shelly crackled on the other end. "Sheriff, the deputies are still on duty, but with visibility dropping to almost nothing, should I activate the Storm Response Protocol? The roads are starting to close, and we've sent out an alert to all residents to hunker down until the storm passes. The highway coming into Evernight is already closed. It's complete white-out conditions out there."

Carter sighed, rubbing the bridge of his nose. "Yes, thanks Shelly. Let the deputies know and liaise with Chief Deputy

Jones to check the generators at the station. I will be at Lillians with the FBI Agents, but if you need me, just let me know. Majority of the townsfolk know the drill by now and will stay inside. Please check with the hospital and the fire dept that they have activated their guidelines as well. Oh, and by the way, when your shift ends, make sure you ask one of the deputies to escort you home safely and Maureen is escorted into her shift."

"Ok, copy that Sheriff." Shelly replied.

He hung up and set the phone back on the table, looking at the group seated around him. Lillian glanced up from a cupboard she was digging in, her expression curious.

"What is it?" she asked.

"Storm's shutting everything down," Carter said. "We are activating the Storm Patrol Guidelines. This means we still have deputies on, but as it is white-out conditions, only life-threatening situations can be attended to. A lot of the roads are closed, which will make it difficult all-round. That said, if something critical comes up, I'll still head out myself if I'm needed. Everyone's been told to stay put until this blows over. Could be 24 to 48 hours, maybe longer. Looks like we're all stuck here for now."

Lillian smiled faintly, pulling a tray out of the cupboard. "Well, it looks like you're stuck with us agents."

"Appreciate it," Beretti said, glancing at Ethan. "If it's okay with you, Ethan, maybe Jacobi and I could use your room tonight. Jacobi can take the floor, and you can have the couch out here. What do you think?"

Ethan's face lit up. "Really? That'd be cool."

Lillian smiled softly, ruffling Ethan's hair. "Looks like it's settled."

With the sleeping arrangements figured out, Lillian moved to the kitchen to start preparing supper. Beretti followed her, rolling up her sleeves. "Need a hand?" she asked.

"Always," Lillian replied with a smile.

In the living room, Jacobi, and Carter settled into the chairs near the TV. Carter flipped through the channels until he found a local news station, which was already covering the storm. "Looks like it's not letting up anytime soon Sheriff," Jacobi remarked, leaning back.

Carter nodded. "Nope. Storms like this are a way of life around here, though. You get used to being snowed in. Sometimes you just have to hunker down and ride it out."

"Are the predictions reliable?" Jacobi asked, glancing at the sheriff.

"Most of the time, but with the way it's coming down, who knows?" He paused, then glanced at Jacobi with an easy nod. "By the way, just call me Carter. Most folks do unless it's a formal setting."

Jacobi nodded. "Sure thing, Carter."

Satisfied, he returned his attention to the weather report, the two men settling into a comfortable silence as the wind howled outside.

Ethan had curled up on the couch with a blanket, the glow from the television flickering across his face.

He hesitated, then looked up at Jacobi curiously. "Have you ever seen one before? Like the wolf thing?"

Jacobi paused for a moment, his expression thoughtful. "Not that exact one, but yeah, I've seen others like it."

"They're pretty scary, aren't they?" Ethan said, his voice quieter.

Jacobi nodded with a small smile. "Yeah, they are. But don't worry, buddy. We'll take care of it."

Ethan's shoulders relaxed slightly, and his small smile grew just a little wider.

Meanwhile, in the kitchen, Beretti, and Lillian worked side by side, chopping vegetables and stirring pots. The aroma of simmering stew filled the air, mingling with the faint sweetness of freshly baked bread.

"You're good at this," Lillian remarked, nodding toward Beretti's precise knife skills.

Beretti smiled. "Comes with the job. When you're out in the field, you learn to cook with whatever you've got."

"Sounds like you've had an interesting life," Lillian said, glancing at her.

"That's one way to put it," Beretti replied, her tone light but carrying a trace of weariness.

Back in the living room, Jacobi turned to the sheriff. "How long have you lived in Evernight?"

Carter leaned back in his chair, his expression thoughtful. "Grew up here. After high school, I joined the military, served a few tours, and then came back. Settled down here again. It's home."

Jacobi nodded. "I can see why. It's got that quiet, small town charm. Though I bet it gets less charming when things like this happen."

Carter gave a small, knowing smile. "It's not always this crazy. Most days, it's just the usual small town drama. But when things get bad, the people here pull together. You don't find that everywhere."

The two men fell into a comfortable silence, the crackling of the TV and the occasional clatter from the kitchen filling the room.

FORTY-EIGHT

Nick sat on his bed, the faint glow of his phone illuminating his face as he scrolled aimlessly. The storm outside had trapped him indoors, and the monotony was starting to wear on him. A message popped up from Ryan:

Ryan: *What are you doing?*

Nick: *Just reading some comics.*

Ryan: *I'm so bored. My dad's at work, and Mom's passed out on the couch. You know how she is. Want to come over?*

Nick frowned, glancing at the snow piling up outside his window. The thought of braving the blizzard wasn't exactly appealing.

Nick: *Dude, it's a blizzard out there.*

Ryan: *So? We'll be inside. My dad got some more fireworks for Christmas. We should try some out... just the small ones. We can go in the barn.*

Nick hesitated. Fireworks in the barn sounded like the kind of reckless fun Ryan always managed to talk him into. The idea sparked enough intrigue to make him reply:

Nick: *In the barn?*

Ryan: *Yeah. It's perfect. Light a couple, have some fun, and head back in. Just sneak out. Nobody will even notice.*

Nick sighed, biting his lip. His parents wouldn't be happy, but the thought of breaking the boredom won him over.

Nick: *Fine. Be there in 10.*

Ryan: *Sweet! Bring your gloves. It's freezing.*

Nick slid his phone into his pocket and started layering up. Pulling on his boots and jacket, he moved quietly through the house. His parents were in the living room, the sound of the TV masking his steps as he slipped out the back door.

The wind hit him immediately, the icy sting forcing him to tighten his hood. Snow swirled in the air, coating the neighborhood in a thick blanket of white. The trek to Ryan's house wasn't far, but each step was like trudging through a frozen obstacle course.

When he reached the barn, Ryan's flashlight beam waved through the dark. He poked his head out, grinning ear to ear. "You made it! Thought you'd chicken out."

"It's insane out here," Nick said, brushing snow from his jacket as he stepped inside. The barn smelled of oil and cold metal, the air tinged with a faint dampness. Tools and storage bins lined the walls, a workbench cluttered with odds and ends sitting beneath a dim hanging bulb.

Ryan knelt beside a bag on the floor, pulling out a handful of fireworks. "Check these out," he said, holding up sparklers and a few bottle rockets. "He even got sky bombs!"

Nick shook his head, a reluctant grin tugging at his lips. "You're gonna get us in so much trouble."

"Not if we're careful," Ryan said, setting up a metal can to use as a launcher. "Trust me, it'll be fun."

They started small, lighting sparklers that hissed and crackled, casting flickering shadows across the barn walls. Ryan waved one around like a sword, laughing as Nick rolled his eyes.

The first bottle rocket whistled into the air, exploding with a muffled pop against the storm outside. The sound was enough to send a small thrill through Nick, despite his earlier doubts.

Just as they prepared the next round, Nick froze. "What… the hell," he whispered, pointing toward the barn window.

A silhouette moved outside, tall and hunched, its shape distorted by the swirling snow. Nick's stomach tightened as the figure drew closer.

Ryan followed his gaze, his bravado vanishing. "Holy crap."

The silhouette stepped closer to the window, revealing its monstrous form.

"The wolf is back. We need to hide. Now," Nick hissed, his voice barely audible.

Ryan nodded, the color draining from his face. Nick grabbed the bag of fireworks from the ground, clutching it tightly as they scrambled up the wooden ladder to the loft. His hands slipped once before he caught himself, the bag thudding lightly against his side.

At the top, they ducked behind a stack of storage bins,

their breathing quick and uneven as they fought to stay quiet.

Below, the barn door creaked, the handle rattling before it slowly swung open. The boys froze, their wide eyes fixed on the opening. The creature stepped inside, its massive form filling the doorway. It moved with unnerving precision, each step careful as it sniffed the air.

Ryan clutched the edge of the bin, his hands trembling. The sound of the creature's claws clicking against the wooden floor made his skin prickle with dread.

Nick's voice was barely a whisper, his words trembling with fear. "It's gonna kill us."

Ryan shot him a panicked look but said nothing as he fumbled in his pocket, pulling out a handful of flash crackers. His fingers shook as he lit one, tossing it toward the creature. The loud pops and bursts of light filled the barn, but the Dogman barely flinched. It turned its glowing eyes to the loft, a low growl rumbling deep in its chest.

"Shit. It's looking at us," Nick whispered, his voice cracking.

Nick fumbled in the bag, his hands brushing against a sky bomb in the bag. He handed it over urgently. "Light it!! It's coming!"

Ryan struck the lighter, the small flame dancing unsteadily before it caught the fuse. He hurled the firework toward the creature, the sizzling fuse drawing its attention.

The sky bomb erupted in a deafening explosion, sparks and smoke filling the barn. One fiery projectile ricocheted off the wall, striking the Dogman square in the back.

The creature howled, a high-pitched scream that made the boys clap their hands over their ears. It thrashed wildly, colliding with the walls and knocking over tools and storage bins.

Finally, it bolted out of the barn, its massive frame disappearing into the storm.

Nick and Ryan stayed frozen, their hearts pounding. "Is it gone?" Nick whispered, his voice shaking.

"I think so," Ryan replied, his voice barely audible.

Neither of them moved, their bodies too paralyzed by fear to do anything but wait.

FORTY-NINE

Lillian stood at the sink, the warm soapy water soothing her hands as she methodically scrubbed the last dinner bowl. Jacobi leaned casually against the counter next to her, a dish towel slung over his shoulder, drying the dishes she handed him.

"So, where did you grow up, Jacobi?" Lillian asked, passing him a dripping glass.

Jacobi looked up. "I'm an L.A. boy. So all of this snow and quiet? Definitely not my usual scene."

"I imagine not," Lillian replied.

Beretti stepped into the kitchen, leaning casually against the doorway. "Dinner was delicious, Lillian. Thank you." She glanced at Jacobi, her lips quirking in a grin. "And I see you've got Jacobi well trained. Drying dishes and everything."

Jacobi rolled his eyes playfully, holding up the towel like a trophy. "What can I say? I'm a team player."

"Sure you are," Beretti teased, grabbing a glass of water before heading back into the living room.

Lillian turned to Jacobi, her tone curious. "So, how long have you been in this line of work?"

"Long enough to know there's always more to learn," Jacobi said with a small chuckle. "What about you, Lillian? Have you always lived..."

Suddenly, a loud, echoing boom reverberated through the air. Lillian nearly dropped a glass, her hand trembling as she froze mid-motion, her eyes darting toward the window.

"What the hell was that?" Jacobi exclaimed, his head snapping toward the kitchen window.

Before Lillian could respond, something outside caught her eye. Through the falling snow, a large figure darted across the yard. It moved with unnatural speed, its dark form barely visible through the swirling white. But what made her gasp was the flickering flames trailing from its back.

"Oh my God," Lillian gasped, her hand clutching the edge of the counter. "Did you see that?"

Jacobi nodded, his face set in disbelief. "Yeah. I sure did."

In the living room, the sheriff bolted upright, his instincts on high alert. "What's going on?" he called out, already reaching for his jacket.

"The Dogman just ran through the yard," Jacobi said. "On fire."

Beretti stood up quickly, slipping her gloves on. "We need to find out what caused that boom. Sheriff, you coming?"

Carter nodded, already pulling on his coat. "Lillian, stay here with Ethan," he instructed as he headed toward the door. "We won't be long."

At the front door, Carter unlocked the drawer safe and retrieved his handgun, securing it in his holster. Beside him, Jacobi crouched to unlock a portable safe they had brought into the house. He and Beretti each pulled out a Ruger Super Redhawk (.454 Casull), a powerful revolver that was a necessity in their line of work.

Ethan sat up straight, his eyes wide with both fear and curiosity. "What happened?" he asked.

Lillian crossed the room and knelt beside him. "They'll take care of it," she said gently, though her own heart was pounding. "Just stay inside and keep warm, okay?"

Jacobi and Beretti followed the sheriff out into the storm, the cold taking their breath away the moment they stepped outside. The wind howled fiercely, and the falling snow obscured much of their surroundings.

"Which way?" Beretti shouted over the roar of the wind.

Jacobi pointed toward the barn, its dark silhouette barely visible through the storm. "It came from that way... I think near the barn. Let's check it out."

Carter led the way, his flashlight cutting a narrow path through the swirling snow. They moved cautiously but quickly, Beretti and Jacobi staying close to the Sheriff. As they reached the barn, Carter pushed the door open, the hinges creaking loudly in protest.

Inside, the barn reeked of smoke, burnt hair, and the pungent stench of wet dog and urine. The foul odor clung to the air, making Beretti instinctively breathe through her mouth. Her gaze swept the space, landing on spent fireworks scattered across the dirt floor and a faint patch of charred fur near the entrance.

"Someone's been here," Beretti said, her voice low but steady. She glanced upward and caught a flicker of movement in the loft. "It's safe to come down now," she called. "We're here to help."

There was a rustling sound, followed by a small, nervous voice. "It's us... Ryan and Nick."

Carter's expression softened, though his tone remained firm. "Boys, get down here. Now."

Nick and Ryan climbed down the ladder hesitantly, their eyes wide with fear. As soon as their feet hit the ground, Nick's parents burst into the barn, having followed the commotion.

"Nick Michael Davis! What are you doing out here?" his mother demanded, her face a mixture of anger and concern.

"We didn't mean... we just..." Nick stammered, looking to Ryan for support.

"We lit some fireworks," Nick admitted quietly. "We didn't think it would... you know... attract something."

Carter stepped forward, "You two are lucky to be alive. What exactly happened here?"

Ryan took a shaky breath. "We were messing around with some fireworks, and then… it showed up. It was huge, the same wolf that chased us. It came into the barn and… we tried to hide. I threw one of the fireworks at it, and it ran out."

Beretti exchanged a glance with Jacobi. "That explains the flames you saw. The creature must have been hit by the firework."

Nick's mother shook her head, her anger giving way to fear. "I… I can't believe this. Nick, you're grounded. Do you hear me?"

Carter held up a hand. "Let's save the punishment for later. For now, everyone needs to get back inside. This thing could still be out there."

Jacobi looked at Ryan. "Where are your parents?"

Ryan hesitated, his face reddening. "My dad's at work, and my mom… she's, uh, passed out on the couch."

Nick's mother sighed, clearly exasperated but refrained from commenting. "Ryan, you can come with us," she said firmly. "You're not staying alone in that house tonight."

Ryan nodded quickly, his relief evident.

Jacobi added, "Keep your doors locked. We'll deal with this, but no one's safe outside right now."

Beretti, Jacobi and Carter stood near the barn, watching as the boys and Nick's parents made their way back toward their home. The storm seemed to intensify around them, the wind whipping through the trees as if carrying an unspoken warning of the danger still lurking in the shadows.

FIFTY

As they headed back to the house, Beretti, and Jacobi stopped at their SUV. They retrieved their high-powered rifles and extra ammo, as snowflakes danced around them.

"You really think this thing might come for the house tonight?" Jacobi asked, glancing toward the woods.

"Always better to be prepared," Beretti replied. "If it had no problem entering the barn, the storm won't stop it."

Jacobi chuckled lightly, though there was no humor in it. "Great. A blizzard and a monster. What else could we ask for?"

Beretti shot him a sidelong glance. "You forgot the ghost in the bedroom."

Jacobi shook his head. "You know, most people would quit this line of work after one case like this."

"And yet, here we are," Beretti quipped, slamming the SUV's trunk shut. "Besides, you live for the drama and action, Jacobi."

Jacobi grinned and nodded. "Guilty as charged. It keeps life interesting."

When they walked back inside, they set their gear down in Ethan's bedroom before returning to the living room. Carter settled back into his chair, and Lillian took hers, while Ethan, Beretti, and Jacobi sat on the couch. The glow of the TV filled the room as they watched a late-night sitcom, its light-hearted humor offering a brief respite from the tension of the day.

After a while, everyone began to wind down. Beretti excused herself to brush her teeth, and Jacobi stretched, letting out a yawn. "Alright, I'm calling it a night," he said, heading toward Ethan's room. Lillian turned off the TV and said goodnight as she and Carter headed to their rooms.

Ethan stayed in the living room, stretching out on the couch. He grabbed a quilt from the back of the chair and pulled it over himself, curling up as the warmth of the room offered a small sense of comfort. The storm outside continued to swirl in the darkness, but inside, the house gradually fell silent.

When Jacobi came back into the bedroom after using the restroom, Beretti glanced up and immediately had to slap a hand over her mouth to keep from laughing out loud. He was wearing pajamas with a cartoonish Bigfoot pattern on them.

"Nice pj's," she said, her voice muffled by her hand as she tried to suppress her laughter.

Jacobi grinned and struck a mock pose. "Yeah, I only bring them out for special occasions. Consider yourself lucky."

Shaking her head, Beretti chuckled as he closed the door behind him and moved toward his cot. "You're full of surprises, Jacobi."

"Hey," he said casually, his tone shifting slightly, "that was a smart move earlier, trying to connect with Ethan by mentioning your parents."

Beretti's smile softened. "It wasn't a move. It just felt right. Poor kid's been through enough. I figured he could use someone who gets it."

Jacobi nodded, his expression thoughtful. "Well, it

worked. You could see him relax a little. He needs that."

Beretti shrugged lightly. "We'll see. He's still carrying a lot, but I hope it helps him open up."

Jacobi sat down on his cot, his face more serious now. "Between the two of us, I think we've got this. And Carter seems solid too. We'll figure it out."

"I think so too," Beretti agreed. "Kids like Ethan need to know they're not alone. It's a hard thing, losing your parents at that age."

Jacobi tilted his head, curiosity flickering in his eyes. "What were they like? Your parents. I mean."

She hesitated for a moment, then answered. "My dad was in the army, so of course he was strict, disciplined, always protective but hard to connect with because he was away so often. My mom was a school teacher. Tough but fair, and she had the biggest heart. She was such a beautiful woman and a truly giving soul."

Jacobi nodded thoughtfully. "Sounds like they balanced each other out. Guess that's where you get your mix of heart and grit."

Beretti smirked. "You're just saying that because you're

stuck in a room with me for the night."

Jacobi laughed quietly, adjusting under the blanket. "Maybe. Anyway, get some rest. I'm sure tomorrow will be another day full of surprises." He paused, glancing at her with a grin. "And don't take a picture of me in these pajamas while I'm asleep. I'd never live it down."

Beretti chuckled, shaking her head. "I'll try not to, but no promises."

Jacobi shook his head with a smile, settling in. "You're the worst."

Beretti lay back, staring at the ceiling as Jacobi's breathing slowed into a steady rhythm. She wasn't surprised he had fallen asleep so quickly; he had a knack for switching off when needed, even in the weirdest circumstances.

An hour or so later, the room was silent, save for the faint sound of the wind howling outside. Despite the exhaustion of the day, sleep eluded Beretti. Her thoughts circled the strange case, the Dogman outside, and the strange occurrences inside this house. She sighed and closed her eyes, willing herself to relax. But then, she noticed something odd. The temperature in the room had dropped sharply, and her breath puffed out in a visible cloud. She opened her eyes, her body tense.

Something was wrong.

She tried to sit up, but her body wouldn't respond. Panic rose in her chest as she realized she couldn't move. It was as though an invisible force was holding her down. Her breathing quickened, shallow and rapid, as though her lungs refused to fully expand. Her heart hammered like a drumbeat of panic, and a cold, creeping dread gripped her mind. Every instinct screamed at her to move, to fight, but her body remained rigid, a prisoner of an invisible force. She was gripped by a terrifying fear that made her wonder if she was dreaming or awake.

Out of the corner of her eye, Beretti saw it. A shadow, darker and denser than the surrounding room, forming near Jacobi's cot. It grew rapidly, twisting and shifting until it took on the unmistakable shape of a Dogman. The figure loomed tall, its head nearly brushing the ceiling, its presence suffocating as it hovered over Jacobi, who was still sound asleep.

Beretti's body refused to move. Every muscle was frozen as she stared at the creature, unable to look away. The shadow turned its head toward her. Even though it had no discernible facial features, Beretti could feel its gaze boring into her. A cold dread filled her, unlike anything she had ever experienced. Along with the paralyzing fear, a wave of helplessness and an overwhelming sense of not belonging washed over her, as though the room itself was rejecting her presence.

The shadow tilted its head, almost as if it were studying her. Then, its gaze shifted downward to Jacobi. It leaned closer, its massive frame looming just above his chest.

Jacobi stirred, letting out a soft groan as his eyes fluttered open. The moment his gaze landed on the hulking figure above him, he flailed his arms in blind panic and bolted upright, yelling, "What the fuck!"

The sound shattered Beretti's paralysis. Her chest heaved as she sucked in a quick breath, her hands clutching her chest. The shadow began to dissolve, its dark form breaking apart into curling tendrils of smoke.

Beretti watched, her heart pounding, as the smoke swirled briefly in the air before drifting toward the bookshelf. The tendrils seeped into the dark wood, vanishing completely as though the creature had never been there.

Jacobi scrambled off his cot, as he tried to catch his breath. "What the hell was that?" he demanded, his voice cracking.

FIFTY-ONE

A loud knock echoed through the room just moments after Jacobi's startled yell. "Everything alright in there?" Carter's voice came from the other side of the door, calm but laced with quiet concern.

Jacobi rubbed his face, exchanging a glance with Beretti before opening the door. He met Carter's steady gaze. "Sorry for the noise, Carter," he said. "The Dogman ghost made its presence known."

Carter's expression remained collected, though his eyes narrowed slightly. "Really?"

Beretti nodded. "Yeah. It was brief, but it freaked us out for a second. It's gone now."

Carter took a moment to absorb the information, then gave a single nod. "Alright. It's cold in this room. Do you still want to stay in here?"

"Yes," Beretti said without hesitation. "We'll handle it. Sorry again for waking you."

Carter's mouth twitched into a faint smile. He glanced down at Jacobi's pants, raising an eyebrow. "Nice pajamas."

Jacobi straightened slightly, a grin on his face. "FBI-issued official pajamas. Very exclusive."

Carter shook his head, a quiet chuckle escaping him. "Whatever works," he said before walking back down the hall, closing the door behind him.

Beretti glanced at Jacobi with a smile. "FBI-issued, huh? Tactical and stylish?"

Jacobi grinned, sitting on the edge of the bed. "Absolutely. They keep you warm, blend in with the shadows, and apparently make great conversation starters."

Beretti chuckled softly, careful not to wake anyone else. "Well, they've certainly lightened the mood."

Jacobi leaned back, letting a smile play on his lips.

"Exactly what they're meant for."

"But seriously, has that shit ever happened to you before?" Jacobi finally asked, his voice edged with disbelief.

Beretti shook her head. "No," she said quietly, her tone carrying both fear and frustration. "Not like that. Not...whatever that was."

Jacobi let out a low whistle, stopping in his tracks to face her. "I've seen some weird things, but a shadow Dogman? That's new. What did it do to you?"

"I couldn't move," she responded. Couldn't even scream. It was like I wasn't even in control of my own body anymore." Her voice dropped as she added, "And for a moment, seemed like I didn't belong here. Like the room itself wanted me gone."

Jacobi ran a hand through his hair, letting out a shaky laugh. "Well, if it makes you feel better, I was awake for the part where it decided to hover over me. I couldn't breathe for a second. And then...poof." He gestured toward the bookshelf. "Gone. Just like that."

Beretti let out a humorless chuckle. "I'm not sure what's worse: seeing it or knowing it was standing over you and I couldn't do a damn thing."

Jacobi resumed his pacing, his feet thudding softly against the floor. "What do you think it wanted?"

Beretti exhaled deeply and leaned back against the wall. "I don't know. Maybe it's tied to this place. Or to Ethan. It's not just random. It was…targeted."

"Targeted how?" Jacobi pressed, crossing his arms as he leaned against the desk.

"Think about it. It didn't go after anyone else. It's always been focused on this room." Beretti's brow creased as she spoke. "First Ethan, now us. And it's not just haunting, it's interacting."

Jacobi frowned. "You're saying it knows what it's doing?"

"I'm saying it's more than just some residual spirit or energy," she replied. "This thing's aware. And it's watching."

The room fell silent, save for the faint howl of the wind outside. Jacobi tapped his fingers against the desk, his gaze distant. "Okay, so let's assume you're right. How does that connect to the Dogman outside? Two different entities, both tied to the same place? Seems too much of a coincidence."

Beretti stood, the movement sudden and decisive. "It's not a coincidence," she said firmly. "We just don't have the full picture yet. But whatever's happening here, it's escalating."

Jacobi nodded, his earlier humor now fully replaced by a grim seriousness. "Well, at least we're not bored."

Beretti shot him a dry look. "Thanks for the silver lining."

A faint creak echoed from the hallway, drawing both of their gazes to the door. Jacobi's hand instinctively reached for his gun on the desk, fingers wrapping around the grip. Beretti moved silently to the window, peering out into the snowy yard. Nothing but swirling white met her gaze.

"Probably just the house settling," Jacobi said, though he didn't sound convinced.

Beretti turned back to him. "I am starting to think it is not tied to Ethan. It is something about this room."

Jacobi sighed, running a hand down his face. "Great. What do we do about that?"

"Not sure yet," she said. "But, we'll figure it out."

FIFTY-TWO

The next morning, Beretti woke to the dim gray light filtering through the curtains, the sound of the wind howling outside a constant reminder of the storm that continued to rage. She blinked a few times, her breath visible in the chilly room. Jacobi was still asleep on the pull-out cot, sprawled in his usual careless fashion, his mouth slightly open.

Beretti quietly pulled on her jacket, slipped into her boots, and made her way outside. The cold air hit her like a slap, jolting her fully awake. She stood on the porch, shielded from the worst of the snow, and took a deep breath. The air was crisp and clean, carrying the muffled sounds of the storm, a swirling chaos that blanketed everything in sight.

As she pulled out her phone to type an update to ASAC Ward, her gaze caught a flicker of movement across the street. A crow landed silently on a tree branch, its dark form stark against the snowy backdrop. It sat there quietly, its head tilting slightly as it watched her. Beretti glanced at it briefly before turning her attention back to her phone. She quickly typed out an update detailing the events of the previous night: the incident at the barn, the ghostly apparition in Ethan's room, and the continued signs of the Dogman's presence.

As she hit send, her phone buzzed almost immediately with an incoming call. She swiped to answer.

"Ward," she greeted, her voice low, not wanting to disturb the household.

"Beretti," Ward's gravelly voice came through. "Just read your message. You've had quite the night. What's your status now?"

Beretti leaned against the porch railing, her eyes briefly flicking back to the crow, which still sat on the branch, its dark eyes fixed on her. "The storm is still going strong, but we're managing. Jacobi and I are holding tight at the house with the sheriff and his partner. Ethan's the focus here. Something's tied to him or his room. And then there's the

Dogman outside. We still don't know how they're connected, but this is escalating."

Ward exhaled audibly. "You mentioned a ghost. That's new territory, even for us. Any theories?"

"Not yet," Beretti admitted. "It's not just residual energy. This thing is aware. It paralyzed me last night, and it's been fixated on Ethan's room. Jacobi…he saw it too. Whatever it is, it's not random."

Ward was silent for a moment before responding. "Stay on it. If it gets worse, we'll send reinforcements. But right now, keep gathering intel. We need a complete picture before we move further."

"Understood," Beretti said, her tone steady. "I'll keep you updated."

"Stay safe," Ward said before hanging up.

Beretti pocketed her phone and lingered on the porch for a few more moments. The crow remained on the branch, its quiet presence almost calming as the snow swirled around it. After a while, it flapped its wings and flew off into the storm.

Shaking off the cold, Beretti turned and went back inside, shutting the door firmly behind her.

The warmth of the house was a stark contrast to the chill outside. The smell of frying bacon greeted her as she stepped into the kitchen, where Lillian was already bustling about, cracking eggs into a bowl and flipping pancakes on the griddle.

"Morning," Beretti greeted.

Lillian glanced up with a faint smile. "Good morning. Sleep well?"

Beretti hesitated for a beat. "As well as could be expected. Need a hand?"

"No thanks, I've got it under control," Lillian replied, waving her off with a spatula. She gave Beretti a quick look. "I hope you weren't out in the cold too long."

"No," Beretti said with a small smile. "The cool air wakes me up fast. I actually enjoy it first thing in the morning."

Lillian nodded approvingly. "Well, as long as it works for you."

"I'll take a quick shower, if that's okay," Beretti asked.

Lillian replied, "Of course, dear."

As she headed down the hall to the bathroom, the sound

of sizzling bacon and the hum of Lillian's quiet movements followed her. Beretti's thoughts remained focused on the mission. The storm outside mirrored the storm brewing within the house, and she knew they were running out of time to piece together the puzzle before someone else got hurt.

FIFTY-THREE

As Beretti stepped out of the bathroom, the inviting aroma of freshly brewed coffee drifted from the kitchen. Carter was at the counter, pouring coffee into two mismatched mugs. He glanced back at her. "Coffee?"

"Please," Beretti replied, pulling out a chair at the well-worn kitchen table. She watched as he set a mug in front of her and slid into the seat opposite.

Lillian was busying herself at the sink, tidying up. Beretti cupped the mug in her hands, savoring the warmth before speaking.

"How long have you lived in this house, Lillian?" she asked.

Lillian paused, her hands stilling briefly before she resumed rinsing a pan. "It's been close to 40 years," she said thoughtfully. "Ethan's mother grew up here."

Beretti nodded, letting the statement settle before continuing. "In all that time, have you ever experienced anything unusual? Strange noises, shadows, or things out of place?"

Lillian glanced over her shoulder, her expression tightening. "Not personally," she said quietly, "but I know why you're asking. Ethan's told me about what he's been seeing and hearing in his room."

Beretti leaned forward slightly. "What about your daughter? "Did she ever mention anything strange? Anything like what Ethan's been describing?"

Lillian's hands gripped the counter behind her as she thought for a moment. "Now that you mention it... just before she moved out, she asked me something odd. She asked if I thought the house felt... strange. If I'd ever seen or heard anything unusual at night."

"What did you say?"

"I told her no," Lillian said, shaking her head slightly. "Because I hadn't. At least, nothing like what she was talking about. But the way she asked… I guess it stayed with me. She seemed uneasy. A week or two later, she packed her things and moved out. She never brought it up again.”

Beretti took a slow sip of her coffee, considering her next question carefully. “After she moved out, did anyone else stay in that room?”

Lillian shook her head immediately. “No. I left it empty for a long time. My daughter and I stopped communicating for a number of years, so Ethan had never stayed over. I just used it for storage of odds and ends. I guess, if anything, when I did go in there, the room did seem a little colder than the rest of the house. I had long forgotten what my daughter had asked until you brought it up.”

Beretti absorbed the response, her mind churning over the implications. “Did your daughter ever say why she moved out so abruptly?”

“No,” Lillian replied softly. “She just said she needed a change, and I didn’t press her on it. I thought it had to do with a boy, something she didn’t want to talk about.”

“You think this is connected to what Ethan’s been experiencing?” Lillian asked finally, her voice tinged with worry.

Beretti set her mug down gently on the table. "I don't know yet," she said truthfully. "But it's worth looking into. Sometimes these things aren't just coincidences."

Carter, silent until now, shifted uncomfortably in his seat but didn't speak.

Lillian crossed her arms, her expression resolute despite the concern etched into her features. "Whatever it is, Ethan doesn't deserve this. None of us do."

Beretti gave her a small, reassuring nod. "That's why we're here. We'll figure this out."

The pieces weren't all there yet, but they were starting to fall into place. Beretti could sense the house's past creeping into its present, intertwining the memories of those who had lived there with the traces of something that seemed to linger long after they'd gone.

FIFTY-FOUR

The sound of the shower running filtered through the quiet house as Beretti, Lillian and Ethan sat around the kitchen table. The warmth of the breakfast spread, bacon, toast, and scrambled eggs, helped stave off the chill that lingered in the air. Carter had already finished his meal and stood by the door, buttoning up his thick winter coat.

"Thanks for breakfast," he said, smiling as he leaned down to give Lillian a quick kiss on the cheek. "I'm going to try and make it to work. Hopefully, the snow isn't too bad further out."

Lillian looked out the kitchen window, her brow creasing at the sight of swirling snowflakes whipping against the glass. The storm outside had built steadily through the night, piling snow in thick drifts. "Be careful," she said, resting a hand lightly on his arm.

"I'll take it slow," Carter replied. "If it's too bad, I'll turn back. Don't worry." With that, he stepped out into the frigid air, the door closing firmly behind him.

Beretti tore a piece of toast into smaller bits, watching Ethan as he played with his food, avoiding eye contact. "Sleep okay, kid?" she asked.

Ethan said looking up. "Yeah, much better than being in my bedroom."

The quiet lingered until about fifteen minutes later, the sound of the front door opening and closing caught their attention. Carter reappeared in the kitchen, taking off his coat and rubbing his hands together to warm them. His expression was grim.

"No luck?" Lillian asked, setting her coffee cup down.

Carter shook his head. "The road's completely blocked about a mile up. Two big trees are down, and there's no way to get around them. Visibility is maybe twenty to thirty feet, tops. I called it in, but in this weather, I doubt anyone's coming to clear it anytime soon. Looks like we're stuck here for the foreseeable future."

Lillian sighed, her shoulders sagging slightly as she turned back to the stove. "I'll keep the coffee coming. You'll need it," she said, offering a faint smile.

The sound of the shower stopped, and a few minutes later, Jacobi appeared, his hair damp and his shirt slightly wrinkled from being pulled on quickly.

"I kept your breakfast warm," Lillian said, motioning to the plate she had set aside.

Jacobi smiled appreciatively as he sat down. "Thank you. I could get used to this," he said before beginning his meal. Beretti shifted her focus back to Ethan, leaning forward slightly "Ethan, can I ask you more about what's been happening in your room?"

Ethan glanced at her hesitantly, his eyes flitting to Lillian for reassurance. She gave him a small nod, encouraging him to speak.

"Okay," he said softly.

"Does the shadow in your room speak to you?" Beretti asked.

Ethan shook his head quickly. "No. It doesn't talk. Just growls."

Beretti exchanged a brief glance with Jacobi, who had paused mid-bite. "Does it happen every night?" she asked.

"No," Ethan replied, shaking his head again. "Not every night. Some nights it's… quiet. But the room is always cold."

Beretti nodded, taking a moment before asking her next question. "What about the Dogman outside? Did that start before or after you saw the one in your room?"

Ethan's fingers twisted at the edge of his napkin as he thought, his face scrunched in concentration. "The one inside came first," he said finally.

Beretti leaned closer. "Ethan, I want you to know something. You don't have to sleep in that bedroom until we've sorted this out, okay? You can stay out here in the living room where it's safe."

Ethan's eyes widened slightly, relief washing over his face. "Really? I don't have to go back in there?"

Beretti offered a reassuring smile. "Not until we've figured this out. You don't need to worry, it seems to be confined to the bedroom. You're safe here."

Ethan nodded, his shoulders relaxing for the first time since the conversation started.

"There's one more thing," Beretti added, her tone softening. "I want you to know that I believe you. I did before, but last night Jacobi and I saw it."

Ethan's eyes widened again, his expression a mix of surprise and validation.

"Because we've seen it, Jacobi and I can start figuring out how to deal with it," Beretti continued. "We're not going to stop until we solve this, Ethan. I promise."

Lillian placed a comforting hand on Ethan's shoulder, squeezing lightly. "We're all here for you, sweetheart," she said.

Ethan nodded but remained quiet, his fingers fidgeting with the napkin in his lap. He hesitated, his gaze flickering toward the table as if gathering his thoughts. "There's something else I've been thinking about," he finally admitted.

Beretti's brows lifted slightly. "What's that?"

He took a deep breath. "A crow. It was there... squawking when the Dogman was chasing us in the field." His voice was quiet, but certain. "And another time, when I was walking to Nick's place. It just kept cawing like crazy."

Jacobi leaned back slightly, exchanging a look with

Beretti. "That's interesting," he muttered.

Beretti tapped her fingers lightly against the table. "I noticed a crow watching me a few times since I have been here," she admitted. "But it was quiet, just watching."

Ethan looked up at her, his expression questioning. "I've seen it just watching me from the window too. Do you think it means something?"

Beretti studied him for a second before nodding. "Maybe." She leaned forward slightly, her voice softer now. "My mother was Native American. She told me when I was younger that crows can symbolize a warning."

Ethan's eyes widened. "Like... warning me about the Dogman?"

Beretti nodded. "It's possible. Some believe crows can be messengers, signs of danger or change. If it was there both times before the Dogman showed up, maybe it was trying to warn you."

Ethan swallowed, his mind turning over the thought. "So... it wasn't just a regular bird?"

Beretti offered a small smile. "I don't know for sure, but it's something we should pay attention to."

Jacobi exhaled, rubbing his jaw. "That's definitely not a coincidence."

Ethan stared down at the table, processing everything. The crow had been there more than once. Was it really just watching, or had it been trying to tell him something all along?

FIFTY-FIVE

Ethan's bedroom was strangely still, the air dense and unsettled. Beretti stood at the center of the room, her eyes scanning every corner. The morning light filtering through the curtains seemed unable to push back the darkness clinging to the space.

Jacobi fidgeted by the door, appearing uneasy. "What ya doing?" he asked quietly.

"The Dogman ghost doesn't show itself anywhere else. Not the yard, not the living room. It's confined to this bedroom." She crossed her arms, frowning. "That means something. We just don't know what yet."

Jacobi nodded. "And it was dormant for years, right?

Until Ethan started sleeping in here?"

"Right," Beretti said. "Years since Diana left this room behind. Then Ethan shows up, and it starts again." She glanced at Jacobi. "And then it showed itself to us."

Beretti motioned for Jacobi to start searching. "Look everywhere. Closets, drawers, under the bed. Anything that seems out of place."

Jacobi moved to the closet without protest, while Beretti approached the bookshelf. It was cluttered with the usual collection of a teenager. Dog-eared novels, tangled cords, gaming magazines, a scattering of trophies. As her eyes scanned the spines, she spotted a thick hardcover jutting out slightly, its placement just a little off.

She slid the book out, revealing a smaller, leather-bound book tucked behind it.

"What is it?" Jacobi asked, leaning over her shoulder.

Beretti turned the journal over in her hands. "It's a journal," she said, flipping open the cover. A large, yellowed tooth slipped from between the pages and hit the floor with a dull clink.

Jacobi bent down, picking it up carefully. "What the hell

is this?" he asked, holding it up for her to see.

Beretti frowned, her eyes lingering on the sharp, curved edges of the tooth. "It looks like a large canine tooth," she said, her voice uncertain. She shook her head, her gaze drifting back to the journal. On the inside cover, her eyes landed on the name written there. "Diana."

Jacobi straightened. "Ethan's mom?"

Beretti nodded, already flipping through the pages. The entries were typical at first, full of teenage angst and rebellion. Complaints about school, fights with her mom, and notes about boys she liked.

Beretti read aloud:

I'm so over this place. Mom doesn't get me at all. I can't wait to get out of here.

She skimmed further, pausing at another entry and reading it aloud:

Sometimes, I think I hate her. She's always on my case about everything. What I wear, who I hang out with, even the music I listen to. It's like she doesn't even want me to have my own life. I fucking hate it here.

Beretti flipped another page and found Todd's name.

Surprise, surprise. Mom hates Todd. She's hated him since the second I introduced them. She says he's trouble and that I shouldn't be with him. We had this huge fight last night, and now she's banned him from the house! Seriously, who does that? It's so freaking unfair.

"Sounds pretty normal," Jacobi said.

Beretti turned a page, pausing when she spotted an entry written in a much lighter tone.

Todd found something cool by the river today. We were skipping rocks when he saw a tooth, just lying there in the mud. It's huge! He gave it to me and said it might bring good luck. I brought it home and put it on my dresser. I think I love him but I don't want to say it first.

"That's interesting," Beretti commented, continuing to flip through the pages. The tone shifted after that entry, the handwriting growing uneven and frantic.

Jacobi read over Beretti's shoulder:

I hear things at night. Scratching on the walls. Breathing when no one's there.

Beretti turned another page. The entries became more fragmented. Diana described shadows moving in the corners of the room, a low growl that woke her in the middle of the night.

"Here's one," she said, reading it aloud:

It doesn't leave the bedroom. It watches me, waiting. I think it's angry, but I don't know why. Yesterday I woke up with scratches all over my arms. It is starting to really freak me out.

Jacobi's expression shifted as the realization hit. "This all started after she brought the tooth home."

Beretti nodded, flipping back to the earlier entry. "'*I brought it home and put it on my dresser*,'" she repeated under her breath. "She didn't know what she was bringing with her."

Jacobi frowned. "And then what? She left the room and the ghost behind? That's why it went dormant?"

"Seems like it," Beretti said. "But now Ethan's in here. Maybe the ghost sees him as a replacement or maybe he woke it up somehow. Either way, it's active again."

Jacobi crossed his arms, his voice uneasy. "What do we do

with the tooth?"

Beretti pulled the jagged canine from her pocket, holding it between her fingers. "Logically? If it came from the river, returning it might break the connection. It could appease whatever this thing is."

She hesitated, her eyes narrowing as she turned the tooth in her hand. "But... I keep thinking about last night."

Jacobi raised an eyebrow. "What about it?"

Beretti stared at the tooth, her voice lowering. "When it appeared... I felt something. It wasn't just fear. It was... sadness. Like it was lost. Like it didn't belong here anymore, but it didn't know where else to go."

Jacobi shifted uncomfortably. "You think it's trying to leave?"

"Maybe," Beretti said. "Or maybe it's looking for something, or someone, it lost. Maybe Diana. Maybe the tooth. I don't know yet."

She slipped the tooth back into her pocket. "But if this tooth is its anchor, we need to get it out of here. And soon."

FIFTY-SIX

Beretti and Jacobi joined Lillian and Carter at the kitchen table, where the two had been quietly chatting over their coffee. "We found something," Beretti said after a moment, breaking the silence.

Carter raised an eyebrow. "What's that?"

"In Ethan's room," Beretti explained, glancing at Lillian. "We found Diana's journal."

Lillian looked up at Beretti. "Her journal?" she echoed, her voice soft. "I didn't even know she kept one."

"She did," Beretti said. "It was tucked behind some books on the shelf. And inside it… we found a tooth."

Lillian's eyes widened, and she set her mug down carefully. "A tooth?"

Beretti nodded. "And not just any tooth. It matches the size of a Dogman's tooth."

Carter straightened in his chair. "You're saying Diana found a Dogman's tooth?"

"She mentioned it in her journal," Beretti said. "Her boyfriend Todd found it by the river when they were teenagers. He said it was just lying in the mud, so she brought it home. That's when the strange things started happening in her room."

Lillian pressed her hand to her mouth, her face white. "She never told me any of that," she whispered. "I… thought she was just going through a phase. But she was scared, wasn't she?"

"Yeah," Beretti said softly. "It seems like she was. And when she left, the activity stopped. Until Ethan moved into that room."

Carter leaned forward, his fingers tapping against his mug. "So you think the tooth is why the ghost Dogman thing is tied to the room?"

"It makes sense," Beretti said. "It feels… attached. Almost like the tooth is an anchor, keeping it here."

"That would explain a lot," Carter said, shaking his head. "All this time, and it comes down to something she picked up as a kid."

"The question," Jacobi said, his voice measured, "is what do we do about it?"

Beretti sighed, running a hand through her hair. "The long-term solution is simple: the tooth needs to go back to the river. But for tonight? I'm going to take it outside."

Jacobi straightened. "I'll come with you."

Beretti stood, tightening her jacket before retrieving the tooth from her pocket.

The cold wind rushed in as they stepped onto the porch. The storm raged on, snow swirling in the air and piling high against the trees and house.

"Where do you want to bury it?" Jacobi asked.

"Right here," Beretti said, crouching near the edge of the porch. She buried the tooth in a drift of snow, packing it down tightly.

As she stood, Jacobi's gaze darted around the street. "You feel that?"

Beretti scanned the street, her senses on high alert. "Yeah," she said. "We're not alone."

"Let's go back in," Jacobi said.

Beretti nodded, and they retreated into the house, shaking the snow off their boots before they stepped inside.

"Well?" Carter asked, his eyes flicking between them.

"It's done," Beretti said, brushing her hands together. "We'll see if it makes a difference."

Lillian nodded, though her expression was still tight with worry. "I hope it helps."

"Me too," Beretti said, sitting back down.

The group sat in silence for a moment, as they sipped their drinks. In the living room, the faint sound of Ethan laughing at the movie drifted through the air, a small reminder of normalcy amid the chaos.

But even as they rested, the gravity of their decision lingered. The tooth needed to go back to the river. And soon.

FIFTY-SEVEN

The fire engine rumbled down the snow-covered road, its red lights flashing faintly in the gray afternoon. Heavy snow fell steadily, blanketing everything in sight and reducing visibility to barely thirty feet. Inside the truck, the firefighters welcomed the break from monotony. It wasn't every day the public works department called for their help, but with the storm wreaking havoc across the area, every agency was stretched thin.

"I guess we're public works now," said Elias, the youngest and newest on the team, leaning forward in his seat. His breath fogged the glass as he squinted into the swirling snow.

"Just trees, rookie," Lucas said, smirking as he glanced at him from the passenger seat. "Don't get too excited."

"Hey, it beats sitting around the station," Elias replied.

"Depends on how bad the block is," Franklin said from the back.

Captain Pelletier, behind the wheel, kept his eyes on the road ahead. "Eyes up. Storm like this can turn routine into trouble fast."

The truck crested a hill, its tires slipping briefly on the packed snow, before the blockage came into view: a massive tangle of trees sprawled across the road, their thick trunks splintered and jagged where they'd been torn from the earth. Snow clung to their branches, and the surrounding forest loomed dark and shadowy, pressing in on the narrow road.

"Damn," Lucas said.

"Worse than I thought," Captain Pelletier said, bringing the truck to a stop a safe distance from the pileup. The engine idled, ensuring the heater kept the cabin warm while they worked. "All right, Franklin, Lucas… chainsaws. Elias, you're on cleanup. Clear any branches or logs they cut up and toss them off the road."

Elias nodded. "Got it, Cap."

The men stepped out into the storm as the wind whipped

around them. Franklin and Lucas moved to the back of the truck, pulling out the chainsaws. The machines roared to life as they turned to face the first fallen tree.

Elias grabbed a pair of gloves and stepped into position, careful to stay clear of the chainsaws. He bent to pick up a solid branch, its jagged edges coated in ice and dragged it to the side of the road where the growing pile of debris was stacking up. The snow clung to his boots with every step, slowing him down, and the freezing wind cut through his jacket like a blade.

The work was grueling. Every time he straightened, he found himself scanning the nearby forest.

"Everything good, rookie?" Captain Pelletier asked from his position near the truck. His focused gaze never stopped scanning the woods.

"Yeah," Elias said quickly, forcing himself to focus on the task.

As he turned back to the tree line, movement caught his eye. A crow swooped down and landed on the fire engine, its black feathers stark against the snow-covered red paint. It sat there, motionless, staring into the woods.

A crack echoed through the air, sharp and unnatural.

Captain Pelletier stiffened, his head snapping toward the sound.

"Hold up!" he barked.

A sudden silence fell as the roaring chainsaws stopped. Franklin straightened, his gloved hand gripping the handle of his saw tightly.

"What is it?" Lucas asked, his voice cautious.

Captain Pelletier didn't answer immediately. Another crack came, closer this time, followed by a low, rumbling growl.

"Something's out there," Elias whispered.

Lucas forced a nervous laugh. "Probably a tree shifting under the snow. Happens all the time."

"Trees don't growl," Franklin said.

Before anyone could say another word, the crow abruptly launched from the fire engine, its wings beating hard as it shot upward into the storm-gray sky. It circled frantically above the treetops, cawing madly, its cries urgent and relentless, an alarm.

Then the forest erupted.

A monstrous shape tore from the tree line, massive, hunched, and impossibly fast. Snow exploded beneath its claws as it charged, its glowing predatory eyes locking onto Franklin.

"Jesus Christ!" Elias shouted, stumbling backward into the truck.

Franklin barely had time to react before the Dogman was on him. Its claws slashed across his stomach with horrifying force, tearing through his jacket, and spilling his guts into the snow. Franklin staggered back, his eyes wide with disbelief as he looked down at the steaming mass spilling from his abdomen. His gloved hands moved instinctively to try to hold his entrails in place, but his legs gave out, and he collapsed into the blood-stained snow.

"Franklin!" Lucas roared, revving his chainsaw, and swinging it at the creature.

The Dogman twisted away with terrifying speed, the blade missing by inches. It snarled and turned to Lucas, its intense eyes fixing on him. Lucas swung again, the chainsaw screaming through the air, but the Dogman sidestepped with unnerving agility.

Instead of retaliating against Lucas, the Dogman turned

back to Franklin, pouncing on him with a bone-chilling growl. The creature slammed its claws into his chest, tearing into him with savage ferocity. Franklin let out a strangled cry before falling silent.

"Get in the truck!" Captain Pelletier bellowed, shoving Elias toward the vehicle.

The men scrambled into the cab, slamming the doors shut just as the Dogman turned and sprinted toward the vehicle. Captain Pelletier gripped the wheel as the Dogman launched itself at the rear door of the truck.

Its claws smashed through the back window, sending shards of glass flying into the cab.

Elias screamed as the Dogman's claws raked across his leg, slicing through his pants, and leaving a deep gash. He lashed out instinctively, kicking at the creature with his steel-capped boots. The kick connected with its snout, and the Dogman recoiled slightly, snarling in frustration as it tried to force its claws further inside.

"Hold on," Captain Pelletier ordered, throwing the truck into reverse.

The tires spun for a moment before catching traction, and the truck lurched backward. Captain Pelletier eased off the gas, carefully maneuvering the truck. The snow piled high on either side of the road left little room for error, and Captain Pelletier adjusted the wheel with precision.

"Hurry!" Lucas shouted.

Captain Pelletier brought the truck to a stop, shifted into drive, and turned the wheel hard. The truck groaned as it pivoted into a three-point turn, the tires digging into the packed snow.

The Dogman clung to the broken window, its claws scraping against the frame.

"Get down!" Lucas yelled, twisting in his seat, and leaning back with the fire extinguisher.

With a hiss, the extinguisher released a thick cloud of white foam, engulfing the Dogman's head and claws. The creature roared, choking, and coughing as it lost its grip and tumbled into the snow.

"Go! Just drive!" Lucas shouted.

Captain Pelletier straightened the wheel and hit the gas. The truck surged forward, speeding down the road and leaving the bloodied scene behind.

Inside the cab, silence fell as the men tried to catch their breath. Elias, still trembling, turned, and vomited onto the floor of the back seat.

Captain Pelletier didn't flinch. He just stared at the road ahead. "That was not a freakin' wolf," he said.

Lucas wiped his mouth with the back of his hand, his voice hoarse. "Then what the hell was it?"

Captain Pelletier didn't answer as the truck roared forward into the white void.

FIFTY-EIGHT

Light snow continued to fall, swirling in the truck's headlights and reducing visibility to a mere twenty feet. Inside the cab, the air was thick with tension, as it hurtled toward the hospital.

"Slow it down, Cap," Lucas said, his voice strained. "The last thing we wanna do is crash and get stuck out here… not with that thing."

Captain Pelletier's hands tightened on the wheel. "I know," he said, easing his foot off the gas. The truck slowed, its movements steadier but still precarious as the snow piled higher.

In the back seat, Elias shifted uncomfortably, wincing as

his legs throbbed. He had bundled his jacket against the gash on his thigh, the makeshift pressure slowing the bleeding but doing little to dull the pain.

"You okay back there?" Lucas asked, glancing over his shoulder.

Elias hesitated before replying, "I think my legs are torn up pretty bad… but nothing crazy. I'll be fine." His voice wavered slightly, betraying the fear still coursing through him.

Lucas nodded. "Good. Keep the pressure on it. We'll get you patched up at the hospital."

Elias swallowed hard, his throat dry. "What… what are we gonna do about Franklin?"

The question hung in the air. Captain Pelletier's grip on the wheel faltered for a moment, and the truck swerved slightly before he corrected it.

"I…" Captain Pelletier began, his voice trailing off. He cleared his throat, trying again. "I didn't even think to call it in."

Lucas frowned, glancing at Pelletier. "Well, you should now. They need to know what's out here."

Captain Pelletier reached for the radio but stopped, his hand hovering over it. "I don't know what to tell them," he admitted. "What am I supposed to say? That a massive mangy wolf, or whatever the hell that was, just tore Franklin apart? They'll think I've lost my mind."

"Call the sheriff directly," Lucas suggested.

Captain Pelletier nodded slowly. "Yeah… once we get to the hospital, I'll do that. I can explain it to him better than some dispatcher."

Elias leaned forward slightly, concern etched on his face. "What if Franklin's still alive?"

The cab fell silent. Captain Pelletier's eyes flicked to the rearview mirror, meeting Elias's worried gaze.

"There's no way," Captain Pelletier said finally. "That creature tore out his stomach. The amount of blood he lost… he passed out within seconds. He's gone."

Elias sat back, his stomach churning. He wanted to believe otherwise, but the image of Franklin lying motionless in the snow, his blood pooling beneath him, was burned into his mind.

Lucas shifted in his seat, as he stared out the window.

"That thing… it must be the wolf creature that attacked those two ladies."

Captain Pelletier's glanced at Lucas. "It has to be. But that ain't no wolf. I've seen wolves. I've hunted wolves. That thing… it looked more like…" He hesitated, as if saying it out loud would make it real. "More like a werewolf."

Lucas nodded grimly. "Yeah… yeah, it did. The size, its face… the way it attacked. That wasn't a normal animal."

"It's like something out of a nightmare," Elias mumbled from the back seat.

The truck's cabin fell into an uneasy silence, broken only by the rhythmic sound of the windshield wipers.

Elias stared out the window, the dark outlines of trees whipping past in the storm. Every shadow, every flicker of movement made his heart race, his mind conjuring images of the creature stalking them, waiting for an opportunity to strike.

"Do you think it's following us?" Elias asked quietly.

Lucas and Captain Pelletier exchanged a glance.

"No," Captain Pelletier said after a moment. "It got what

it wanted. It's probably back there… with Franklin."

The words hit Elias like a blow. He closed his eyes, trying to push the thought away, as a tear fell down his cheek.

"Let's just focus on getting to the hospital," Lucas said, his voice firm. "One thing at a time."

After what seemed like an eternity, a large green sign emerged from the storm ahead. The reflective letters read: **HOSPITAL - 1 MILE**. The sight brought a small measure of relief, though none of them dared to voice it.

Captain Pelletier slowed the truck as they neared the hospital, the large building casting a stark silhouette against the swirling snow. He pulled into the emergency entrance, bringing the truck to a stop with a loud sigh.

"We're here," he said quietly.

Lucas turned to Elias. "Let's get you inside."

Elias nodded, his movements stiff and slow as he swung his legs out of the truck. Lucas supported him as they made their way toward the entrance, leaving Captain Pelletier alone in the cab. He stared at the dashboard for a long moment before reaching for his phone.

The sheriff needed to know what was out there.

FIFTY-NINE

The storm raged outside, but inside Lillian's house, there was a calm, yet tense atmosphere. They watched the news but only half-listened, the broadcast dominated by updates on road closures and hazardous conditions across the county.

Carter stood by the window, his phone in hand, peering out into the swirling snow.

Ethan sat nearby on the floor, engrossed in his iPad. His small face was illuminated by the device's glow as he scrolled through a game, his finger darting across the screen. Occasionally, he frowned or said something under his breath, but he didn't seem to notice the worry in the room.

"Sandwiches are almost ready," Lillian called out from the kitchen, her voice carrying a forced cheerfulness as she tried to maintain a sense of normalcy.

"Thanks, Grandma," Ethan replied absently, his eyes never leaving the screen.

Jacobi nudged Beretti. "You think the storm will let up tomorrow?"

Beretti shrugged. "I hope so."

'Before Jacobi could reply, Carter's phone buzzed in his hand. He glanced at the screen and frowned. "It's Pelletier," he said, answering it immediately.

"Carter," Captain Pelletier's voice came through, tense and gravelly. "I need to report something… unusual."

Carter's stomach sank. "Go ahead."

Captain Pelletier's voice dropped, as he tried to find the words. "We got called out to clear trees blocking the road. Me, Lucas, Franklin and the rookie, Elias. It was right at the end of Lillian's road." He paused, exhaling heavily.

"What happened?" Carter asked, his voice firm.

"We didn't finish," Captain Pelletier admitted.

"Something came out of the woods. A... creature. It was massive, wolf-like but... not natural. It attacked us. Franklin didn't make it. We had to leave him behind."

Carter froze, his eyes darting toward Beretti and Jacobi. "You left him behind?"

"Our hands were tied," Captain Pelletier sighed, his voice thick with regret. "That thing... it tore him apart. I couldn't risk the others. We barely made it out ourselves."

Carter clenched his jaw. "Did you call it in?"

"Not yet," Captain Pelletier admitted. "I... I was in shock and figured you'd know what to do with this better than dispatch. This... this isn't something we've dealt with before, Carter. Not even close. Hell, I still can't believe what happened."

Carter nodded to himself, though Captain Pelletier couldn't see him. "Alright. I'll take it from here, bud."

Captain Pelletier hesitated. "Be careful, Carter. I have never seen anything like it before."

"I will," Carter said before hanging up.

Beretti and Jacobi got off the couch and followed Carter

into the next room, away from the living room where Ethan might overhear. Carter turned to them, his expression grim. "That was my old friend, Captain Pelletier from the fire department," he began quietly. "They were out clearing the road at the end of the street when the Dogman attacked them. One of their team, Franklin, is dead."

Beretti's posture stiffened, her expression hardening. "Dammit."

Carter nodded as he rubbed his jaw. "He was a good, family man. Pelletier said it was too dangerous to stay. They had to leave Franklin behind."

Jacobi didn't hesitate, already moving toward the door. "How long ago?"

"An hour. Maybe less," Carter said.

Jacobi glanced toward the window. "We've got maybe thirty to forty minutes of daylight left. If Franklin's still out there, we need to check."

Beretti was already grabbing her rifle. "Agreed."

Carter hesitated for a moment, his eyes flicking toward the kitchen where Lillian was arranging sandwiches on a tray. He exhaled deeply before nodding.

"Lillian," he called, stepping into the kitchen.

She looked up from the tray, a frown creasing her brow. "What's wrong?"

"We're going to take a quick walk around the neighborhood. Just checking on a few things," Carter said, keeping his voice calm.

Lillian's frown deepened. "You sure it is safe?"

Carter forced a reassuring smile. "Just making sure everything's fine. We won't be long."

Lillian studied him for a moment before nodding reluctantly. "Alright. Be careful out there."

"We will," Carter promised.

The trio grabbed their rifles, jackets, and flashlights before heading for the door.

SIXTY

The wind howled across the open road, whipping up flurries of snow that blurred the edges of visibility. The street and houses looked like a ghost town, chimneys releasing thin trails of smoke into the frigid air as families huddled inside. Despite the eerie stillness, a few windows cast a warm glow against the encroaching darkness, the only signs of life in the otherwise silent neighborhood.

Beretti, Carter and Jacobi moved steadily through the frozen quiet, their flashlights cutting through the dense haze. The fading daylight added to the urgency pressing on them with every step.

Beretti and Jacobi each carried a rifle while Carter was carrying his trusty 12-gauge shotgun.

The first sign they were nearing the location was a dark patch of red staining the snow near the bend in the road.

"There," Carter said, his flashlight illuminating the blood.

The trio approached cautiously, their beams converging on the scene. The crimson stain stood out starkly against the snow, spreading outward in dark rivulets that had already begun to freeze. Nearby, the chainsaw Franklin had been using lay discarded where it had fallen during the attack, half-buried in the snow, its metal slick with frost. It was a grim reminder of how quickly everything had gone wrong.

"Blood," Beretti said grimly.

Carter knelt beside the patch, his flashlight sweeping across the area. "A lot of it," he said.

Jacobi pointed his flashlight toward the tree line. "There's more. Over here."

Beretti and Carter joined him, their lights catching the unmistakable trail of blood leading from the pool toward the dense woods. Broken branches and trampled snow marked where Franklin's body had been dragged, the trail disappearing into the brush.

Beretti swallowed hard. "It pulled him in there."

Jacobi's gaze remained fixed on the woods. "That's as far as we're going."

Carter straightened, frowning. "You don't want to check?"

Jacobi shook his head firmly. "Not with this snow. We'd barely be able to move, let alone see what we're doing."

Beretti nodded in agreement. "He's right. We'd be completely exposed, too. No cover, no clear line of sight. And with the light almost gone…"

Carter hesitated, his jaw tightening. "I don't like leaving him."

"Neither do I," Jacobi said. "But going in there's a death sentence. If the Dogman is still nearby, it'd have the upper hand in seconds."

Carter sighed. "Alright. Once the storm lets up, we'll come back. With more people and better gear."

The three of them stood in silence for a moment, their flashlights casting long beams across the blood-stained snow. The woods loomed dark and foreboding, the dense underbrush impenetrable to their light.

Beretti glanced toward the trail one last time, with a deep sense of helplessness. "This is the right call," she said quietly. "We'll come back for him."

Carter gave a reluctant nod. "We will. Let's get moving. I'll take the chainsaw home for safekeeping."

The walk back felt harder than the walk out. The snow fell faster now, piling higher with each passing minute and erasing the footprints they had just made.

Beretti kept her flashlight sweeping across the road, her rifle resting in her other hand.

"This storm's working against us," Jacobi said, his voice tight. "If it keeps up, it'll bury everything out here. Including the trail."

Carter nodded grimly. "We'll have to act fast once it clears."

Beretti tried not to think about Franklin's fate, but the image of the blood trail disappearing into the woods lingered in her mind. It was impossible to ignore.

They reached the edge of the neighborhood just as the last traces of daylight disappeared, plunging the area into darkness. The warm glow of Lillian's house came into view, a beacon of safety against the storm's relentless assault.

Carter placed the chainsaw at the end of the porch before the trio hurried inside, slamming the door shut behind them and locking it.

Lillian looked up from the kitchen, concern etched across her face. "Everything okay?"

Carter forced a smile. "Yeah. All good."

Beretti and Jacobi exchanged a glance but said nothing.

The truth could wait.

For now, they were safe.

SIXTY-ONE

The smell of toasted bread and melted cheese lingered in the air as the small group finished their modest dinner. Lillian tidied up the kitchen, glancing occasionally toward the living room where Ethan lay sprawled on the floor, fast asleep under a blanket. His iPad sat on the coffee table, its screen dark.

Lillian glanced at the group and asked, "Would anyone like a scotch?" Her voice was light, but there was a faint edge of weariness to it.

Everyone shook their heads. "I'm good, thanks," Beretti said as she leaned back on the chair.

Jacobi, glancing briefly at Lillian, added, "I'm good too."

Lillian poured herself a small glass, the sound of the amber liquid filling the quiet room. She sat at the table, her fingers idly tracing the rim of her glass.

The television flickered with images of storm updates and weather warnings, the sound turned low. The anchors spoke about road closures and power outages, but no one was really paying attention. Jacobi stared at the screen, lost in thought, while Beretti got up and walked into the kitchen to pour herself a glass of water.

As Beretti leaned against the counter, sipping her drink, Lillian broke the silence. "I feel terrible," she said softly, her voice trembling slightly. "About Diana... and the tooth. I should've known about it. Maybe if I had..." She trailed off, her eyes welling with tears.

Beretti turned, setting her glass down, and took a step closer. "You couldn't have known, Lillian," she said gently.

Lillian shook her head, her gaze fixed on the table in front of her. "I regret so much about how I handled things with Diana. When she left... I was so hurt." Her voice cracked, and she took a sip of her scotch before continuing.

Beretti pulled out a chair and sat down across from her. "Why were you hurt?"

Lillian sighed, her shoulders slumping as memories she'd tried to bury surfaced. "It was Todd," she said finally. "His father wasn't a good man. When I was young, I dated him. He was controlling… abusive. I was lucky to get out. When Diana started seeing Todd, I worried he'd be the same. I tried to warn her, but she didn't want to hear it."

"What made you think Todd was like his father?" Beretti asked softly.

"I noticed things," Lillian said, her hands gripping her glass tightly. "He could be controlling, didn't like when Diana spent time with her friends or family. I called him out on it a few times, and Diana got defensive. She said I was overreacting." Lillian's voice trembled as she continued, "We argued so much. I just wanted her to see what I saw, but it only pushed her further away."

Beretti nodded, listening intently as Lillian spoke.

"When she left, we barely talked for years," Lillian said, wiping at her eyes. "She got pregnant, and Todd was in and out of the picture. Then, not long after Ethan was born, they broke up for good." She paused, her fingers trembling as she took another sip of her drink. "A year later, Todd was killed in a hunting accident. It was… sudden."

Beretti placed a hand on Lillian's arm, grounding her. "You've been carrying this for a long time."

Lillian nodded. "I just wish I had handled it differently. Maybe if I'd been more supportive, Diana wouldn't have shut me out. I don't know." She exhaled shakily, staring into her glass.

"You did what you thought was best," Beretti said gently. "You were trying to protect her."

Lillian looked up, her eyes glassy but filled with a hint of gratitude. "Thank you," she whispered.

In the living room, Carter stretched in his chair, "Sorry guys, but I think I am gonna head to bed. I'll lock up for the night," he said, standing.

Jacobi nodded. "I'll check the back door."

The group moved through the routine of locking doors and checking windows, ensuring every latch was secure. When they were satisfied, Carter leaned against the counter. "Time to call it a night."

"Good idea," Lillian said. "It's been a long day for everyone."

Carter nodded. "Let's hope tomorrow brings better weather."

SIXTY-TWO

Lillian walked into the bathroom, closing the door behind her. The house was warm, the soft murmur of conversation drifting from the kitchen where Carter, Beretti and Jacobi were saying their goodnights. Ethan was asleep on the floor under a warm blanket.

She reached for her toothbrush, ran it under the tap, and smeared on a line of toothpaste. As she lifted it to her mouth, the rhythmic strokes of brushing became a mindless routine, her thoughts already drifting.

As she looked at her reflection in the mirror, a deep, raspy growl resonated from the window.

Lillian froze mid-brush, her breath locked in her chest.

She didn't want to look.

Didn't want to confirm what every nerve in her body already knew.

But out of the corner of her eye, through the reflection of the darkened glass, she saw them.

Amber eyes. Watching her.

Lillian's pulse pounded in her ears. A sick, sinking dread curled in her stomach. She placed the toothbrush down with trembling fingers, every muscle in her body screaming at her to run. But she told herself, *don't look. Don't look. Don't look.*

Heart hammering, she turned, forcing herself toward the door. The moment she hit the hallway, control snapped, and she nearly ran.

"Carter!" she called, her voice louder than she intended. "The Dogman. It's at the bathroom window!"

Beretti, Jacobi and Carter spun around at the sudden commotion, reacting instantly to Lillian's panicked state.

"Stay here," Carter told her as he passed.

The three of them moved quickly, closing the distance to the bathroom in seconds. Carter stepped inside first, his gaze locking onto the window.

Nothing.

The night pressed against the glass, endless and empty.

Jacobi edged in behind him, his eyes scanning the reflection. His hand hovered at his hip out of habit, but his weapon was still locked in the safe by the front door.

Beretti reached for the blind and yanked it down with a snap.

"Well, now it's got nothing to look at," she said.

Carter lingered a moment longer, listening. The wind howled outside, whipping against the house, but beyond that, silence. No shifting of leaves, no crunch of snow. The dogman was gone. For now.

They turned back toward the living room.

Lillian stood frozen near the couch, arms wrapped around herself, shaking, with Ethan now awake and standing beside her, his eyes wide with fear.

Carter walked over to her, his voice low and steady. "You're okay," he said, reassuring her with a hug. "It's gone."

She nodded, but her breath still came fast, her eyes darting toward the hallway as if the thing might be standing there.

SIXTY-THREE

Beretti moved swiftly, leading the way to where she and Jacobi had stored their portable safe near the front door. She crouched, entered the code and yanked it open. The dull gleam of their Ruger Super Redhawk (.454 Casull) revolvers greeted her, the familiarity of them reassuring as she handed Jacobi his.

"I'm not taking any changes tonight," she said, securing hers into her hip holster.

Jacobi gave a quick nod, mirroring her actions. "Yeah, I have a bad feeling about it."

They didn't waste time. Moving in unison, they strode toward Ethan's bedroom where their rifles had been stored earlier. Beretti flicked on the light, scanning the room as if expecting to find something lurking in the corners. Jacobi stepped to his rifle case first, unfastening it and checking the magazine and chamber before slinging the rifle over his shoulder, his movements quick and efficient. Beretti did the same, ensuring her weapon was ready to fire at a moment's notice.

Satisfied, they returned to the living room. Carter was already at his own safe, the steel door swinging open as he reached inside. He pulled out his 12-gauge shotgun and racked a shell into the chamber. He turned to the front door, peered through the peephole onto the porch, then stepped back.

Jacobi checked the back door again, fingers tensing on the handle as he peered through the glass. He double-checked the lock before stepping back.

Lillian sat on the couch, her arms wrapped protectively around Ethan, who had tucked himself tightly against her side. Both of them were anxious, their eyes flickering toward the windows as if expecting something to crash through at any moment.

She glanced at Carter, her voice hushed but tense. "Do you really think it will try to come inside?"

Carter met her gaze, his expression firm. "We're not taking any chances."

He then knelt slightly to meet Ethan's eye level. "Kid, listen to me. We're prepared for this. You're safe. But right now, I need you to focus on something else, alright?"

Beretti stepped forward, softening her tone. "Ethan, why don't you put your headphones in and keep watching your videos? It'll help keep your mind off things."

Ethan hesitated, but after a brief glance at Lillian, he nodded. Slowly, he reached for his iPad, pulled his headphones over his ears, and pressed play. Lillian mouthed "thank you" to Beretti, who nodded in return.

Each of them took position by a window, scanning the night outside. The storm had worsened, thick snow obscuring their vision, but they could still make out the silhouettes of trees swaying in the distance. The world beyond the glass was a haze of white, quiet but deceptively so.

SIXTY-FOUR

A tense silence gripped the house. The only sound was the occasional howl of the wind as the storm continued its relentless assault outside. The dim glow from the lamps barely pushed back the shadows creeping along the walls.

Carter stood near the front window, his shotgun in hand, eyes scanning the darkness beyond the glass. Jacobi and Beretti remained at opposite ends of the room, their rifles ready.

Suddenly, they heard a soft thump overhead.

Subtle, barely more than the wind, but enough to grab everyone's attention.

Everyone froze, their gazes snapping upward.

Another thump. Heavier this time.

Then came the unmistakable sound of footsteps.

The ceiling creaked under something massive moving above them. Each step sent faint vibrations through the walls.

Ethan pulled his headphones off, eyes wide. "What is that?" he whispered.

Lillian pulled him closer, her fingers gripping his arm. "Put your headphones back on," she said gently but firmly.

Ethan hesitated but nodded, slipping them back over his ears and turning up the volume.

It moved again, crossing from one side of the roof to the other.

"Where is it now?" Lillian whispered.

Beretti kept her eyes on the ceiling, listening. "Pacing. Like it's thinking."

A beat of silence. Then a horrible cackling noise echoed from above.

It wasn't a growl. It wasn't a snarl. It was something

worse. A twisted, mocking laugh. It had a warped, unnatural edge, as though the creature was trying to mimic something it had heard before.

Lillian flinched. "Oh my..."

The sound crawled through the ceiling, settling deep in their bones. It wasn't just some mindless beast. It was enjoying this.

Carter clenched his jaw and adjusted his shotgun. "Screw this."

He moved toward the front door, but Jacobi stepped in front of him. "That's exactly what it wants."

Carter stopped, his grip tightening on the shotgun. "We can't just sit here and let it taunt us."

Jacobi kept his voice steady. "We don't. We wait for it to make a mistake."

The cackling stopped abruptly. The silence that followed was worse. The quiet made it clear it was waiting for their next move.

A loud thud shook the ceiling as something landed hard near the center of the roof. Dust trickled down from the rafters. The creature exhaled loudly, its breathing a harsh, rattling sound that vibrated through the wood.

Beretti's fingers curled tighter around her rifle. "Only shoot if it breaks through."

Carter nodded, his shotgun steady.

The next few moments stretched painfully.

Another step creaked above them. Then another. The Dogman prowled the length of the roof again, circling, waiting.

Then, without warning, the noise stopped.

Complete and utter silence.

Lillian barely breathed. "Where did it go?"

No one answered. No one moved.

SIXTY-FIVE

The living room was silent. No more footsteps above. No more cackling. Just the sound of their own breathing and the wind howling outside.

Carter kept his shotgun ready, his eyes trained on the ceiling. Beretti gripped her rifle, shifting slightly as her gaze flicked between the door and the windows. Jacobi stood near the back of the room, his posture rigid.

Lillian sat with Ethan on the couch, her arms still wrapped around him. His headphones were on, but his eyes darted around, sensing the tension thick in the air.

Then, from the chimney, a sudden whooshing sound.

A dark blur shot straight down the flue.

BOOM!

Ash and embers exploded outward, a thick cloud of soot blasting into the living room. Sparks danced across the floor, the heat momentarily flaring as the dying embers scattered.

Lillian yelled as she grabbed Ethan, yanking him off the couch, his iPad hitting the floor. She bolted for the kitchen, shielding him as they huddled near the table.

Carter and Beretti rushed forward, stomping out the glowing embers before they could catch on the rug or furniture. Smoke curled upward, swirling into the air as the last bits of ash smoldered and died.

Jacobi, coughing through the dust, stepped toward the fireplace, rifle raised. He peered into the hearth, where something heavy had thudded against the bricks.

Jacobi froze, his expression darkening. He didn't move for several seconds, just stared into the fireplace.

Beretti, still near the embers, wiped soot from her sleeve and looked up. "What is it?"

Jacobi didn't answer. He took a slow step back, his face blank.

Carter moved closer, narrowing his eyes. "Jacobi?"

Jacobi finally turned toward them, grim and pale. His voice was flat, almost detached when he spoke.

"You don't want to know what it threw down the chimney."

Lillian's face dropped as she quickly placed her hands over Ethan's ears. He pressed his face into her shoulder, his small body trembling against her.

Beretti's stomach tightened. "Tell us."

Jacobi exhaled slowly through his nose, gripping his rifle.

"A half-eaten human leg."

Lillian gasped, holding Ethan even tighter.

Carter swore under his breath and stepped closer to Jacobi. "Are you sure?"

Jacobi nodded grimly. "You want to take a peek?"

Nobody did.

Carter exhaled slowly, then shook his head. "We're not staying here. Not if it's escalating like this."

Beretti immediately turned to him, her expression tightening. "Where exactly would we go?"

Carter ran a hand over his head. "Anywhere but here. This thing is playing with us. We need to move before it decides to take the game to the next level."

Jacobi scoffed. "You mean head out into the blizzard? Where we can't see five feet in front of us? Where it's bigger, faster, and stronger than us?" He gestured toward the front window. "That's a suicide mission."

Beretti nodded. "We leave this house, we lose every advantage we have. The walls, the doors, the guns. It's safer in here than out there."

Carter's shoulders tensed. "Safer? With that thing dropping body parts into the damn chimney?"

Beretti didn't back down. "Going outside makes us easy prey." She pointed at the fireplace. "This was meant to scare us, to get us to do something stupid."

Jacobi nodded. "Like running straight into its territory."

Carter let out a long breath, then ran a hand through his hair. "I just want to keep everyone safe. This thing is toying with us, and I hate just sitting here waiting for its next move."

Lillian, still clutching Ethan, watched them anxiously. "The roads are blocked anyway," she said suddenly. "We're not getting out tonight."

Jacobi glanced at Beretti, then back to Carter. "We bunker down. We keep our eyes open. We don't do exactly what it wants."

Beretti nodded. "We wait for daylight."

Carter exhaled, his shoulders dropping slightly. After a moment, he gave a reluctant nod. "Alright. This whole thing is getting to me. Sorry I lost it for a second. I'm not used to dealing with… monsters."

Beretti offered a reassuring look. "It's alright. We get it. These situations are tough, but we stick together. No matter what."

SITXY-SIX

Jacobi grimaced as he crouched by the fireplace, gripping the half-eaten, charred leg with his gloved hands. The stench of burned flesh and decay filled the air, making his stomach churn. He worked quickly, pulling the grotesque remains free from the ash.

"Shit," Carter mumbled, turning away.

Beretti grabbed an old towel from the nearby basket and held it out. "Wrap it up. We'll put it in the laundry tub for now."

Jacobi wrapped the leg and carried it down the hall to the laundry room, dropping it into the deep sink with a dull thud. He ran the faucet, letting cold water wash away some of the soot and blood, though it did little to ease the horror of what had just happened.

Now that the fire had died down, the living room was growing cold. Lillian shivered, rubbing Ethan's back absentmindedly as she moved toward the thermostat. She cranked up the central heating, ensuring the house stayed warm despite the winter storm outside.

Ethan hesitated before looking up at Carter, his voice small. "What if it comes down the chimney?"

Carter crouched slightly to meet his eyes, his tone steady. "It can't fit, bud. Don't worry. You're safe in here."

Beretti moved to the window, rifle in hand, scanning the snow-covered yard. She noted a crow perched on the fence post, barely visible through the swirling snow. It sat motionless, watching her with dark, unblinking eyes.

She glanced away for just a second. When she looked back, the crow started squawking loudly, wings twitching as if warning her. Unease settled in her gut.

A loud knock echoed from the back door.

Everyone froze.

Carter straightened but didn't move from his spot, gripping his shotgun tightly. Jacobi and Beretti exchanged a quick glance before moving toward the hallway, rifles raised.

The knocking came again. Steady. Insistent.

Beretti didn't take her eyes off the back door when she said, "Remember, don't shoot unless it comes in."

Jacobi gave a tense nod, his focus locked on the back door.

The knocking continued. A deliberate, rhythmic sound.

Lillian held Ethan close, whispering softly to herself to breathe.

Then, as suddenly as it had started, the knocking stopped.

Silence stretched through the house, as they waited.

Jacobi exhaled slowly. "It's still out there."

Beretti glanced back toward the window, but the crow was gone.

SIXTY-SEVEN

The house had been eerily quiet for the past hour. No more thuds on the roof, no scratching at the windows, no growls carried by the wind. The only sound was the steady hum of the central heating and the wind rattling the windows.

Carter, Beretti and Jacobi sat in the living room, their guns within arm's reach. The unease from the night's earlier events hadn't faded, but for the moment, nothing stirred outside.

Lillian sat on the couch, gently stroking Ethan's back as he lay curled up, half-dozing under the thick quilt. He hadn't spoken much, but his breathing was even, his body finally allowing itself some rest.

Jacobi exhaled quietly and leaned forward, resting his elbows on his knees. "Maybe it finally got bored," he muttered, though he didn't sound convinced.

Beretti, sitting near the window, shook her head. "Doubt it."

From outside, the sharp cry of a crow shattered the stillness.

Beretti stiffened. "It's coming," she said to the others.

Another squawk. Urgent.

A dull *thump* echoed from the front porch.

Everyone froze.

Another *thump.*

Footsteps.

Slow.

The wooden planks of the porch groaned under a massive weight.

Lillian tensed, her fingers tightening against Ethan's shoulder. His eyes fluttered open groggily, and she hushed him with a gentle touch.

Carter, Beretti and Jacobi were already on their feet, weapons in hand, eyes locked on the front door.

Step. Creak.

Step. Creak.

Then silence.

Something stood just outside.

No movement. No sound. Just waiting.

Beretti and Jacobi raised their guns. Carter took a slow step closer, gripping his shotgun. The air was suffocating, the stillness stretching unbearably.

The door handle started to turn.

It moved slowly, testing the lock.

Ethan sucked in a breath, his body stiff under the quilt. Lillian pressed a reassuring hand against his back, though her own heart pounded painfully.

The handle jiggled again, firmer this time.

Beretti steadied her revolver, bracing herself. If that lock gave, she wasn't hesitating.

Then, just as suddenly, it stopped.

For a long moment, nothing.

A shadow passed the front window.

It was enormous, stretching impossibly tall against the glow of the porch light filtering through the closed blinds. A broad silhouette, distorted by the storm, loomed for just a second before shifting away.

They barely had time to register it before a heavy *thud* landed in the snow.

Jacobi slowly stepped closer to the window. The snowfall blurred everything beyond the glass, but the way the wind shifted told him something was still moving out there.

"Son of a bitch," Carter mumbled, lowering his shotgun slightly but keeping his grip firm.

Jacobi swallowed hard, his voice barely above a whisper. "It was testing us."

The room remained silent, every single one of them listening, waiting.

SIXTY-EIGHT

Lillian woke after a restless sleep, her body stiff, and her mind still burdened with worry. She sat up slowly, the faint ache in her back a reminder of how little rest she'd managed to get on the living room couch, next to Ethan. She glanced around the room, taking in the quiet stillness that had settled over the house.

Beretti and Jacobi were still awake, their postures rigid despite the calm. Beretti sat near the armrest of the couch, her rifle leaning against the side, while Jacobi was angled in a chair, his gaze intense and focused. Carter, however, had nodded off in his chair, his chin resting against his chest, one hand still near his pistol.

Lillian sighed and pushed herself to her feet, wrapping

her shawl tighter around her shoulders. She glanced toward the window, briefly smiling as she noticed the world outside.

The storm had finally stopped. The snow, which had seemed endless through the night, now lay still and undisturbed, a thick blanket glistening faintly under the soft light of dawn. The wind had calmed, reduced to a gentle whisper brushing against the house.

She moved quietly through the kitchen, the familiar hiss of the coffee pot breaking the silence. No one had gotten much sleep except for Ethan, who was still soundly asleep on the floor, curled under a cozy blanket. She glanced at him with a mixture of exhaustion and relief.

She placed mugs on the counter, her movements careful not to disturb the fragile peace in the house. The night had been long, filled with the constant unease of the Dogman's taunts, but the last hour had been thankfully quiet.

As she opened the fridge, the creak of a chair drew her attention. Carter stirred slightly but didn't wake. Jacobi stretched, rolling his shoulders before glancing toward her.

"You're a saint for making coffee," he said quietly.

Lillian gave a small smile and reached for the coffee pot. "I figured we could all use it."

As the coffee pot gurgled to a stop, she poured the steaming liquid into the mugs and handed one to Jacobi. "Here. Strong enough to wake the dead."

Jacobi took it gratefully. "Exactly what I need."

Beretti accepted a mug next, nodding her thanks as she wrapped her hands around it to soak in the warmth.

Carter finally stirred, rubbing his face before blinking blearily at the coffee. He exhaled a slow breath. "Morning."

"Morning," Lillian said, handing him a cup.

He took a sip and sighed heavily with exhaustion.

Jacobi tilted his head. "Storm's finally passed, huh?"

Beretti nodded. "Looks that way. We've got clear skies now, which works in our favor."

After finishing her coffee, Beretti stood and stretched, rolling out the stiffness in her shoulders. "I'm going to grab a quick shower. I need to wake up properly."

Carter nodded. "Go ahead. We'll keep watch."

She made her way to the bedroom first, placing her rifle back in its secure case before heading toward the bathroom.

The bathroom was mercifully warm, the hot water easing the tightness in Beretti's shoulders and washing away some of the fatigue of the night. She lingered under the stream for a moment, letting the steam clear her head, before stepping out and drying off.

When she returned to the living room, Jacobi stood, stretching his arms over his head. "Anyone need the bathroom before I go?" he asked, glancing around. When no one spoke up, he gave Beretti a nod. "My turn," he said, heading to the bedroom to secure his rifle and grab his bathroom kit.

Beretti sat back down, pulling her rifle closer. Lillian had begun tidying the kitchen, moving with nervous energy. Carter remained at the table, his gaze fixed on the yard outside.

Ethan stirred on the couch, rubbing his eyes and sitting up. "What time is it?"

"Morning," Lillian said gently, moving to sit beside him. "It's 8am. The storm's over."

Ethan's face brightened slightly. "Really?"

When Jacobi returned, he dropped into his chair and stretched out his legs again. "Hot water still works. Small miracles."

Beretti smiled. "It does."

Jacobi glanced at her. "What's the plan for today?"

She straightened in her seat. "The storm's passed, which means we've got daylight and better visibility. I want to check on Franklin's remains. If the Dogman dragged him off, we might be able to recover something."

Jacobi tilted his head. "And the tooth?"

Beretti nodded. "We'll need to take it back to the river, too. We can't put that off any longer. With the weather clearing, people will start heading out again, and the last thing we need is this thing killing anyone else."

"You think now is the time to meet it head on?" Jacobi asked.

Beretti met his gaze. "Yeah. We've been reacting this whole time, playing defence. That's not going to cut it. We need to take control of this situation."

Jacobi nodded firmly. "Agreed. Let's get moving after breakfast."

Carter exhaled and nodded. "Count me in. I'd like to help

the residents out after the storm without having to watch my back."

As Lillian set out bowls of cereal and toast, the group sat down for breakfast. The simple meal was a small comfort after the long, harrowing night.

The sun had risen higher, casting bright light over the snow-covered yard. The forest beyond stood silent, its branches sagging under the remnants of the storm.

Ethan, now fully awake, pulled his blanket tighter around himself. "What are we going to do today?"

Beretti glanced at him, her expression softening. "We're going to take care of some things. But you don't need to worry about that, okay? You just focus on relaxing today."

Ethan nodded, his face calm but tired.

SIXTY-NINE

The living room was unusually calm as Beretti and Jacobi sat at the coffee table, playing a game of cards with Ethan. The boy had finally started to relax after the tense, sleepless night, though his wide-eyed curiosity still lingered.

"Got any threes?" Ethan asked, peeking over his hand at Jacobi.

Jacobi chuckled and handed over a card. "You're ruthless, kid."

Ethan grinned as he added the card to his growing pile. "Your turn, Agent Beretti."

Beretti glanced at her hand, narrowing her eyes in mock suspicion. "Got any kings?"

Ethan sighed and handed over a card, his competitive streak faltering for a moment.

Jacobi chuckled. "Tough break, kid. She's got the instincts of a bloodhound."

Ethan shrugged, grinning. "That was brutal ma'am."

Beretti raised a brow, though her tone was light. "Call me Beretti, remember? No need for ma'am."

"Oh, right," Ethan said sheepishly. "Sorry."

Jacobi smirked, leaning back. "She just doesn't want to sound old, kid."

"Keep it up, Jacobi," Beretti said, deadpan. "See how far that gets you."

The sound of shuffling cards and Ethan's occasional giggles provided a strange but welcome reprieve from the stress that had gripped the house for days.

Carter returned from a quick shower, yawning as he made his way to the dining table. He glanced over at them, a faint smile tugging at the corner of his mouth as he watched Ethan laugh.

But the peace was short-lived.

Carter's phone buzzed against the table, drawing everyone's attention. He grabbed it quickly, glancing at the screen. Department of Public Works.

"Sheriff Carter," he answered, his voice steady.

The man on the other end sounded tense. "Sheriff, it's Dave Bierko from Public Works. Morning."

"Morning, Dave. What's going on?"

"Well, I'll get right to it. We heard about what happened to the firefighter... that wolf creature. Everyone's talking about it, and, uh, the guys are spooked. They don't want to go out there to clear the trees alone."

Carter glanced toward the others before responding. "You want us to come out there?"

"Yeah, if you can. Just for protection while we work. The guys are already jumpy, and I don't blame them. We can't afford another... you know."

Carter leaned back in his chair, exhaling slowly. "No problem. Text me when you're on your way, and we'll meet you there."

The relief in Dave's voice was clear. "Thanks, Sheriff.

Really appreciate it. We'll be heading out in about thirty minutes."

"Got it," Carter said before ending the call.

Carter set his phone down and looked at Beretti and Jacobi, who had already stopped their game to listen.

"That was Public Works," he said. "They want us to meet them at the downed trees and provide some protection while they clear the road. They're spooked after what happened to Franklin. Don't want to risk being out there alone."

Beretti exchanged a glance with Jacobi, then nodded. "Smart call on their part."

Jacobi set his cards down. "Agreed. No sense taking chances."

"They're heading out in thirty minutes," Carter added. "We'll meet them there."

Jacobi patted Ethan on the shoulder as he stood. "Sorry, kid. We've got to get ready now."

The house shifted into quiet preparation. Beretti and Jacobi moved to the bedroom to retrieve their rifles. Their pistols were already holstered at their sides, but they each pulled out their rifles and began their routine checks.

Jacobi inspected the magazine, cycled the bolt, and tested the safety with practiced efficiency before slinging the rifle over his shoulder.

Beretti retrieved her own rifle, double-checking the scope and barrel before securing the strap. She glanced briefly at Carter, who retrieved his shotgun from the cabinet and gave it a quick but thorough inspection.

As Jacobi adjusted the strap on his rifle, Beretti glanced at him. "Don't forget sunglasses. The glare off the snow will fry your eyes."

Jacobi smiled, reaching for his aviators. "I always look better in sunglasses, anyway."

Beretti didn't miss a beat. "Is that because they hide half your face?"

Jacobi clutched his chest in mock offense. "Wow. That's cold." He paused, smiling again. "But honestly, that was a good one. You're getting funnier."

Beretti gave a rare grin. "It's not hard when you're the target."

Their laughter filled the room, cutting through the lingering unease like a welcome reprieve. Even Carter smiled, shaking his head at their banter.

Across the room, Ethan laughed along with them, his shoulders relaxing.

Jacobi turned to him with a grin. "See? At least someone appreciates my suffering."

Ethan chuckled again, shaking his head. "It was pretty good."

Beretti chuckled lightly. "Glad you think so, kid."

The light-hearted moment eased the strain in the room, bringing a much-needed sense of relief, even if only for a little while.

Exactly thirty minutes later, Carter's phone chimed with a text. He picked it up and read the message: **"Leaving now. ETA 10 minutes."**

"They're on their way," Carter said, slipping the phone into his pocket.

The three of them pulled on their jackets, the thick winter layers insulating them from the sharp chill outside. As they stepped onto the porch, the frigid air jolted them awake instantly, biting at their skin and filling their lungs with an icy sting. The sun cast a blinding glare off the snow-covered landscape, the trees standing motionless in the crisp morning light.

Beretti paused as her gaze wandered to the spot where she had buried the tooth the night before. Something about the snowbank didn't look right. She stepped off the porch, her boots crunching against the snow, and narrowed her eyes.

"Jacobi," she called, her voice laced with suspicion.

He turned and followed her, his footsteps loud in the stillness. "What is it?"

Beretti gestured toward the disturbed snowbank. "That's where I buried the tooth last night."

Jacobi knelt, brushing away the light layer of fresh snow to reveal clawed markings and uneven impressions in the icy crust beneath. "Looks like something dug it up," he mumbled, straightening to meet her gaze.

Beretti's expression darkened as she scanned the surrounding woods. "The Dogman. It must've taken it."

"You're sure?" Jacobi asked, his voice low.

"What else could it be?" she said, her voice thoughtful. She paused, the pieces clicking together in her mind. "Maybe it wasn't Ethan it was after. Maybe it was drawn to whatever was in the room with him. And now that the tooth is gone... that has to mean something."

Jacobi tilted his head, his brow tense with thought. "You think that's why it's been hanging around?"

Beretti nodded slowly. "At least part of the reason. Maybe not all the attacks, but it's clear it wanted the tooth. That's the connection. It was drawn to him because of it."

"So it's gone now?" Jacobi asked, his voice hopeful but cautious.

Beretti exhaled, her breath visible in the frosty air. "If the tooth is what it wanted, it might leave us alone now. But there's no guarantee. We have to stay on guard. It's still a Dogman, after all."

Their walk continued in silence, heavy with unspoken thoughts. The sleet in the last few hours helped compact the snow enough to walk on.

As they neared the clearing where the trees had fallen, the rumble of a diesel engine reached their ears.

The Department of Public Works truck came into view, its orange lights flashing against the white backdrop. The vehicle stopped a short distance from the blocked section of the road, and four men climbed out, bundled in thick jackets and hats.

Carter raised a hand in greeting. "Morning."

"Morning, Sheriff," one of the men called back.

The workers looked nervous, their eyes darting toward the tree line as though expecting the creature to leap out at any moment.

Beretti and Jacobi exchanged a glance, their rifles already in hand as they took up positions near the group.

"Let's get this done," Carter said.

The workers nodded and began unloading their chainsaws and equipment, moving with a quiet urgency that hinted at their unease.

SEVENTY

The sound of the Department of Public Works truck faded into the distance, the rumble of its engine swallowed by the stillness of the snow-covered landscape. The road was finally clear, the massive fallen trees cut into manageable sections and pushed aside.

Carter, Beretti and Jacobi stood at the edge of the woods, watching the truck's orange lights disappear around the bend.

"Well," Carter said, breaking the silence, "at least that's one problem taken care of."

Beretti nodded, her gaze shifting to the dense forest ahead. "I want to check for Franklin's remains while we're here," she said. "We won't go far, just a quick look around to see if anything's visible. If the body's buried under the snow, we might have to come back later."

Jacobi adjusted his rifle strap. "Makes sense. Let's take a look."

Carter scanned the tree line, his shotgun held loosely but ready. "The snow would've covered any tracks by now, so we're not likely to see much."

Beretti agreed but added, "It's worth checking."

"Always," Jacobi said, already stepping toward the woods.

The forest was quiet, the fresh snowfall muffling their footsteps. The occasional creak of a branch or rustle of snow dislodging from above was the only sound, and it set all three of them on edge.

Jacobi walked a little ahead, his rifle at the ready, while Beretti followed, her eyes darting all around as Carter brought up the rear, keeping a steady but cautious pace.

"There's nothing," Jacobi mumbled, his voice barely audible. "It's like the whole place is asleep."

Beretti glanced at him, her eyes narrowing. "Silence

always worries me in the woods. It usually means something's watching."

Jacobi's mouth twitched, but he didn't reply.

They moved slowly, their eyes scanning the ground and the surrounding trees. The snow lay pristine, undisturbed, as though nothing had dared to cross the forest since the storm.

After several minutes of searching, Beretti came to a stop, crouching down to inspect an area where the snow looked slightly uneven. She brushed it aside with gloved hands but found only a cluster of frozen leaves.

She sighed and stood, brushing off her gloves. "Nothing here. If the remains are here, they might be buried under a drift, and we're not going to find them without more time."

Jacobi shifted his weight, the snow crunching softly beneath his boots.

The sound made Beretti glance at him, her brow raising. "And chew your gum quieter please," she whispered.

Jacobi blinked, then smirked sheepishly. "Sorry."

Carter chuckled quietly from behind them. "You've got good ears, Beretti."

"Once you hear it…," Beretti replied, her tone dry.

Beretti scanned the area. "If Franklin's body was dragged this way, it could be buried too deep for us to spot. The snow's not making this easy."

Jacobi glanced around, his eyes hidden behind his sunglasses. "So, what's the call?"

"We head back," Beretti said, her voice firm. "No point pushing further in right now. We'll try again when the snow settles more."

Jacobi nodded, though his grip on his rifle didn't relax.

As they turned back toward the road, their pace quickened slightly, though none of them wanted to appear rushed.

The crunch of their boots against the snow sounded impossibly loud, and each step was like it might provoke a response from the unseen predator they all feared.

Jacobi kept his head on a swivel, his aviators masking his sharp gaze as he scanned the tree line. Beretti's eyes darted between the ground and the forest ahead, her senses hyper-aware of every sound. Carter brought up the rear, his hand gripping his shotgun tightly as his gaze flicked behind them.

"Quiet," Beretti whispered, though no one had spoken.

The three of them stopped simultaneously, listening intently. The silence was deafening.

A distant thud, soft and muffled, broke the stillness.

"What was that?" Carter whispered.

Beretti shook her head. "Could be snow falling from a branch."

"Or it could be the Dogman," Jacobi said.

Beretti glanced at him but said nothing, her focus on moving forward.

When they finally broke through the tree line and stepped back onto the road, a collective tension seemed to ease from their shoulders.

Beretti turned to look back at the woods. "Nothing out there. For now."

Jacobi nodded, his posture still guarded. "I doubt the Dogman has gone far. Probably watching us right now."

Carter adjusted his grip on his shotgun, his expression grim. "We'll try again later. I just feel so sorry for Franklin's family. One of my deputies let them know last night and understandably, they were devastated. I'd like to give them something to bury."

Jacobi looked over at Carter with a mix of compassion and reassurance. "We'll find him sheriff."

Beretti gave him a curt nod, though her gaze lingered on the forest as they began the walk back to the house with their heads on a swivel.

SEVENTY-ONE

The walk back to Lillian's house was quiet, but none of them let their guard down. Beretti and Jacobi kept their rifles at the ready, while Carter gripped his shotgun, his eyes scanning every dark corner and flicker of movement around them.

"I've never looked at the woods with so much suspicion," Carter admitted, his gaze drifting to the tree line that bordered the neighborhood.

Beretti's eyes swept the distance, her voice calm but laced with vigilance. "In our line of work, the woods hold a lot of secrets."

Jacobi nodded, his breath visible as he spoke. "This kind

of quiet always puts me on edge."

Carter rubbed the back of his neck, a faint scowl crossing his face. "I don't envy you two. One of the reasons why I haven't asked what else is out there. I'd rather stay a little ignorant, thanks."

Jacobi gave him a faint smile. "Can't blame you, Carter. Some things are easier to deal with when you don't know the details."

A high-pitched giggle suddenly broke the quiet, freezing all three of them in place.

"Where did that come from?" Jacobi asked.

Beretti pointed. "Over there."

Just ahead, a child no older than five was playing in their backyard. The little boy flung snow into the air, his laughter ringing out as it scattered around him.

A parent stood a few feet away, bundled in a thick jacket and holding up a phone to record the moment. They smiled and laughed as they focused entirely on the child.

Beretti noticed a crow land on a nearby fence. It squawked loudly, the sound loud and urgent.

Her stomach dropped. "Eyes up," she said urgently. "The Dogman is here somewhere."

Without hesitation, the three of them started moving quickly toward the parent and child.

Carter's grip tightened on his shotgun as Jacobi's gaze swept the area.

"They're too far from the house," Beretti said urgently. "Too exposed."

Then, Beretti's eyes narrowed, locking onto a spot in the woods as her instincts screamed that something was wrong. "Ahead, ten o'clock," she said, her voice urgent.

Jacobi followed her gaze and felt his stomach drop.

From the woods behind the house, a massive shadow emerged, moving fast and low to the ground. The Dogman.

"Get inside!" Beretti screamed, her voice cutting through the air like a whip.

The parent turned, startled, and froze as they locked eyes with Beretti.

"Get inside now!" Beretti yelled again, running forward.

The parent still didn't move, confused and unsure of what was happening. Finally, they grabbed their child, scooping them into their arms, but their focus remained on Beretti, not the woods behind them.

Jacobi had already broken into a sprint, his boots throwing up snow as he charged toward the family. "Go! Get down!"

The Dogman burst through the snow, its massive form moving with frightening speed despite its injuries. Even from a distance, the scorched, patchy hair along its back was visible, exposing raw, blistered skin beneath.

The parent screamed as Jacobi reached them, tackling both mother and child to the ground just as the Dogman leaped. The creature sailed over them, its claws slicing the air inches above their heads.

Beretti raised her rifle, her heartbeat thundering in her ears. She tracked the Dogman as it skidded in the snow, pivoting to face them with a snarl that seemed to echo from the depths of hell.

"Jacobi, move!" she shouted.

Jacobi rolled off the parent and child, grabbing them and pulling them to their feet. He shoved them toward their house. "Go! Run!"

Beretti exhaled slowly and steadied her aim. The Dogman lunged sideways just as she fired, the crack of the rifle shattering the air. The bullet struck its leg, tearing into muscle and sending a spray of blood onto the snow.

The creature howled in pain, as it landed awkwardly.

It locked eyes with Beretti, its amber gaze burning with fury, before it turned and bolted toward the woods, its injured leg dragging slightly but not enough to slow it much.

Jacobi didn't hesitate.

He surged forward, picking up his rifle as he sprinted after the retreating figure.

"Jacobi, wait!" Beretti screamed.

But he didn't listen.

"Damn it!" Beretti said, already running after him.

Carter was right behind her, his shotgun raised as he shouted, "Jacobi, stop! Get back here!"

But Jacobi didn't stop.

The snow made running a challenge, each step sinking slightly into the crusted surface, but Beretti pushed forward, her legs burning as she followed Jacobi's trail.

"Why doesn't he ever listen?" she said under her breath, her frustration mounting with every step.

Jacobi had the Dogman in sight, but the creature was fast, even with its injured leg. It weaved through the trees with unsettling speed, its movements fluid and precise, as if it anticipated every step.

Beretti glanced over her shoulder at Carter. "Stay close! We can't lose him!"

"I'm right here!" Carter shouted back, his breath visible in the cold air.

Jacobi's voice echoed through the trees as he yelled after the Dogman, his tone a mix of rage and adrenaline. "Come on! Come at me, you bastard!"

Beretti gritted her teeth as she pushed harder. She could hear Carter's labored breathing behind her but kept her focus on the trail ahead.

The forest grew darker the further they ran, the thick canopy above blocking out much of the sunlight. Snow clung to the branches, occasionally falling in clumps as the wind passed through.

Up ahead, Jacobi disappeared behind a cluster of trees, his figure swallowed by the shadows.

"Jacobi!" Beretti screamed.

When they reached the spot where Jacobi had vanished, Beretti skidded to a stop, her rifle raised as she scanned the area.

"Jacobi!" she called again, her voice echoing through the trees.

Carter came to a stop beside her, his shotgun at the ready. "Where is he?"

Beretti's eyes darted between the trees, her heart pounding. "I don't know. But he was right here."

A faint rustling sound drew their attention.

Carter motioned silently with his hand, and Beretti nodded, stepping forward carefully.

SEVENTY-TWO

Jacobi ran through the woods, his lungs burning in the freezing air as he tried to dodge deep snow. His heart pounded, adrenaline surging through his veins, driving him forward as branches clawed at his jacket and face.

The Dogman's trail was erratic, its tracks weaving between trees and through clusters of undergrowth. Even with its injured leg and scorched back, the creature moved with an agility that defied its size.

Jacobi slowed, his rifle gripped tightly as he scanned the forest ahead. The tracks were harder to follow now, blurred and faint where the snow had settled deeper.

Where the hell are you?

The haunting silence that followed the chase made his heart beat harder. The woods were too quiet. No wind, no rustling branches, nothing but his own labored breathing.

He crouched behind a thick tree trunk, his eyes darting from tree to tree. The faint calls of Beretti and Carter echoed faintly in the distance.

"Jacobi! Where are you?" Beretti's voice was sharp with urgency.

Jacobi clenched his jaw, his instincts screaming at him to stay silent. If he called out, the Dogman would hear him.

Stay low. Stay quiet.

The bark of the tree was rough against his gloves as he steadied himself. He shifted slightly to peer around the trunk when a twig snapped behind him.

Jacobi froze, every muscle in his body tensing as the sound echoed unnaturally loud in the stillness.

He turned and stood slowly, his rifle raising as his pulse quickened. His finger hovered over the trigger as he scanned the trees.

Another sound. A rustle of snow.

It's here.

Jacobi's grip tightened on the rifle, his eyes darting to every possible angle. The surrounding forest was a maze of shadows and faint movement, every tree, and branch a potential hiding spot for the predator stalking him.

Suddenly, there was a deafening crash of snow and branches.

The Dogman burst from behind a downed tree with astonishing speed, its massive form colliding with Jacobi before he could fire.

The impact sent Jacobi sprawling, his rifle flying from his hands as he hit the ground hard. A painful gasp escaped his lips as the air left his lungs, his chest rising and falling heavily.

The Dogman snarled, its blazing eyes filled with rage as it loomed menacingly over him.

Jacobi, reacting on instinct, scrambled to his feet as fast as his body would allow. He barely had time to get upright when the Dogman's clawed hand lashed out.

The force flung him into a nearby tree, his back crashing against the rough bark with a bone-jarring impact. His left arm hit hard, twisting awkwardly as it absorbed the brunt of the blow. An intense, searing pain shot from his shoulder down to his fingers, and his vision momentarily blurred from the shock.

Jacobi slumped against the trunk, his breath coming in ragged gasps. His chest burned, and his arm throbbed with a deep, relentless ache. Blood seeped through his torn jacket, staining the snow beneath him in dark patches. He tried to push himself upright, but a fresh wave of pain radiated from his arm, forcing him to grit his teeth. His back throbbed from the collision, every breath sending a sharp pulse of agony through his ribs and chest.

He struggled to move but each attempt to push himself up was met with a searing reminder of his injuries.

Through the haze, he heard a gunshot ring out, the crack splitting the silence.

The Dogman snarled and darted to the side, its sudden movement turning what should have been a fatal shot into a miss that struck a nearby tree.

Beretti's second shot grazed the creature's shoulder as it shifted again, moving with startling quickness and lethal accuracy.

"Damn thing's too damn fast," Beretti said under her breath, her frustration clear as she tracked its movements.

The Dogman leaped upward, landing on a low branch of a nearby tree.

Jacobi blinked, his dazed mind struggling to process what he was seeing. The Dogman clung to the branch with ease, its glowing eyes locked on Beretti as it crouched like a predator ready to pounce.

The momentary reprieve gave Jacobi the chance he needed.

Summoning every ounce of strength, he staggered to his feet, clutching his injured arm to his chest as he stumbled backward. The pain was blinding, but adrenaline pushed him forward.

"Jacobi, move!" Beretti yelled, her rifle still aimed at the Dogman.

The creature, positioned between them, cut off his direct path to her. Jacobi had no choice but to dart in the opposite direction, veering deeper into the woods. His boots sank with every step, the effort of running made harder by the burning pain in his chest and shoulder.

The Dogman snarled again, its muscles tensing as it tracked Jacobi's retreat. It crouched, ready to leap, but another shot from Beretti cracked through the air. The bullet hit the Dogman in the forearm, forcing it to hesitate. Its claws dug into the bark, and its eyes snapped toward her, rage brimming in their amber depths.

"Stay back!" she yelled, squeezing the trigger again.

At the last second, the Dogman shifted, and the bullet tore through its ear instead of striking its head. A spray of blood hit the snow as it let out a furious snarl before leaping from the tree and vanishing into the dense brush.

"Jacobi!" Beretti called out, already sprinting after him.

Carter shouted to Beretti as he was chasing close behind. "Where is it?"

"Took off that way after Jacobi," Beretti pointed, not slowing her pace.

Carter nodded, as he ran up beside her.

SEVENTY-THREE

Jacobi sprinted, his fitness working in his favor despite the agony searing through his chest. Blood trickled from the cuts, each step jolting fresh pain through his body. But he didn't slow. Sheer determination and willpower kept him moving, his mind singularly focused on one thing: staying alive.

The forest blurred around him, branches clawing at his jacket and face as he crashed through the undergrowth. He clutched his injured arm to his chest, his boots slipping slightly on the crusted snow.

Behind him, he suddenly heard it. The heavy, rhythmic thud of footsteps.

It's coming.

The Dogman was close. Jacobi could feel it in the way the air seemed to shift, in the way every instinct in his body screamed at him to run faster.

He burst through a dense patch of brush, branches snapping loudly as he stumbled onto a wide, open expanse of white.

A frozen lake.

Jacobi hesitated for only a moment, his boots skidding slightly as he stepped onto the ice. It was slick, and he struggled to keep his balance as he moved away from the bank. Each step sent a faint cracking sound beneath him, the ice protesting under his weight.

He cast a quick glance over his shoulder and saw the Dogman emerging from the trees, its eyes focused on him.

I'm not going one-on-one with that thing, Jacobi thought grimly, his chest heaving as he slid further out onto the ice. *Not without a rifle.* He had his sidearm on him but with an injured arm, it was useless.

The ice groaned beneath him, and he winced, but his decision was made. He'd take his chances here rather than face the Dogman head on.

The Dogman stepped onto the ice, its claws clicking against the surface as it moved cautiously forward. Its head lowered, its nostrils flaring as it sniffed the fear emanating from Jacobi.

Sliding further out onto the lake, Jacobi kept moving, his boots slipping slightly with each step. He could hear the faint groans and cracks of the ice beneath him, but he didn't stop. He couldn't stop.

The Dogman stalked him, never taking its eyes off him. Blood dripped from its wounds, leaving a red trail on the ice as it closed the distance.

Jacobi turned to face it, his chest heaving as he fought to calm his breathing. His heart pounded in his ears, drowning out everything but the sound of the Dogman's growl.

I can't run forever.

The Dogman moved closer, its muscles rippling under its blood-soaked fur. The amber glow of its eyes seemed brighter against the stark whiteness of the lake, and Jacobi could see its teeth glinting as it bared its fangs.

It shifted its weight slightly, and the ice beneath it let out a sharp crack.

The Dogman's ears twitched at the sound, its gaze flicking briefly to the ice before returning to Jacobi.

The cracking grew louder as the creature stepped forward, its massive weight pressing down on the fragile surface. Jacobi took a cautious step back, his boots slipping as he tried to keep his balance.

The Dogman growled low in its throat, its body crouching slightly as though preparing to pounce.

Jacobi tensed, his free hand instinctively moving toward his sidearm. His injured arm hung useless at his side, and he knew he'd only have one chance to draw and fire.

Not ideal, but better than nothing.

Before he could act, a sudden yell shattered the tension.

"Jacobi! Down!"

Beretti burst out of the trees, her rifle raised, with Carter close behind her. Jacobi's head whipped toward them, relief flooding his face for a brief moment.

"Lie flat!" Beretti shouted again, her voice loud and commanding.

Jacobi didn't hesitate. He dropped to his stomach, spreading his weight across the ice as Beretti aimed her rifle at the Dogman.

The creature snarled and turned toward her, its muscles tensing as it prepared to charge.

Beretti squeezed the trigger, the crack of the rifle reverberating across the lake.

The bullet struck the Dogman square in the chest, jerking its massive body back slightly. It let out a deep, guttural growl as it staggered.

But then the ice let out a deafening crack.

The Dogman froze, its ears flattening against its head as the sound reverberated around the lake. It scrambled to move, its claws scratching frantically against the ice as cracks spider-webbed beneath it.

Beretti kept her rifle trained on the creature, her finger hovering over the trigger.

The Dogman took one more step, and the ice beneath it collapsed.

The creature plunged into the freezing water with a loud

splash.

It thrashed violently, its claws raking at the edges of the ice as it tried to pull itself out. The water churned around it, dark and frigid, soaking its fur as it fought desperately to escape.

Jacobi watched from where he lay, his chest heaving as he desperately hoped the water would claim the Dogman.

Beretti and Carter moved closer to the edge of the lake, her rifle still aimed at the struggling creature.

"It's not going to make it," Carter said, his voice low.

The Dogman snarled and growled as it clawed desperately at the crumbling edge of the ice. Each attempt to pull itself free only broke more ice away, sending it crashing back into the freezing water.

"It's suffering," Beretti said.

The creature's strength was visibly waning, its movements growing slower, more labored. Its snarls turned into low, guttural moans, filled with pain and desperation.

Beretti raised her rifle, taking a steadying breath as she aimed. "I'm ending this."

The Dogman's eyes lifted toward her, filled with rage and a glimmer of something almost pleading. Before it could slip beneath the surface, the crack of Beretti's rifle echoed through the clearing. The bullet struck the creature cleanly in the eye, silencing it mid-growl. Its massive frame went limp, the water lapping against its fur as it sank beneath the surface.

They watched in silence as the ripples smoothed out, the ice creaking faintly around the edges of the hole.

Jacobi exhaled shakily.

"Jacobi!" Beretti called out, her voice firm. "Stay flat and crawl back. Slow and steady."

Jacobi nodded, gritting his teeth as he carefully shifted his weight, using his uninjured arm to drag himself toward the shore. His other arm dangled at his side, throbbing with each movement, while every inch forward sent sharp stabs of pain through his chest. A faint trail of blood marked his path, smearing against the ice and blending into the frozen landscape.

Carter crouched near the edge, his hand outstretched. "You're doing fine. Just a little further."

When Jacobi finally reached the shore, Beretti crouched

down to help him up, gripping his good arm firmly. Carter joined her, grabbing Jacobi's other side to steady him.

"You're insane," Beretti said, shaking her head as she supported him.

Jacobi gave her a weak grin. "You're welcome."

Carter chuckled, as he helped Jacobi up. "You're one crazy son of a bitch."

"I had to end it," Jacobi said.

Beretti nodded, her eyes lingering on the jagged hole in the ice where the Dogman had vanished. After a moment, she turned and began helping Jacobi back toward the forest, Carter supporting him on the other side.

SEVENTY-FOUR

Pain radiated through Jacobi's body as he watched the nurses move about the small hospital room, their efficiency both comforting and disconcerting. The overwhelming smell of antiseptic lingered in the air, mixing with the quiet hum of machinery. He sat on the edge of a hard examination bed, his shirt discarded in a bloody heap on the floor. His chest and arms were crisscrossed with fresh stitches, the gashes raw but clean.

A nurse carefully worked on his right shoulder, her gloved hands moving with steady care as she secured it in a sling to stabilize the injury. There were no broken bones, but his shoulder and back were mottled with deep bruises, a painful reminder of the impact.

Beretti's sharp eyes didn't miss the way the nurse's gaze flickered, not just to the wounds but to the defined muscle beneath the fresh stitches. The faint pink on the nurse's cheeks and the slight tremor in her hands as she adjusted the sling betrayed her nerves.

With faint amusement, Beretti leaned against the wall, arms crossed. Jacobi, even covered with bruises, scratches across his face, and a stitched-up chest, still managed to have that effect on people.

She was thankful he was alive and grateful he was upright and even throwing out the occasional joke but watching him unintentionally fluster someone trying to do their job was a distraction she hadn't anticipated.

"You know," she said finally, "you can't keep running off like that. We're partners, Jacobi. You don't get to take those risks without me."

Jacobi winced as the nurse moved his arm, then gave Beretti a sheepish grin. "I know. But I saw it running, and my instincts just kicked in. I thought I could..."

"That's the problem," Beretti interrupted, her voice firmer now. "You thought *after* the fact. You're always reacting, Jacobi. You don't stop to think first. You're lucky this time. You could've been killed."

Jacobi held up his good hand in mock surrender. "Alright, point taken. No more solo heroics. I'll try not to be so reckless next time."

Beretti sighed, shaking her head.

Jacobi glanced at her, his usual playful demeanor softening. "I'll be smarter next time, I promise."

EPILOGUE

As Beretti and Jacobi pulled up outside Lillian's house, the scene was one of quiet recovery. Neighbors were out shoveling snow, clearing driveways, and tidying up after the storm. Despite the cold, there was a sense that things might finally be getting back to normal.

Jacobi glanced out the window, watching someone scrape ice from their windshield. "I hope whatever spirit was attached to that tooth is at peace now," he continued as they got out of the SUV and walked up the driveway. "Not just for its sake, but so Ethan can finally enjoy his bedroom."

Beretti nodded. "Agreed. As long as the FBI doesn't retrieve the tooth along with the Dogman come spring, all should be fine."

Jacobi grinned, glancing at her. "Good point."

Jacobi and Beretti knocked on the door, and within seconds, it swung open to reveal Ethan, his face lighting up with excitement. "You're back!" he said, practically bouncing on his feet. "Come in!"

As they stepped inside, the change was immediate. The air felt lighter, no longer weighed down by the unease of the past few days. The comforting scent of something sweet filled the house, and in the kitchen, Lillian was pulling a tray of cookies from the oven.

She glanced up as they entered and smiled warmly. "Well, look who's back," she said. "How are you feeling, Jacobi?"

Jacobi smirked. "A little sore, but it won't hold me back."

Lillian gave him a knowing look as she set the tray down. "Didn't think it would." She dusted her hands off on a dish towel and joined them at the table. "Carter's out helping clean up some of the storm damage," she said, settling into a chair. "He did drop the 'package' off at the morgue first, though."

Jacobi and Beretti both nodded.

Ethan wasted no time grabbing Beretti's sleeve and tugging her toward the table. "Come on! I've been practicing.

I think I'm finally going to win this time."

Beretti sat beside him, arching an eyebrow. "Oh yeah? We'll see about that, kid."

They played cards late into the night, their laughter, and conversation filling the home with a long-overdue sense of normalcy. The warmth of the fire and the friendly competition between them was a welcome change from the fear and uncertainty they had endured.

At one point, Ethan hesitated, his fingers idly tapping against his cards. Then, almost shyly, he admitted, "My room doesn't feel so scary anymore."

Beretti and Jacobi exchanged a glance before Beretti ruffled Ethan's hair. "That's great to hear," she said softly.

Feeling more excited than he'd been in a while, Ethan grinned and dealt the next hand.

****

The next morning, as they prepared to leave, the entire family gathered to see them off.

"Thank you," Carter said, his voice full of gratitude. "For everything."

Lillian gave them both a warm smile. "You'll always be welcome here. And thank you for keeping us safe."

Beretti smiled back warmly. "Thank you to all of you for your hospitality. It's been a long few days, but you made it easier for us."

Jacobi nodded. "Yeah, thanks for putting up with us. We appreciate it."

Ethan looked up at Beretti and Jacobi, his hands wrapped around a warm mug of cocoa. His eyes, still holding traces of everything he'd been through, softened with gratitude.

"Thanks," he said quietly.

Jacobi gave him a nod, a small smile tugging at the corner of his mouth. "Anytime. You're one brave kid, you know that?"

Beretti ruffled Ethan's hair lightly. "You take care of yourself, alright? You have my number if you ever need to text me."

Ethan smiled. "Okay."

As Beretti and Jacobi climbed into their SUV, Carter turned to Lillian and Ethan. "I'll be right back," he told them before heading down the steps.

Jacobi rolled down his window as Carter approached, his expression thoughtful.

"I know I said I wouldn't ask," Carter said, "but it's been driving me crazy."

Jacobi arched an eyebrow. "What's that?"

Carter glanced over his shoulder, then leaned slightly toward the window. "Is Bigfoot real?"

Beretti smirked, while Jacobi grinned.

"Does it snow in Maine?" Jacobi replied.

Carter huffed a quiet laugh and stepped back as the SUV pulled away, shaking his head as he watched them disappear down the road.

****

At the airport, just as they were waiting to board their flight, Beretti's phone buzzed. She pulled it out and saw a text from Carter.

Franklin's remains were found. Memorial planned for next week. The town is healing.

She showed the message to Jacobi, who nodded solemnly. "Good. He deserves that."

Beretti tucked the phone away and adjusted her bag. "I agree."

Jacobi leaned back in his chair, his usual grin softening slightly. "What about us? You still game to head out on the next job with me?"

Beretti looked at him for a long moment before cracking a faint smile. "That depends. Are you actually going to listen to me this time?"

Jacobi chuckled, wincing at the movement. "I'll try. No promises."

Beretti rolled her eyes. "Figures." But there was warmth in her voice as she added, "Yeah, I'm still in. Somebody's got to keep you alive."

Their flight was called, and they stood, grabbing their bags. As they walked toward the gate, Jacobi quipped, "Guess that makes you the boss."

Beretti smiled. "Don't forget it."

ABOUT THE AUTHOR

 Luka T. Jacobs, an author from the picturesque Illawarra region south of Sydney, Australia, is passionate about cryptids like Sasquatch and Dogman. She lives there with her partner and their dog, Finnigan.

Luka's love for animals and adventure fuels her storytelling. With a background in Graphic Design and Art, she adds a unique visual flair to her work. An avid traveler and explorer, she draws inspiration from the wild, eager to share her imaginative worlds with readers.

Luka T. Jacobs

Stay connected and join the conversation! *Follow me on Facebook to interact and share your thoughts, explore my books on Amazon, and visit my website for more information about my works and upcoming releases. Don't forget to sign up for my newsletter—you'll be the first to hear about new books, exclusive content, and special offers!*

FB: https://www.facebook.com/lukatjacobs

A: https://amazon.com/author/lukatjacobs

W: http://www.LukaTJacobs.com

JOIN CRYPTID HORROR CENTRAL

Join my email list and get first access to new releases and download my **FREE** short story *"The Dogman of Coldwater Creek"*.

WWW.LUKATJACOBS.COM

Dear Reader,

Thank you for diving into my book amidst a sea of choices—
it truly means the world to me.

If you enjoyed the story, I'd love it if you shared your
experience with others and left a review. As an
independent author, your voice helps bring these tales
to life for more readers, and every recommendation
makes a tremendous impact.

Thank you again for joining me on this journey.
I'm so grateful to have you as a reader!

SNEAK PEAK:
FOREST OF THE
SASQUATCH: THEIR
TERRITORY, THEIR RULES

The forest breathed its ancient rhythm. High above, the towering pines swayed in the fall breeze, their needles whispering secrets carried through ancient shadows. Sunlight filtered through the dense canopy, dappling the forest floor in patches of amber and gold.

Hidden deep within the Superior National Forest, near Devil's Track Lake, where the trees cast the deepest shadows, lay a place untouched by humans, the clan's secret sanctuary.

Even the animals of the forest seemed to sense the boundary of this sacred ground, avoiding it entirely. Deer grazed near its edges but never crossed into its heart. Birds flew above the cliffs but rarely landed near the cave's entrance. The natural world seemed to understand what the hairless ones could not: this place belonged to the Sasquatch alone.

Thick, unyielding walls of thorny thicket and dense brush surrounded the area, growing so tightly together that even the smallest creatures struggled to pass through. Towering trees formed a natural barrier, their twisted roots and low-hanging branches weaving into an almost impenetrable maze. Beyond the thicket, a sheer cliff face rose abruptly from the earth, its jagged surface streaked with moss and lichen. At its base, hidden among boulders and shadows, was the entrance to a vast cave system, cool and damp, where the clan had lived for generations.

The caves were a place of safety, a haven where the family slept, gathered, and raised their young. Here, in this untouched wilderness, the Sasquatch thrived, living in harmony with the forest. But their peace was fragile. The hairless ones had grown bold, venturing deeper into the forest, leaving trails of destruction in their wake.

Aluk crouched low beneath the brush, his eyes glinting as he watched a pair of hairless ones far below. He and his brother Matto had left the sanctuary to patrol the edges of their territory, as they often did when the hairless ones grew too bold. What they saw now made Aluk's fists clench.

The two hairless ones had arrived in a roaring metal beast, its tires gouging deep ruts into the soft earth. They had parked it at the edge of a clearing, its bulk looming like an unwelcome guest. One of them, a tall hairless one in a bright orange jacket, was crouched over the lifeless body of a deer, its glossy eyes staring blankly into the dirt. The hairless one's hands were red with blood as he hacked at the carcass with a hunting knife, his movements rough and careless.

The second hairless one, stocky with a scruffy beard, stood nearby, gathering sticks. "Told you this spot was good," he said, his voice carrying across the clearing. "Nobody comes out this far."

"Think they'll notice one less deer?" the tall hairless one asked, his laugh sharp and grating.

Aluk growled softly, his breath steaming in the cool evening air. His eyes darted to the thunder stick lying in the dirt near the stocky one's feet. A weapon capable of death from a distance, one the clan had learned to fear.

The deer was theirs. The clan depended on these woods for food. The hairless ones had not only invaded their sacred ground, they had stolen from it.

Matto placed a hand on Aluk's shoulder, his claws brushing against the coarse hair there. Through gestures and images, Matto conveyed his thoughts: *Hold. Wait. The Elder forbids this.*

Aluk's response came in a flood of sharp, vivid images: the hairless ones' bloody hands, their trash scattering across the sacred ground, the machine scarring the earth. *They destroy. They take. How much longer will we watch?*

Matto hesitated. He shared Aluk's anger, but the Elder's warning rang in his mind. The Elder had long insisted on secrecy, on patience. But patience had not stopped the hairless ones from encroaching farther each year.

Hidden in the tree line, Aluk and Matto crouched, watching as the hairless ones built their red-breath. The breath licked high into the sky, casting flickering shadows on the trees. One of the hairless ones stood and stretched, letting out a loud belch.

"I'm gonna take a piss," he said, stumbling toward the forest's edge.

The men wrinkled their noses as an awful stench wafted toward them. It was rank and overpowering, like garbage left out in the sun for days, layered with a heavy musk that clung to the back of their throats.

"Geez, what is that smell?" one of them mumbled, turning his head away.

Aluk's massive body tensed. He glanced at Matto, who

raised a hand in warning. The elder's unspoken message was clear: *hold back. Watch, but do not act.*

But Aluk's mind surged with defiance. He sent an image of the hairless ones laughing, their red-breath consuming the sacred ground, the machine scarring the earth. *Enough.*

As the hairless one staggered toward the trees, Aluk shifted silently from his vantage point, slipping through the thick underbrush. His movements were precise, his hulking frame ghostlike in the moonlight as he circled closer. The rustle of the leaves, the crack of twigs, sounds that would have betrayed a human, blended seamlessly with the forest's natural rhythm.

The hairless one stopped a few feet from the tree line, fumbling with his belt. Aluk waited, crouched just beyond the brush, his eyes locked on his target.

Before Matto could stop him, Aluk lunged forward.

The hairless one barely had time to gasp before Aluk's hand clamped over his face, silencing him. In one swift motion, Aluk dragged the hairless one into the thickets. There was a muffled cry, then silence.

Back at the red-breath, the second hairless one looked up, frowning. "Derek?" he called, squinting into the darkness.

"Quit screwing around, man."

He heard a faint rustling from the direction Derek had gone. Then, the snapping of branches. A silhouette moved at the edge of the firelight, massive and looming, too large to be anything human.

A wave of panic washed over him, accompanied by a deep, unsettling fear. He stumbled back toward the clearing, nearly tripping over his own feet. His eyes darted around, trying to pierce the blackness. "Derek?" he called again, his voice trembling now.

When no response came, he turned and sprinted toward his four-wheeler parked near the fire. His hands fumbled as he started the machine, the engine roaring to life. The noise echoed through the forest, jarring and unnatural.

"Not sticking around for this crap," he mumbled, his voice shaking as he gripped the handlebars and gunned the throttle. The four-wheeler lurched forward, kicking up dirt and leaves as it sped down the narrow trail towards the clearing's edge.

The trail was dark, lit only by the pale beams of the machine's headlight. The hairless one's pulse quickened, the trees seeming to converge, their shadows alive with an unseen, unsettling presence. He glanced over his shoulder, expecting to see something chasing him.

As he glanced back at the trail, his eyes widened in disbelief.

Standing in the middle of the path was a towering figure, its hair gleaming faintly in the four-wheeler's headlights. The creature's glowing eyes locked on him, and its massive form blocked the trail entirely.

"Jesus Christ!" the hairless one screamed, shifting his weight as he jerked the handlebars in a frantic attempt to avoid the creature.

The four-wheeler skidded out of control, its tires losing traction on the dirt. The hairless one's panic made him overcompensate, and the machine careened off the trail. It slammed headfirst into a tree with a sickening crunch, the force throwing the hairless one forward.

His body hit the tree with brutal force, a sharp thud reverberating in the woods. He crumpled to the ground at its base, groaning in pain. Blood poured from a deep gash on his forehead as he tried to crawl away, but his body betrayed him, too stunned to respond.

Aluk and Matto emerged silently from the darkness.

The brothers towered over the injured hairless one and the machine that had defiled their sacred forest. Aluk's lips curled back in a snarl as he sent an image to Matto: the machine broken, destroyed, its noise silenced forever.

Matto stepped forward first, his massive hands gripping the four-wheeler. With a guttural roar, he lifted the machine as though it weighed nothing and slammed it into the ground. Metal crumpled and shattered under the force.

The hairless one whimpered, struggling to drag himself away. His effort was futile.

Aluk advanced, his eyes cold. His massive hand reached down, cutting off the hairless one's final, strangled scream.

When the forest fell silent once more, the brothers walked back toward the clearing.

The red-breath still burned faintly, casting flickering light across the remains of the deer carcass the hairless ones had stolen from the woods. Aluk crouched beside it, running his massive hands over the animal's body. Its spirit belonged to the forest, not to the hairless ones who had taken it without care or honor.

With a series of deliberate gestures and vivid shared images, Aluk, and Matto came to an agreement: the deer would not be left here to rot. Nor would the bodies of the hairless ones remain to poison the sacred ground.

Matto hoisted the deer across his shoulder with ease, its lifeless form dangling against his broad back. His gaze lingered on the thunder stick lying in the dirt, its metal surface gleaming faintly. With a deliberate motion, he bent down, picked it up, and secured it alongside the deer. He had no idea what he was going to do with the weapon, but he knew he couldn't leave it behind for other hairless ones to find and use.

Aluk carried the bodies of the two hairless ones, their weight inconsequential against his immense strength. The brothers cast a final glance at the campsite and disappeared into the forest.

****

As the first light of dawn painted the horizon, the brothers returned to the sanctuary. Matto laid the deer at the center of the main cave, where it would be divided among the clan. Aluk turned to face the Elder, his chest heaving with the weight of his anger and pride.

The Elder's amber eyes flicked from the bloodied brothers to the deer and back again. Aluk's shared images depicted the events: the hairless ones stealing what was not theirs, the loud machine ravaging the land, and the brothers' swift retribution.

The Elder's expression remained unreadable, but his thoughts were firm. *You have acted without permission. You risked exposure.*

Aluk's response came quickly, sharp, and unrelenting: We protected the forest. The hairless ones are no longer. The deer is ours again.

Matto added his agreement, showing an image of the clan gathered around the deer, nourished by what had been stolen. *This is our duty. To guard. To provide.*

The Elder stared at them for a long moment before turning toward the depths of the cave. His final thought was projected to the whole clan: *You have risked more than you know. But tonight, the forest has been restored.*

Only available at Amazon.com.